C000048991

PRAISE FOR THE WORK OF
GEORGE WILLIAMS

"George Williams writes with an electric energy, unpredictable inventiveness, and deft ear for dialogue that makes him one of the most exciting and compelling writers of his generation."
—Richard Burgin, author of *Don't Think*

"Recommended to adventurous readers, who will surely enjoy Williams's wildly irreverent inventions."
—*Library Journal*

"George Williams, a self-described 'recovering anarchist,' writes a hyper-controlled, smart and taut prose that goes beyond the spare exactness of the Moderns. The sentences seem so easy, but their accretion is sly: William's prose unveils a tough and dense vision, the steady shock of a live snapping wire."
—Stephen D. Geller, author of
Jews in the Bosom of the Big Bang

"George Williams is one of the finest minds and writers of our generation."
—Eric Miles Williamson, author of
East Bay Grease

THE LAST FAMILY

BOOKS BY GEORGE WILLIAMS

GEORGE WILLIAMS

THE LAST FAMILY

Copyright © 2020 by George Williams

All rights reserved. No part of the book may be reproduced in any form or by any electronic or mechanical means, including information storage and retrieval systems, without permission in writing from the publisher, except by a reviewer who may quote brief passages in a review.

Down & Out Books
3959 Van Dyke Road, Suite 265
Lutz, FL 33558
DownAndOutBooks.com

The characters and events in this book are fictitious. Any similarity to real persons, living or dead, is coincidental and not intended by the author.

Cover design by Jeremy Medoff

ISBN: 1-64396-159-4
ISBN-13: 978-1-64396-159-0

For Chloe and Basil, Edwin and Rosalba

It will be very long, I trust, before romance-writers may find congenial and easily handled themes, either in the annals of our stalwart republic, or in any characteristic and probable events of our individual lives. Romance and poetry, like ivy, lichens, and wall-flowers, need ruin to make them grow.

—Nathaniel Hawthorne

I

I walk home from the F train and lunch at Puglio's, a Little Italy dive, with a girl I met a month ago at CBGB's. Her name is Becky. She has freckles and an orthodontic smile and probably graduated *summa cum* from Sarah Lawrence but to compensate she wears black leather and claims her nipples are pierced. Over a dollar bottle of wine I bet her fifty bucks they aren't. We are headed to settle the bet when we bump into a Western Union man on Water Street, right outside the Brooklyn warehouse whose top floor five of us have come to call home.

"Webb Clayborne?"

Becky looks at me.

"Clayborne?"

"Nobody by that name," I say. "Webb?" The messenger looks at the telegram and back.

"Yes," I say.

"Close enough. Sign here."

Up on the seventh floor Becky and I flop on my mattress in a far corner. Power tools hang from the rafters: nail gun, Skilsaw, jackhammer. An air compressor leans on an old tire.

"Who else lives here?"

"Anybody who can take it." I tack up the blanket that partitions me from the rest of loft. At the end of the large warehouse room is a steel communal dining table courtesy of The State of New Jersey and Rahway, next to a makeshift kitchen of hot plates

and a round bear of a refrigerator circa 1957, which rumbles
day and night. The rest of the loftmates have sheetrocked two
by fours into sleeping quarters with pre-fab windows curtained
with burlap. A transient here, I sleep against the wall, beside a
welding tank and a garbage can of 35mm film from the Golden
Age of Porn, part of a Hunter College installation one of the
sculptors has been completing for months now. He cuts up the
three reels of film into slide-size squares and pastes them to a
High Gothic triptych of bevelled glass. "Stained Glass," he calls
it.

I open the telegram. It is uncharacteristically to the point:
Dear Webb:
Docie very ill.
Come home.

"What about our bet?" I ask.
"Who's Docie?"
"My sister."
"I'd better go."
"You don't believe me."
"Randolph? Clayborne?"
"Webb's fine. What about our bet?"
"You have fifty dollars?"
"Minus 49.50."
"Deal." She opens her leather shirt.

I chase her down seven flights of stairs and out onto crooked,
cobbled Water street, below the industrial dinosaur of the
Manhattan Bridge.

"Where's my fifty bucks?"

She drops down the stairs for the F train back to town,
laughing gleefully. I figure I might see her again.

With Becky gone I sit at the steel table and wonder how on
earth Mother found out where was holed up. Momentarily my
heavy heart gladdens. Alabama in the late spring evokes images

of pastoral rejuvenation, the sweet Saturday morning sound of mowers on the greening grass, hazy links stretching into the horizon, bourbons on dusky patios where the crickets churr, whatnots and sentimental gimcracks cluttering the mahogany hallways, antique rooms and family histories and heirlooms that weigh on the house like a tomb of ghosts, and all the rest of the rot that has made my mother's side of the family miserable for generations. But my heavy heart lightens anyway, even with the news of Docie who, if she is sick, is therefore well, her histrionic agonies no doubt heightened by now to newer enormities.

I always called my eldest sister Dora, because Docie sounds bovine, and if there's one thing she is not it's cowlike. Her proper name is Eudora, but even the December I left for New York she threw one of her personality fits we'd hoped she'd outgrown, pulling at her locks like they were crazy snakes and making sounds like those swine Jesus filled with the devil and sent crashing into the sea, all the while breaking windowpanes with her penny loafer and blaming Mother and her father for her birth name and the curse of physical beauty and cold sores before Saturday night riot and naturally blond hair and a figure that stoked every boy in Birmingham like a Bessemer steel mill, and winding down her tantrum with an inventory of every other indignity of good fortune she's endured since birth, summed it up with a soggy Nutty Buddy flung at an ancestral portrait of a Revolutionary guerilla in rolled stockings bag wig and embroidered waistcoat. It stuck on his distinguished forehead, cone-up. Mother fainted clean away.

Dora's thirty-two and I suspect no more grown now, because if she's sick there's really only one explanation for it, she's checked herself into a private rest home for the mentally infirm, where a whey-faced doctor squat in a swivel chair crows some psychological bullcock about how *she's* the most important person in the world and how it's the fault of the way she was raised—not *reared*, as Mother maintained we say—because nothing's her fault if only she could learn to accept and perhaps adore herself a little more, and so on and on. I always had the impression Docie loved herself more than she loved anyone else, and that it was a waste of family money to pay nutpicks to tell us what she and everybody up the block already knew. Besides, the doctors were numbskulls, and she knew it. They were blind as newts to Dora's goldbricking. In fifteen minutes she could pantomime a list of symptoms and birdlime a whole staff into believing not even Freud himself saw such a made-to-order-item, whether borderline, hysterical, paranoid, manic or plain neurotic, while I'm sure what most of them hoped she suffered from was simple nymphomania, curable as tick fever or heat rash. Dora goosed them all, and for that I give her credit. I imagine she's out in a lawn chair right now, out by the croquet wickets, smoking, counseling some homely depressive on how to be more forward with men, while an attendant in a white jacket feels his eyes bob like boiling eggs as he looks up and down Dora's legs and chesty blouse. No, Dora's not sick; she's just tired of working.

Bill, the stained-glass artisan, comes out of his cubicle in a Japanese robe.

"Have a drink?" he asks.

"No, thanks."

He pours vodka on ice and resumes clipping the movie.

"How's the project?" I ask.

"Great thing about the Seventies," he says absently.

"What's that?"

"No breast implants."

"I hadn't thought of that."

"Big primordial bushes too. No landscaped gardens. Beautiful hearts of darkness." With tweezers he holds up a square of film and with one eye squint examines it through a magnifying glass, his open eye as big as a golf ball.

"I got a telegram," I say, "from Birmingham."

"No kidding." He scratches his gray beard.

"My mother says my elder sister is sick."

"Runs in the family, no?"

"No."

"Are you leaving?"

"Probably. Depends on what Rosa says."

"Don't forget to pay your rent."

"Rosa's my guardian angel."

He tweezers another frame of cut film. "I'll need it by next week."

"She'll bring it by."

"Who?"

"Rosa."

"Have I met her?"

Bill clips and pastes. I take a nap. I wake up when the door slams. Bill stands at the refrigerator with a beer. Next to him is a streetwalker in red hot pants wearing an Afro wig.

"I don't carry rubbers buddy."

"Webb, you got any?"

"Fresh out."

"Twenty-five for a hand job."

"Webb, are you sure?"

"Sorry."

He runs down to the bodega, leaving the girl with me. She can't be older than nineteen.

"Whatta you guys do?"

"Construction."

"Weird. I mean all this stuff." She points to a hatchet buried in a dartboard, a smashed T.V., rebar sticking crazily out of shotcrete.

"They're sculptors."

"No kidding."

For the last five years I've called myself *Randolph*, Edmund Webb, most recently hailing from The Heart of Dixie, B'ham, a town that strives to be as desperately glamorous as Atlanta which, in turn, apes New York, the megalopolis where I've been bolopunched, dropkicked, and bootsoled from the lowest to the lowest jobs the city has to offer. New York's fine, but if you were on a cruise ship you wouldn't want to spend your vacation in the engine room.

Along with the telegram came a money order for a solid yard, so despite the fact that I was little rattled—I haven't heard from a soul in The Magic City since I ducked out of town and switched surnames—my spirits steadily rise. I can pay off my roommates and get out from under New York for good. Work for Princeton's Physical Plant. Join the Jehovah's down the street. Drive a Mack truck cross-country. Sell Bibles door to door. Lately I'm sick at heart from stumbling over homeless folk who sleep on our doorstep, and the heavy aroma of drunks that clutches at my face every morning is enough to demoralize a wild dog.

Don't misunderstand me about The Big Apple. It's the one city *guaranteed* to tell you everything's a question of perspective. A few summers ago I was accidentally invited to a film company barbecue at the top of a forty-story building in mid-town Manhattan. On the spacious penthouse patio, where gaffers and gofers were rotissing a plump brown pig over a half-barrel of coals, I stood by the railing and nearly fainted. A thousand feet up, helicopting on expensive whiskey over the canyon glories of Manhattan, not on the hot tar and baking sidewalks of the street below, I finally *saw* New York. Shortly I was asked to leave; a permanent wave rock star on his way over to review some rushes phoned from his limo with his hackles up, saying he wanted the unvites ushered. The friend I came with, who worked there, asked me to use the stairs. Back on the street, I looked up, somewhat dizzily. Up forty stories, you could fly from those clustered peaks and climb even higher. From below, the buildings looked like pile drivers.

For a long time I've lived beside the Brooklyn Bridge, Brooklyn side (then declasse), on the top floor of a hundred-year-old warehouse, with a group of sculptors with whom I work construction, a euphemism that carries over to their studios. One sculptor jackhammers concrete and shoots nails into wood and bends reinforcement rods and pours plaster over everything and calls it Drop Dead, a talismanic confusion meant to drive off the ghosts of suicides who haunt the legendary span. It was inspired by a genuine jumper spied from the roof one summer night, a distant stick who fell with his arms methodically flapping, to no avail. Choppers with spotlights circled the murky waters. He was history. We wondered if we knew him.

Another sculptor knifes gatefold girls to planks and wraps them in Saran Wrap and suspends them from the ceiling. A numbered series, all zeros in whatever language has a sign for cipher. Another puts little wooden houses on two-by-four ledges and calls them Little Wooden Houses on 2 x 4 Ledges. They all believe Western Civ is circling the drain. One evening the nail gunner, Stanley, said art was its velocifier. They agreed, and we smashed bottles against the wall all night long, dancing like fullbacks to kamikaze punk.

I met them on a sheetrock job and moved into a corner of the seventh floor of the warehouse when the lower East Side dive I was holed up in was bought for renovation. On the floor below, heavy machinery stamped out filing cabinets from sheet metal, so I woke every day to what felt like an earthquake. I figured out soon why the sculptors gave me shelter. I have a strong back and their installations had a lot more mass than sense, so I helped them haul and lift.

The sculptors liked me because I too had a collision-sport relation with my father. Plus, for the nihilistic Marxists, I was too big a target to miss, dough-white ex-college football and Golden Gloves boxer, not merely a Southerner of descent, which meant worlds to them, but an ex-Richie Rich to boot, scion of Old Virginians fattened by Tidewater *Nicotiana*, as exotic to the Randolphs as opium hashish, since no one but my sole Randolph aunt smoked the divine, rare, devilish, damned, incomparably sublime and filthy weed whose fumes, according to King James, nearest resembled the Stygian smoke of bottomless Hell, the distinctly American vice of plugs, pipes, cigars, butts, snuff, and finally Virginia Slims. These lucrative products bore me sweetened with naïveté into the thundering world, conceived with gold already in my pockets; the pungent copper brown of cured leaves hanging from plantation rafters translated into post-bellum trusts, trees with Grants waving in the wind lined the Randolph landscape, no small Confederate irony, since *our* Randolph branch—the name, with Byrd's, a Virginia first, ramifying from Blackwater to Manassas from the explorer shores of Pocahontas, where no one had a moment leftover for the King's *Counter-blast to Tobacco*—profited from the annihilation of Richmond by its own powder magazine, when capitol officials, in a moment of clarity, staved in the city's whiskey barrels and poured the golden liquor into the gutters, to keep it free of Yankee gullets. Thirsty throngs of Confederate patriots surged the streets and dipped it up with cups and pans, or kneeled into the rivers of bourbon with open mouths. In the starved craws of citizens the whiskey worked an instantaneous magic. The war-drunk Rebels, armed with firedogs and rusty muskets—ladies and gentlemen alike—sacked their own city, and fought in the streets over burning loot. Soldiers torched the tobacco warehouses along the James, from which sparks, carried by Union winds, ignited the Confederate arsenal. The city went off like a bomb. The red glare of caroming artillery shells filled the night sky. Midnight looked like noon, and vice versa. The sculptors knew all this, because I claimed to be a beneficiary of disasters greater than fortunate birth. I told them Confederate Randolphs raked in dough post-war like carpetbaggers, and asked them to consider the continuing drama. Black Friday sold more cigarettes than Bette Davis. What was a co-ed acid trip without blankets under a moonless sky and the orange glowworm of cigarette trails? Coke and crack were indirectly tarring more lungs than pot smoke. Packets of toot and a carton of menthol Merits. Who needed food? And now a billion Asians lighting out for Marlboro country.

So I became the sculptors' heavy bag for wordy abuse. They opposed everything they think I stood for: brand-name loyalty, institutional violence, corporate restaurants. "I wrote myself out of the Randolph will," I explained, striking a philanthropic pose, but nobody bought it. "How can you do that?" Bill, the Japanese-American sculptor asked, flinging an empty quart of Bull at the broken-brick wall. I showed them all my savings—a coffee can of change—and they laid off, grudgingly, but one Saturday morning when I came back from the bodega down the street with a can of high-profile orange juice, I was brought before the loft tribunal—a triumvirate led by a sculptor whose specialty was burning holes in doors with a blowtorch—where I was tried as a petty bourgeois fascist ideologue and condemned, the column of juice ceremoniously glopped into the proletarian chamber pot, a hole in the warehouse floor where once an American Standard had stood. One of the sculptors had unbolted it one early winter morning and vanished into the night. The commode resurfaced in an installation on Broadway, on the second floor of a ramshackle building rented to a nest of porn merchants below, who supported the arts by donating space for exhibitions.

Now for a dusty square of warehouse the sculptors expect their FFV Alabama Crimson Tide Goliath to bail them out of bar fights.

"Why?"

"What do you expect, Queensbury rules? What a gentleman!" Bill said, the first week I moved in. "You fight to win. Suckerpunch. Stab them with keys, bottles, mechanical pencils. Break chairs over their backs. Bite their nuts off if you have to."

"Who?"

"Downtown artists! Soho gallery queens! Village dilettantes!"

"Have you been in a fight lately? People get killed, maimed. Bones break. Teeth fly. It's not pretty."

"Not since Junior High."

"Have you tried to pick one? I mean, with the ones on your

hit list?"

"I showed up drunk at an opening. Pissed on a guy's installation. I figured we'd do the dance, but hell a line formed to the rear. Drenched the piece of concrete shit, artist included. It looked like a urinal anyway. Got a brief write up in *Art in America*. Now you tell me."

"Tell you what?"

Last fall one of the sculptors I genuinely liked hurt himself real bad, and later died. I liked Stanley because he really was insane, and not like most of the bozart clan, hapless posers fleeing the frozen waffles and Colombian bong hits of their privileged upbringings in suburbs across the continent. Privileged, I mean, by his standards.

They were all were drunk on tequila after a five-hour bout in a Tribeca wharf bar, when Stanley shouted "Geronimo" and leapt from the step van as it sped down Canal Street. By the time we turned around and got back through the traffic, a patrol car, its search-beam blazing, had already pulled over to keep any more cars from going over him. He was a real mess, slumped in the gutter. His head, resting on the curb, lay opened like a cantaloupe. He was talking to himself, but I knew in my bones that was it.

"Goliad," he said. "Angel of Goliad."

A cop shined a flashlight in my face.

"You know him?"

"Don't you?" I was crying, beside myself. "Don't you?"

He pushed me back.

"Take me back to Goliad," Stanley said. "Goliad."

"Take it easy, son," the cop said to Stanley. He knelt down, then turned to me. "Nothing you can do now but contact his relatives."

A medic put a sheet over him. There was no one to claim the body, so we chipped in and had him cremated and threw his ashes in the East River from the peak of Brooklyn Bridge, except for a handful I expressed to his hometown Postmaster, with instructions to scatter to the South Texas winds. Cremated remains weigh more than I expected: teeth, vertebrae, dense ash. Ghost burned from the bone.

Stanley was the descendant of generations of Texas oil shooters, crazy dudes who jugged out wells with nitroglycerin. Oil lore had it they found his grandfather's face, fully intact, treetop three hundred yards from a miscalculated blast. Like me, Stanley was a family man, so to speak, and damned to it.

Long before that I rented a room on a houseboat on the Hudson from a retired electrician and his psychic wife, who read horoscopes and analyzed handwriting and gingerly flim-flammed drink money any way she could, while her husband sat astern playing the ponies and point spreads over the phone. She divined by junipermancy—cloudy bottles of Gilby's—which fueled her visionary engines. He lost a lot more than he won. More than several nights I spent on park benches. I babysat plush apartments in the vacationing summer months. One of my last roosts was a flophouse on 43rd, near where I'd answered an ad for bookstore clerk and followed the address with a sinking heart closer and closer to Times Square. I stood squinting like a bag lady in front of a half-story neon sign. I inquired within and because of my size I started work that afternoon as a bouncer for live sex shows. I worked one week. Then I got a respectable job as a file clerk for a private foundation. They had no money, so no one asked for it, so I drank coffee and played pinochle with the other file clerk, who suggested the foundation was a front.

I ask Rosa, my guardian angel, if I should go back to Birmingham, if only for a week. She plucks a hair on my neck, as if to say, *it's your half-sister, dumbass.*

It's unsettling, though, that there's no mention of anyone else. Five years ago I left on fairly bad terms, bent on permanent exile from The Heart of Dixie, but there were Sunday mornings in Brooklyn Heights restaurants overlooking the East River with the sun in the elaborated cables of Brooklyn Bridge and the sunlight just so, a vast and painful clarity in the air when rain had rinsed the perpetual smutch out of the New York sky, the smell of bananas and coffee and bacon and the easeful rustle of Sunday papers, churchgoers fresh and scented, their obligation behind them, reclined in easeful conversation, their children scrubbed bright as dimes, well, some days this got to me in the worst sort of way, and the wind of the wing of homesickness with it.

Let me lay it out straight. Five years ago I left Birmingham because I found out I was legitimately in the condition of bastardy. Or was I an orphan? Anyway, there were married people involved, but I gathered they weren't the right ones. I have three sisters, all older, and a brother, the oldest, and they bear the indelible Clayborne-Randolph stamp. I look like my mother, only in a funhouse mirror, and not so well born as my siblings. All of them, including Father, are average height and medium build. I rolled out of my mother's womb like a stone wheel.

I'm 6'4" and a quarter—6'5" in grass cleats—and weigh 225. I played tight end at Catholic University in Washington, where I became famous for a merciless head-down truck-like attack after the quarterback with a quick flick would dump the ball off on the count of one, and then Webbo's gone, head down like a battering ram. As a boy, I was what they called *accident* prone. I fell from treetops and roofs, tumbled off bluffs, and flipped off swings and ropeladders, not to mention dozens of good whackings from dad. My head bled but never cracked and I suppose the repeated blows to my pate of horseshoes and cinderblocks and whatever else lay in the way of an accident determined to happen toughened my skull, but as a consequence I'm subject to fits of vertigo and visitations from the dead.

At first I played defensive end, but my sophomore year coach Erikson, a sadist of Viking descent, publicly humiliated me during a bull session, by playing back and forth the fourth quarter game film play that reveals me in a lapse of concentration running *away* from a power sweep of exoskeletons from Amherst. My flight cost us the opening contest. He switched me to tight end. I was a natural, with Velcro hands and monumental desire to run people over. I made all-conference my senior year, and got letters and bribes from a dozen scouts, when in my senior year in the homecoming game I got chopped down with a clip at the knee after an intercepted pass and cartilage and tendons tore like a rotten sail and I was stretchered off the field for good. I was sorry not to finish the season, but I had no intention of going pro. At fifty I wanted climb out of bed without crutches.

I'd played to impress girls, which worked, with the wrong ones, but a week after my accident I got a get-well card from a gorgeous studious sort in my astronomy class. She was an astrophysics major from South Carolina. My collegiate persona was sophisticated clod, the best a star athlete could expect from brainy sorts who weren't familiar with the game, so I assumed she never even noticed me.

In my heart I went wild.

I hobbled on my crutches over to her dorm room under a November moon. She signed my cast. We drove to Georgetown and celebrated the end of my career as a musclehead with a bottle of her favorite wine. We had dinner at Four Seasons. Her idea. Broke, we drove around Washington and laughed. That night the federal buildings were a riot. The Department of the Interior sent us reeling. The Supreme Court building justified a kiss. We tried but we were laughing too hard to pucker up. We nuzzled, shaking with laughter.

"I thought you'd think I was clod," I said, taking a breather.

"I do," she said, and started us up again.

We drove by The White House. It nearly finished us off.

Six months later we were engaged. And that engagement to Claire, oddly enough, orphaned me. Or did it bastardize?

Since her mother was dead, and her father—at least regarding me—was as sociable as a crawfish, Claire flew from Charleston to Birmingham to make spring wedding arrangements with my mother. This was seven months after I'd graduated cum laude with an English degree—a useless combination, but what the deuce—and I was dawdling and hawing at home with no prospects of a job and no immediate intention of arranging one. Claire's father owned a newspaper and a radio station, not to mention the real source of his lucre, a handful of hamburger franchises that dotted the Columbia by-ways, and real estate that involved everything from graveyards and shopping strips to baseball diamonds and downtown developments. It was no wonder Claire wanted to study the stars. Anyhow, I figured my father-in-law could get me work, if only as a batboy or newspaper reporter.

I hadn't seen Claire in three months and when I met her at the airport she iced over and crackled like Arctic spit. I'd ballooned to 260 from milk shakes and cheese melts and sausage dogs and from sleeping till noon with television huzzing its white noise of talk shows and Christian aerobics and endless reruns. My head was as soft as dough, my gladiatorial physique gone with it. She was understandably furious. She said she didn't want to marry a goddamn bloated *scumbag*, and to beat all, *unemployed*—language fairly shocking coming from her. On the way back from the airport she made several things even clearer, the worst of which was that her father, as much as he liked me (such a politician, Claire!) had no intention of offering me a job of any sort; I was to strike out on my own, and once I'd proven my mettle, he'd see where, *if* I fit in with any of his businesses.

I was ashamed. It was a dreary cold wet night in early December and when Claire broke into tears I felt like a real slob. The wipers flailed away and hi-beams blinded me. My heart was sodden. Between sobbings she told me she'd lied and told her father I had a job selling insurance. Was it the lying that bothered her, or was she ashamed to offer her father an insurance salesman for a son-in-law? He wanted to marry her Charleston *up*, some judge he made Claire date, with nuptial designs and a visions of a Whopper for a wedding cake. That was in July.

14

I flew out to Charleston, ordering sourmash two by two, and took a cab to his humble mansion, where the Yellow Cab tires crunched on the looping gravel drive. "Wait here," I told the driver. Live oaks sweated in the swampy heat, stockstill beneath the hot pines.

A butler greeted me holding a coat brush.

"Mr. Clayborne to see you, sir," he said over his shoulder.

Mr. Hunter, wearing a smoking jacket and bearing a glass of scotch, ushered me into his *librury*. We sat in somber hidebound wing chairs riveted with upholstery brass aside a monumental marble-mantled fireplace. The air-conditioner went gangbusters while a fire breathed up the flue.

"Could I interest you in a drink?"

"Jack Daniels," I said to the butler. "A double." Mr. Hunter pointed at his glass.

We stared at the fire until the butler brought the drinks.

"Where's Claire?" I asked.

"Son, I understand you wish to have my daughter's hand in holy matrimony. Unless I am laboring under some misapprehension, I believe her hand is already spoken for."

"You are. Where is she?"

"Presently engaged, son."

I leapt out of my chair, spilling watered-down bourbon on an oriental rug.

"*We're* engaged. Claire and *Webb*. *Ask* her." I waved my fist in his face.

He stood up.

"We have nothing further to discuss."

"Dumb grit cracker trash I'll kick your ass back to Bacon County."

"Don *talk* to me thata way, boy."

"*Whut*away?"

"Sumbitch *git*. *Out* of my house."

Mr. Hunter showed me the door, swearing at me in his native Okefenokan, a lapse of his acquired Charlestonian patois. A deep blunder. Even the butler, an ex-rice farmer from the Carolina bottoms, knew the score now. On the washed-gravel drive the butler brushed the drink off my shirt, repressing a triumphant hoot.

I sat in the cab down the street for hours, watching the meter rack up a sixty-dollar tab, while the driver slept. With no sign of Claire I headed back to the airport. Later I found out she was in Columbia shopping.

I never found out why she cried her eyes out that December when she mentioned her father, because the next afternoon when we took our blood tests down to the county license bureau, I was forced to confront a discrepancy that packed my marrying plans down the river of oblivion.

At the graduation night dance in May my heart clamored for Claire in her black strapless dress. Catholic University was pre-Vatican II nostalgic for a while, so at school-sponsored functions Tommy Dorsey was as smoky as the music got. The big band they hired, made up of Virginia Elks Clubs officers and Tidewater retirees and a D.C. pro-am golfer snake-charmer clarinetist, played a Dorsey rendition of "Oh Boy, Look at Him Now," and we wobbled like tops across the gymnasium floor. Like a rich daddy's daughter, she'd taken her ballroom dancing lessons dutifully and gone to cotillion uncomplaining, and that night after several of my left-footed attempts, my knee throbbing like a toothache, she took the lead and sailed me around the room to the joyful brass and sweet trumpets of post-war triumph, until I got too dizzy to stand.

Claire stood a leggy five foot ten. She had a wide bright face her disposition mostly matched and skyey eyes and the finest nose I've ever seen. That night her clavicles looked as wide as angels' wings. Claire also ran track and, swift as Virginia deer, she bolted in the May dark until breathless, and too drunk to mind my buckling knee, I tackled her on the wide lawn beside the chapel, where we deconsecrated the campus. That's all I kept thinking about six months later when we were standing at the county license counter, after Claire had said, looking at my blood test, "They've got the wrong blood type."

"What's wrong with O?"

"Your blood type is B."

"What do you know about that?" I asked.

"Last night your mother and I were looking through boxes of old papers for your birth certificate and there was a hospital record that said Edmund Webb, blood type B."

"But it says O here."

I stood at the counter thinking of nothing but the skeins of moonglow that night unraveling through the ancient oaks overhead, and the radiant sweet dark, and the sense that in our loving rut we were stirring up cyclones that would blow in from the Empyrean the angelic presence of new life. Sorry. I am a lapsed Catholic. Very lapsed, very Catholic. In more modern language, she was ovulating, and ripe for the deep pluck of a zygote's fish-tailed, frog-legged life. Seven weeks later a summer letter and she's five weeks late. A week later a letter; she's miscarried, and so heavy with blood she lay abed two days. When I called her and asked, a touch too angrily, if she'd stopped running when she thought she was pregnant, stonily a silence microwaved from Charleston; when I asked, a little aggressively, if she could tell boy or girl, I heard a plastic *clunk* clear across Dixie. I don't know why I wanted to blame her; it wasn't anyone's fault, only nature's way of voiding unwanteds. I called her back and asked her if we could try again. "Of course," she said, and exploded into tears. For an hour we cradled our misery over the telephone. The next day I flew out. We drove up to the Outer Banks of North Carolina and camping out tried morning noon and night to draw another angel down from the wild blue yonder. One exhausted afternoon I said, "This is a painful job," and Claire said, smiling like I couldn't believe, "But somebody's got to do it." So back down the road to the palace of wisdom we went.

"But I distinctly remember B," she said, adamant.

"I've had a change of heart and a change of blood." I kissed the downy slope where her temple indents, a skull curve that makes her look as smart as she is. "Maybe all those X-rays on my knee scrambled my genes. A,B,O,X, who cares?" I kissed her again. "The doc gave me a clean bill of health. No venereal diseases, no suspicious antibodies. A bit malty from the beer, but otherwise thick and red."

"Still, it said B, not O."

"Let's go home."

Late that night, I woke with a start. Curiosity deep with dread clutched at my chest. I crept down two flights of squeaking neo-colonial stairs and down another steep half-flight into the climate-controlled basement, where family records and Randolph memorabilia going back to Virginia pre-history lay disintegrating in cedar chests and old wooden filing cabinets my grandparents bought from a savings and loan that went belly up in '29. The grand Randolphs could afford them. The Virginia Historical Society had the best and the oldest of the rest of family antiques stored in their cavernous collections in Richmond. Once a year Mother visited to gaze at the dusty reliquiae—cherub-crested mirrors, beech *fauteuils* and William and Mary era American highboys, English commodes, wine chairs, pewter ewers, chocolate pots and sauce boats, tankards, a Georgian setee and Paul Revere teapots, and a Wedgewood Sphinx, as inscrutable and royal as a Randolph—before touring Hollywood Cemetery, where Virginia-born Presidents and Civil War dead and innumerable relations lay sleeping in the monumental sarcophagi, awaiting resurrection to save our troubled Republic.

In the cedar chests I found old photographs and flattened ballroom shoes and corroded trinkets and dance cards and wedding invitations forty years yellowed; books of ancient etiquette and crumbling romance novels; newspaper clippings and dozens of letters from corporals and captains who boasted and begged; lists of the dead or missing through V-E day; and a newspaper photograph of my mother and her sister Clara from the society column dated 1939, Richmond, Virginia. They're standing in front of a single-engine plane. The caption reads, "Randolph Sisters Take to the Skies." They have a quaint pre-war look, untouched by global depression. My mother's sister, ten years older, was wild for those days, and it's no doubt one of her boyfriend's planes they're posed so pleasantly in front of. It's good to know my mother's gaze, even then, was immobile and distant, like Washington's marble expression holding vigil over the Old Dominion from the Rotunda of the State Capitol. My aunt, on the other hand, looks ready to climb aboard the plane and loop the loop in a wild joyride over Virginia, land of Randolphs, a commonwealth of upright forefathers who spoke to my mother from the grave, but whose voices fell deaf on her sister's hellion ears.

As a young woman, my aunt had been a maddening beauty. I remember her with a clarity I can't account for, a great deal older than in the photograph, her drapey dresses billowing like clouds and her black highheels and seamed stockings way out of date, and cigarette smoke like a hazy halo around her head. But she was no angel. Too much booze and too many married boyfriends who swore divorce and too much carelessness fronting the public frowns and she found herself, so I'm told, completely alone. She never married, and went from lonely to crazy, dead-ending as an aristocratic wine-bag with imaginary friends who kept her company on her bench in Byrd Park. The last time I saw her—come to think of it, one of the few times I saw her—I couldn't have been more than seven or eight. She was wizened and pigeon-chested and had a humped breastbone that made me think she was born deformed, but when I saw pictures of her taken when she worked as a fashion plate in New York, I knew she started hearts wherever she went. Then she was rangy, with a bold face full of luster, and in one photograph she's animated enough to make you forget her later reputation. It's easy to see why Mother, mindful of proprieties, never got on with her. I remember Aunt Clara'a face, a trance of bewildered sadness, like a very old child's, when she bent down to look me in the eye.

Mother said by then she was given to wild fits and prolonged and unaccountable sorrows, which she drank to speechless numbness. Earlier, in her forties, time and nature threw the flag on her, and she went from ravishing to ravaged as fast as an equatorial sunset. Already simplified by drink, she sank even deeper with decades of barbiturates and amphetamines, and wound up roaming the streets of Richmond, a blueblood ghost. At sixty she fell through the floor of depression. She sat on her park bench for days without budging, oblivious to changes in weather, and became a ward of the state, until they found her only living near relation, my mother.

After years in a private facility, where her insurance was exhausted by every trick in the medical book, she was carted to a state asylum, where last I heard she hadn't spoken more than a few words in fifteen years. Once a year Mother visited her, after which she faced the collective outrage of my sisters, who wanted their aunt put in a private rest home, paid for by Clara's trust fund, which lay in limbo making money for no one. My mother absolutely refused. She had retrieved her sister from the streets and spared Clara death by exposure to an early autumn freeze and saved herself a trip to the city morgue, and that, in her mind, was all she owed her.

But back to bastardy. Questions mined in my heart like larvae in leaves. For hours I lingered over the detritus of a long dead age that had little or no bearing and held even less interest for me, well, because I *knew* in those filing cabinets and aromatic chests something lay waiting, some jack-in-the-box in the thicket of documents poised to spring in my face and startle me, like a child, into fearful tears. Why was my heart beating in my neck? What was I afraid of? Jewel-eyed Claire had been certain from what she saw my blood type was B; the blood test for the marriage license said O. A laboratory error, then or now? A secretary's mistake, then or now?

I came across the copy of the hospital record Claire had mentioned. When I was seven I put my fist through a doorpane, by accident. I was chasing my sister Amelia around the carport, terrorizing her with my hand-me-down coonskin cap and Davy Crockett flintlock, when she bolted through the back door into the kitchen, slamming it behind her. I put out a good halfback stiff arm from the days of leather helmets, but all I caught was glass. The way in was fine; the reflex return from elbow to wrist turned my arm into ribbons of blood, rivulets and crimson spouts. I passed out. I was vampire-white going to bloodless blue by the time the ambulance pulled up to the emergency room, where in surgery I almost died twice, the first time from blood loss, the second from a mix-up with blood type that sent me into wild-eyed shock.

As Claire had said, the form read blood type B. From a filing cabinet I pulled my mother's hospital and health insurance folder, filled with expired policies and old bills, and found hers, AB; then to my father's, where a copy of a VA check-up read O. I was pre-med for a semester, before I discovered I didn't relish the sight of blood, and I knew at least this much: it is possible for an O and an AB to produce a B type, but not an O. Either the lab or nurse made a mistake 19 years ago or less than 24 hours ago. The most recent mistake seemed the most likely, a typo from a lab tech's scrawl, for instance, so I gathered the documents together and climbed out of the basement and went up to my room on the third floor where, convinced it was an error, I slept not a whit. Twice I got up and looked in the mirror. Who was that looking back? This wasn't an identity crisis, exactly. I was familiar enough with myself. My reflection reminded me of the vase in psychology books that suddenly becomes two profiles, back to back. And some voice in my head was trying to tell me things I knew I never wanted to hear, but for the life of me I couldn't have said what those things were. My reflection wouldn't shift, look as I might. Back in bed I tumbled and scratched and tossed in sleeplessness, and, my nerves frayed like fiberglass, I got up and wandered in the yard.

In the rose and saffron glow of dawn I crept into the guest

room, where Claire lay on her back gently breathing, content as a child, her arms folded in unthinking sleep. Claire has a large angular head, with cheekbones that rise up toward her feline eyes like rosy plums. She lay asleep in a bountiful tangle of brown hair. I kissed her cheekbone plums and she stirred, murmuring, her body poured out into deep pools of sleep, pleading for me to plunge and drown. But my heart was tied up in knots and knurled with uncertainties. I knelt by the bed, thinking and unable to think, and watched her sleep. That was the last time I saw her.

Hours later, I sat in a doctor's waiting room, a ball of cotton pressed in the crook of my arm, thumbing through magazines, my lip twitching, an itch in the arch of my foot, my heart pounding like a war drum. A young and attractive nurse entered the waiting room. "Mr. Clayborne," she said, and motioned me to an examination room. I stood dizzily beside a table of tongue depressors.

"There's no doubt about it. Blood type O."

"What if I were given blood transfusions for B when my blood type is O?"

"Probable extinction," she said. Why was she joking? She looked hungover from some late night dancing and for the moment enjoyed a giddy fatigue. I understood. Still, how could she trifle with my life blood? "But it depends on how much blood you lost," she added.

"Yes, it does."

She looked at me expectantly.

"Well, how much did you lose?"

"All of it," I said.

I punched the gas all the way home, and rounded the winding drive like an ambulance driver. I walked slightly staggered through the living room of antebellum daguerreotypes of Randolphs and tarnished imitation Paul Revere silver services—the originals on loan to the Virginia Museum, safe from scions and pawnshops—

and faded crocheted silk coverlets on the lumpy loveseats and all the dust and cave-stale dregs and leftovers of some age long past pathetically dead—in light of what I discovered it seemed plain ludicrous now—and down the dark hall to my mother's wing of the house, where I found her where she usually is, on the phone cross-patching publication dates and paper prices and corporate grant money for the historical quarterly she trustees voluntarily, propped there like a queen amidst a wide bed of shuffled papers and press releases and stacks of manuscripts, autographed biographies of crooners and celebrity diet books for fund raisers and wall calendars of the Huntsville Rocket Center and the Sloss furnace now turned into a corroding and dragonish monument to the slag and poverty and slaves and riots and blood and fire and endless lynchings by which The Magic City flourished—magic indeed!—and built to escape its own smoking ruin the crowning suburb Mountain Brook, while my mother stares to the other wall where a Chamber of Commerce drawing of the first Capitol of the Confederacy in Montgomery looks like some sharecropper's idea of Monticello—oh no, we're not from this godforsaken-old-times-dar-are-not-forgotten state of cross-burning Baptist boll weevils but old Virginnie bluebloods gone to Alabama pot—and she's sitting there talking and I shove wide the door and I see her peek over a stack of unsolicited historical romances while she's listening to some country club bird towhee a book club soiree and or a reading by a professional deadbeat.

She gives me a pleasant quizzical abstracted look when I roar not once but twice, *Who the hell's my father?*

She tells the tennis-and-cocktail polite society lady she'll call her back later. She looks up at me white as a candle.

She opens a pill bottle on the nightstand and takes a nitroglycerin.

"Your father?"

"Who the hell's my father?"

"Young man, who do you *think* is your father?"

23

"You tell me."

"Twenty-one years old and four years of college and you can't say? Your *father* is your father. Why would you think otherwise?"

I hand her the hospital records: pneumonia at three; at seven 200 hundred stitches from the broken window; the two blood tests.

"What makes you think I have time for these fool fantasies? Simply because you've neither felt nor rarely acted like a part of this family? Now you set out to prove it with O's and B's and other such nonsense? An error, young man. A secretary who can't tell one letter of the alphabet from another. Leave it alone. It's not worth it."

"What's not worth it?"

"Pretending you know something you don't."

"Who the *hell* is my father?"

"The man upstairs." She hands back the forms. "Edmund Clayborne, the man I married, the father of his children."

Well, not much else came of the confrontation, except that I bellowed for a while longer, something I am stubbornly wont to do when I get stirred, though it usually passes faster than a summer thunderhead, while she denied everything over and over again, even when I told her what she already knew, who-ever got the low watt notion of changing my blood type to protect someone or something no one would ever know anything about anyway unless they found out because they discovered the blood type had been changed, well, they just've well poured my blood into Jell-O molds because they almost gummed it up for good anyhow, but she said it was a mistake the hospital made in all the excitement and confusion, *I* wasn't the only one seriously injured there, she had seen to it personally the nurse responsible was dismissed, and I said does this form in 1963 say B and the hospital record from 1967 say B and the blood type for the marriage license and she tries to interrupt, but I continue saying why does this form for 1963 say B, but if I hold it up to the light it says O where it's been whited out and typed over? Is this the form you had the presence of mind to take with you when I was lying half dead on the garage floor? And who in hell knows about this besides you and me? I hand her back the forms and her hands are shaking just so and she tells me she understands by saying that she doesn't and I say who does? Maybe Father does. She says *no* like it was knocked out of her but before she can get up and around the mountainous heaps of historical essays overflowing from the bed and running along the walls halfway to the ceiling and cry *no no no no* in a voice I do not recognize I'm out the door, thinking I'll head down the hallway and up two flights of stairs to my father's floor of the house, an office and bedroom and makeshift monastery, where I'll blast the door open with a left and before he can say a word I'll say Who are *you* and he'll say What? and I'll say Who *are* you and he'll put down a folder of insurance vouchers and stand up but I'll knock him with a punch to the solar plexus back into his wooden Depression-era bank chair and head down the stairs through the living room into the front hall and out the door, slamming it so hard the doorjambs splinter and now my father, whoever the broom-beating belt-whipping son-of-a-bitch kicker of some other man's son's ass *is*, he'll be mad as hell as he storms out on the front porch with its hollow neo-colonial columns and plywood Corinthian capitals and pre-fab Williamsburg woodwork, where he'll say, Fix the door and I'll say, Fix it? I'll fix it all right, and with a motion I could have only gotten out of a martial arts movie I'll give the solid oak door a sidewinding kick that'll snap it like a melba cracker clean in two, and I'll say See it's fixed and he'll be coming at me now, slowly, mad and afraid, and I say *Who are you* right in his eternal damnation face and he'll grab my shirt with both fists and say Fix the door and before I know it I'll lift him up and toss him off the porch into the boxwoods that front the house and I'll be down the stairs, down the hill, and gone, blind as a rhino.

Instead, I'm nearly flattened by a fit of vertigo, which I get hit with whenever I'm stressed, or overloaded like a cable span, and I can hear my brain joints creaking, and everything yaws and swings, everything going to its own gyroscope, each one at a different tilt. I take jerky, unsteady steps, like a dog on a circus ball, and I make it to the stairwell john without falling down, where I sit with my head between my legs until the blood-rush in my ears slows to a swirl.

I study myself in the mirror.

I hear a faint and desperate *Webb* echoing up the stairs. I plan out what clothes for the duffel bag, and which for the suitcase, and the shortest route to the S & L, and then downtown to the Trailways station, where I guaranteed won't be cuffed by emotional pleas or pains of conscience for fleeing Birmingham, Alabama and the whole damned Look away Dixieland mulefield and suburban swamps of the deep South, since the station's right smack dab in the middle of shantytown, where Mountain Brook's white-as-bare-ass fleece don't dare show their well-grazed hides, as much out of lily-livered fear as guilt that if the loan of blood and fire were called due they'd freeze dead in their tracks and know in their bones it *ought* to go down, that final payment so feared a whole community has buried itself alive with country club luxury and Aunt Jemima maids and Garden club food drives for the downtown honeychiles by means of generations of well-disguised bad conscience now as buck naked as the Emperor on parade and denuded of any relation to reality, from which bus station I'll light out for New York for good, because all I ever heard of New York is it's a surefire place to hole up, honeycomb or catacomb, I didn't care.

Bill sits and clips. The sun goes down. Scott and Mike crash through the door. They've been at Puffy's all Sunday afternoon.

26

"You work tomorrow?" Scott asks me. Scott considers himself the foreman. He finds all the work, so I suppose he should.

"Sheetrock?"

"We leave at five-thirty. Lower East side. Avenue E." He eats a leftover hamburger from the refrigerator and retires to his quarters. He is soon snoring.

Bill says to Mike, "Webb's going back to Alabamy."

"With an Uzi on his knee."

"Pay your rent."

"Check's in the mail," I say.

"Can't take New York, huh?" Mike says.

"Can't take all this art."

"Neither can I." He passes out on the floor, wrapped in a sleeping bag, beside the air compressor.

"When are you leaving?" Bill asks.

"Thursday."

"We'll miss you."

"Need a new loftmate?"

"Got somebody in mind?"

"Becky."

"Some Anglo-Saxon Ivy League ball-cutting manhating feminist harpy?"

"Doubtful. She had lunch with me, didn't she?"

"Temperance League?"

"She likes Chianti. She said her nipples were pierced."

"At least they're not fake."

"She lied."

"She has implants?"

"Heavens no."

"It's the thought that counts."

"Absolutely gorgeous flawless war-worthy gifts from God. If you folks were real artists you'd immortalize her."

"This is the end of the second millennium, Webb. Venus has been in a coma for decades. Beauty doesn't cut it anymore. I mean, Americans love the Big Ugly. Beauty is enough for *me*, but art has got to be *political*. I mean, when two guys simultaneously ejaculate on a porn star's face, and she appears to be in some kind of ecstacy about it, it can't just be an *orgy*. Everybody wants it to mean something significant."

"Like what? Bad form?"

"Oppression. Femicide."

"If you don't believe the theory, then how can you make art about it?"

"Because I'm a hypocrite."

"What about Becky?"

"Let her slum it here for a while. We'll build her a room. If she doesn't mind the occasional violent dancing and bottle smashing we'd love to have her. What does she do?"

"For a living?"

Monday and Tuesday I hang sheetrock in a burned out building. Wednesday night I go to CBGB's to hear a band called The Firebirds. The music is so loud my eardrums crackle like blown speakers. Coming out of the boy's room during a break I see Becky at the bar talking to a skinhead with a fake diamond stud in the side of his nose.

I take her arm.

The skinhead yells, "Back off." His tongue is pierced by a silver diaper pin.

I stand in his face, near a foot taller. He turns around and drinks his beer. I watch and wait and as he swings the bottle around I hit him on the pierced ear with the heel of my hand. He slides down the bar, leaning to catch his balance, and trips over his army boots.

Becky and I go out onto the street. Customized choppers line the gutter, their dense spokes predatory and shiny under the vapor lights.

"You owe me fifty dollars."

"No I don't."

She pulls me around the corner and unbuttons her shirt. I ease my hands inside and we exchange a nearly violent kiss, all teeth and tongue. I bite her neck and she throws a leg around my waist.

"Showtime." An off-duty cop working security watches us.

Becky buttons her shirt.

"Clear out of here," he says. "Pinhead has gone to get his friends."

We take a cab back to Water Street. We approach the Brooklyn Bridge and Becky hands me a vial of white powder.

"No, not coke."

"Better."

From her palm we snort two or three stinging lines.

"What is it?"

The cabbie turns up a wild Hindi music. A picture of Guru Nanak hangs from the dashboard.

"How do you feel?"

"Like a god." I lick her hand.

"Which one?"

"Orpheus."

"Wasn't he torn limb from limb by a bunch of women?"

"With pleasure."

She snorts another line and puts her hands under my shirt and rubs my chest.

"Leaves," she says.

Home I pin up the blanket. We make love, clumsily at first, then drift off as the sun comes up.

The alarm goes off at nine. Below us machines stamp sheet metal.

Becky sleeps. I pack my duffel bag.

"Where are you going?" she asks.

"Home," I say.

"Why?" She's mostly asleep.

"My sister's sick."

"Same old."

"I think she's sick this time. Really."

"How do you know?"

"My guardian angel."

"Her again." She falls asleep.

I sit by a window in the back of the 737. The plane is half-full, with the stern nearly empty. An older woman, as cleanly scented and gently wrinkled as a nun, sits in the inside aisle seat knitting. She has been talking about her niece for forty-five minutes.

"Excuse me," I say.

"Yes?"

"Do you think we could change the subject?"

She laughs out loud.

"Help yourself."

I'm liable to get a fit of the spins when I fly, what with the miles and hours I'm up, with the hush of air ducts, and one lone red light blinking on the wing outside my window, while below, way below, arterial windings of a river lizard-tail into small bays and fishcamp deltas, piney developments tentacled out from every city, their houses like board game real estate randomly attached at rivery nerve ends. Over farm land the roads are caulk lines, and the quilty spring greening is the color of tennis courts. Directly outside, cloud swatches of humpy peaks climb to thunderclouds, and in the distance spiny ribs of cirrus look suspended in currents, though I know they're tossed along at a stormy clip, like the lost souls I read about in catechism class, driven to and fro by every desire, though they look as placid as glass. Now if I look up, my head swims into lightheaded eddies, and the earth wheels away, because above the horizon's blue arc and bow-bend, the wide sky gives into infinity, and that's more than any body can bear.

I say *Rosa, hold on tight,* and the stewardess bringing my Jack Daniels cuts me a sideways look, like I'm fresh because I'm flush with bourbon, but she doesn't know Rosa is my Guardian Angel.

"Rosa used to be my grandmother," I tell the knitting woman, and explain that when she died my regular guardian angel got the afternoon off, so to speak, since to an angel a lifetime must look like a rapidly passing fact, a wink in the face of a number of suns. I've wondered if Rosa always *was* my guardian angel, only I didn't know it until the day she died. In her translated shape, she's airier, for certain, but more focused, like light through a magnifying glass. I could tell that day she was glad to go. Her body was a creaky leaky chuffing old machine, and quarrelsome, with a will of its own to fall apart. She sang her favorite arias from Italian operas, and looked heavenward in mock distress when her voice cracked, because she'd been a tuning fork soprano in her twenties, with recitals in New York before the first World War. She had a knack for turning scientific data into Thomist proofs for the immortality of the soul. One Easter after dinner I asked her what happened when you died, since Jesus had, but hadn't, escaping the jaws of eternal entombment, unlike heretics, I later learned, who lay sealed in molten coffins forever after judgment day, cooked to excruciating consciousness. She took a prism from my Edmund Scientific Kit and threw an arc of the covenant along the wall. I asked her if we changed colors? We go back *through* the prism, she said, and become a beam of light. I believed her. When she started fading, I stayed by her bed for days. Unable to sing, and too feeble to sanctify science, she knew it was time to go—back.

Like other Catholics, I grew up with the idea of a guardian angel. I took the hovering, winged thing for granted, and thought of it as an anonymous kind presence fresh from the snowy upper reaches of eternity, occasionally bid by childish pranks—like altar boys drinking untransubstantiated wine, or chiming the cluster of Mass bells to the Rolling Stones—to thrum a chord of conscience with a You-better-watch-out St. Nicholas riff. But the night she died Rosa came to me in a dream, bright as bright, and said she'd be taking over for a while. I needed a little extra protection, so I wouldn't drive into a ditch, or fall off a plane, so disoriented do I get in the mechanical crunch of the world. She wouldn't interfere, mind you, just nudge me on every so often.

I woke that morning and rang out at the dawn. I was so glad she wasn't *dead*.

My life is no proof, but I believed her. She always said she had visions of the Virgin Mary. Until she died I thought her waking dreams were more manger-and-stable peasant superstition leftover from the old country, or shrinking brain cells, or a chemical imbalance, but that morning some heavenly notion opened up and I haven't felt the same since. Not that I haven't fumbled and blundered big time, but she wasn't supposed to headhunt and find me a corporate sinecure, or play broker for my paramour Claire, but shine a little light into my noggin every so often. So I've gotten into the habit of talking to her, sometimes out loud, without thinking, in public places, but mostly inwardly pleas when I feel a fit of vertigo gaining, like a kid on a roller coaster who knows with every clank of the chain-link the cars climb to that first big drop, and then it's soul rived from bone in a dizzying rush to nowhere, involuntary screams and all.

My family father, Edison Clayborne, is Catholic, so I was raised one—in the South that's no easy feat—because he insisted if his daughters were to be brought up Randolph style, Virginia Anglican aristocrats who say No Can Do to Papal Bulls and Roman Sees and Latin babble, let alone Virgin worship, then his sons would be raised in the best Roman Catholic tradition available, which in America, and in the South, is admittedly not much, but better to his mind that the English-saddle sort of snobbery his wife enhanced the farther away from Virginia she got, a kind of *Town and Country* envy of some now fallen state of family grace. My alleged father is Catholic because his mother, Rosa, was a full-blooded Italian from a farming village in the Monti Lattari, overlooking the Gulf of Salerno and the Tyrrhenian Sea, with a southern view of Vesuvius, where she was born in a manger, my mother once remarked, an Old Country nativity my mother didn't discover until seven years and three children had taprooted her to the Clayborne hearth for the monogamous duration. This was before I was begot, by whomever, but from what I understand she didn't take it very well, because Italian-peasant taint for a First Family blood was akin to miscegenation, her estimation of Southern Mediterranean, who had mixed with the dark tribes of Africa when the Holy Roman Empire fell. Rosa was allowed to visit her grandchildren Thanksgiving, Christmas, and Easter, during which holidays she was treated with an icy cordiality obvious to even an eight-year-old. When Rosa died I was nineteen; my bedside vigil didn't have my mother's approval. Maybe Mother was as surprised by Rosa's nativity as *I* was by my doctored up blood types. She got the full picture when my sister Amelia was born olive swart, with black, gypsy eyes, when her first children had arrived lanoline pale, with the bluest of blood beneath the alabaster skin.

Rosa came over with her parents and ten brothers and sisters in the late 1880's when she was five, and from what I gather there were unwritten laws which governed her Italian relations: you either stuck with blood and built a community and survived by slow assimilation; or, rebelling against the *paterfamilias* you did what Rosa did, marry an Anglo-Saxon and do your best to become one. Given the times, she was lucky she didn't *look* very deep southern wop, meaning Sicilian, according to my mother's international sociology. Though she spoke fluently her native tongue, Rosa uttered it only when she had a longing look, usually praying for her father, long estranged by his daughter's marriage, and now beyond forgiving and forgetting, in moments of reflection during Mass. Her English had no accent, but her Latin was a Gregorian song of lyrical inflection *Italiano*. I was allowed to attend early service with her twice a year. She went every day at dawn.

When she married an architect in nineteen-five and moved to the suburban Bronx, she assumed an American name and life,

Rosa Clayborne, soprano, voice instructor; thus Anglicized, she exiled herself forever from the Ellis Island clan. When one of her brothers was killed in a construction accident, she didn't find out about it for ten years. Only one brother, Annibile, the youngest, showed up at her funeral. He was born in Brooklyn, a complete surprise to his weary mother, and was only seven when Rosa eloped. He admired her; she was a family mystery, a disgrace, an inspiration. He graduated Columbia Law and when I met him he was long retired from practice. He showed me a very old photograph, taken before he was born. There were forty-odd people in the dim picture, aunts uncles cousins and grand-parents who followed the first wave over. He pointed to a ten-year-old girl standing next to a man in a trim jacket, monocle, and slender tie. He has his arm around her. That's little Rosa, he said. They called her little Rosa. I asked him who the man was. Pa*pa*, he said. Annabile hardly remembered his sister, or when she left.

Such estrangement is a lifelong ache, because when she lay dying at ninety-five, she mistook me again and again for her Pa*pa*, whom she begged for forgiveness in twilight delirium. People say I look like him, judging from the photographs we found in Rosa's dresser, but that doesn't make any sense now. In New York, though, before I'd stop and consider, my heart would long for families missed, whole branches never to be known, dozens of Italian cousins and great uncles and god-mothers vanished in one vow three-quarters of a century said. And my father's father, whom I never knew, didn't fare any better in the feuding. My mother claimed that his family bribed, pleaded, threatened, and finally conceded his marriage under one condition, that he never bring any of the half-breeds around, which is as much as saying to any man with a thumbnail of pride to get lost. Which he did. So the Clayborne-Cerusi tree was clipped to a single branch. My paternal grandfather was older than Rosa, and when he died from drink after his business busted during the Great Depression—WPA to blame, according to my putative dad—my surname father and his Americanized mother were left, a middle-class pieta with the Italian blood absorbed in the swab of the Clayborne name, with no one knowing the least thing better, until the forth toss of genetic dice turned up Gypsy Amelia, our dark Cleopatra, and everyone knew, without exactly knowing, some duskier blood had washed ashore in an FFV.

"When I say my guardian angel is my dead grandmother," I say, "maybe you think I'm crazy as a shithouse mouse, but look around you any day of the week and see what notions people entertain, ideas about the world they take as kiss-the-bible-truth. It's the Age of Belief." People will believe anything, I explain. "Alien abductions, voices from Pluto, vegetable souls, but hell, just observe the way people treat each other in public, with the decorum of mating rams, then tell me I've flipped because I believe in angels and devils, or that I belong in the laughing academy because I believe my grandmother is a benign ghost who keeps me from jumping off bridges and stepping into passing traffic, and who counsels me mostly without speaking, telepathically, like the time I chewed peyote and had a conversation with a horse, though we spoke not a word. Or that I'm nuts because I believe she guides me. Never often enough, I admit, about matters of the heart. Easing my stubbornness, keeping me from throwing fists when a word or two will do, and in general preventing the devil from roaring like a lion and knocking down my soul like a bowling pin. In New York, when I was in the mood to break bones, or mostly felt like dancing on the lip of the abyss, with no reason and nowhere to go but the bottom of the Hudson, Rosa set me straight and buoyed me up, occasionally making an airy appearance to let me know I wasn't gripped. Call it superstition. Delusion, if you so subscribe. I only know what I know. It's real enough to me, even if she only comes around when I'm circling the whirlpool, and *still* I don't sail right, by the lights of the ghost ship Catholics call the soul, even if we are, as bunko scientists say, just sophisticated fango, complex chemicals, or protozoa in cosmic pondwater, with the misfortune of being aware of it."

"You are a very troubled young man," the knitting woman says, smiling. "But you'll turn out all right. You've got the right instincts."

"I only rant and rave when I drink."

"Splendid. You'll stop when you need to."

I ask the stewardess for another Jack Daniels.

"We are not permitted to serve more than five drinks to a customer."

"She wants one," I say, pointing to the woman.

"Two," the woman says.

I down those and order two more.

"Absolutely not," the stewardess says.

"Temperance League?"

"Excuse me?"

"Do you have breast implants?"

The knitting woman laughs like an old witch.

When she moves up the aisle I go to the restroom. At the stewardess's station a cart of miniatures sits begging to be unpacked of its mighty burden. I stuff bottles in my jeans pocket.

I turn around and what looks like the co-captain heads my way looking most officious. He's carrying handcuffs.

"You're under arrest."

"What for?" He hasn't noticed the theft. "So I'm drunk. I'm also obnoxious. I was born flatfooted, and obviously stupid. Not to mention suicidally depressed. And a bastard. Let's not forget that. My sister is sick. Understand? I'm having a serious problem here, going back to Alabama. You should sue your plastic surgeon. It's a wonder you can fly a plane."

"I am authorized by federal law to restrain you until we reach our destination meanwhiles."

"What ever you say."

"Rotate one hundred and eighty degrees."

"Likewise."

"He means turn around," the knitting woman says.

He snaps the cuffs on and sits me down.

"I'll watch him," the knitting woman says. The co-captain heads to the bow. The older woman takes a miniature sourmash from my front pocket and unscrews it. She takes a sip. "Open wide," she says.

Below, the outlying suburban lights look like ordered rows of stars. We fly over Shades Valley. My wrists ache. I see the cuckold Vulcan, Birmingham's mascot, still holds his vigil atop Red Mountain. The plane drops abruptly, like a rise in the road that gives the sensation of falling, but this is no illusion, we *are* falling, a controlled crash on asphalt and concrete, wings vying with the wind for a balanced touchdown.

We taxi to the terminal. Up in a cirrus whoosh of thin air, we're liable to feel flung too far for the viscera that dovetails ghost to bone. But back on the stony ground, we feel heavy of heart, overloaded and waiting, like pack animals, for someone to unload us. If we could fly like angels of our own free will, if only over a treetop, we'd put every psychologist in the book out to pasture, where they could chew their cuds and make meadow muffins all the live-long day, to no one's bother.

Co-captain Bob escorts me to the gate, where a crowd of travelers and rides-home watch a beefy burr-cut Birmingham police officer cuff me again and read me my rights. I look around for the knitting woman but she's doesn't appear with the rest of the passengers.

"Do you know Bull Conner?" I ask.

"Shut up," he says.

He shoves me down into the back seat of the patrol car and flips on his light and siren to get around the congested traffic. The CB cracks alive.

"Forty-two."

"Forty-two," he shouts into the microphone. "In transit with

37

the twenty-three. Over and out."

"Pick up a bag of bar-be-*qyoo*."

"Roger."

As we head to the downtown lockup he says, "Boy, you're drunk," again and again, each time with a different emphasis.

"Evidently," I say.

"Best watch your New York attitude. We don't take kindly to *New* Yorkers coming down here kicking up Dixie dust." He says "New" as if to make it rhyme with "Jew."

"But I'm *from* this godforsaken shithole."

"Shut up, boy. I said shut *up*, boy. This is the land of cotton, boy, so don't go *nigger* on me." He whacks the passenger seat with his billy club. "Sonny boy you're drunk. So keep your mouth *shut*."

"Yes sir."

"*Boy*."

"I could whip your fat ass from dawn to Sunday, and you know it. Take off these cuffs. I dare you. Mano a mano. I'll make you piss blood."

The officer, who suddenly reminds me of Gomer Pyle's Sergeant Carter, whips the patrol car off the side of road along a row of warehouses, and leaps out. He opens rear door and hits me one two three four five six seven eight nine times on arm and shoulder.

"*Boy*," he says. "Are you resisting arrest?"

"I'm *under* arrest, you idiot."

He whacks me one two three four more times.

"Goddamn it," I say. "Cut it out. You piece of human shit, cut it out."

He laughs. "I thought you'd see it my way."

"You remind me of someone I know." I wince. Tears of pain fill my eyes.

"I don't know *nobody* from *New* York."

We pull into Plantation Bar-be-que. Painted on the side of the old brick building is a bug-eyed moon-faced Negro wearing a chef's hat and grinning like a dunce, a conversational bubble hand-painted above his head: YES SUH! IT'S COOKED IN DE *PIT!* The arresting officer locks me in the car and returns with a grocery bag of sandwiches.

"Beating a Yankee sure gives a Rebel an appetite," he says, mouthing and tearing at a sandwich while he drives, lights and siren blazing.

"Getting beat too. Mind if I have one?"

"Sure."

He tosses one in the back seat. I open the butcher paper with my mouth and eat the sandwich off the vinyl. I'm sorry to discover it's the best damn bar-be-que sandwich I've ever tasted.

"Thank you suh!" I say between bites.

At the station I'm searched, photographed, fingerprinted, formally charged with drunk and disorderly conduct and put in a holding tank where 30-odd other misdemeaning guests of the city jail— mostly Afro-American—pace miserably and wait for a greasy pay phone to come free so they can arrange their bail money.

"Man what's you white ass doing in jail?" He's drunker than I am, eyes yellow and boiling.

"Drinking."

"*Man.* Driving too?"

"Flying."

"Flying *drunk.* Shit. Don get on *this* dude's plane," he says to the room. A few laughs.

"Got drunk on the plane coming down."

"Now what's wrong with that?"

"You got me."

"I's just walking down the street. Po-lece man said I kep falling down. Bout tore *up* that sidewalk, falling down." He laughs. "Broke up sidewalk with my *head.*"

Around nine-o'clock I call a bail bondsman. I'm assured the paperwork won't be done before three tomorrow afternoon, even if I make bail tonight.

We're locked up in cells with two bunks apiece, more padded board than bed. I climb on the top. I'm alone until two or three in the morning, when another lit drunk is ushered in. He rants and raves about his gun and how the police took it away even though he was on his own property and wasn't waving it at *him*. Then he takes a tremendous foul dump accompanied by such gaseous squeaks and deep methane sighs it almost sounds like an intestinal conversation. The toilet backs up and over-flows, flooding the concrete floor, where a drain takes all of the beastly cuck but the leaves the odor. I sit up and before I can blink I projectile vomit.

"My goddamned .44, my sweet baby .44," the drunk says over and over again, and passes out.

In the morning we are given mops and buckets of hot water and piney disinfectant and asked to swab the cells. Then we are marched into another holding tank, where we are fed a break-fast of peanut butter and jelly sandwiches and thin coffee. My mouth is so dry I can't swallow. Lunch is mashed potatoes and grey meat. I drink water and pee and drink water. Soon I don't feel half as bad as I should. The pain in my arm and shoulder makes me forget about the hangover.

At three-thirty they return our wallets and shoestrings and loose change and spring last night's drunks and D.W.I.'s. I have a court date in ten days.

I shoulder my duffel bag. At a pay phone down the street I make a collect call. I expect Mother or Father.

To my half-sister I say, "Hattie?"

II

Hattie floors her hatchback through the Red Mountain Roadcut. It's dusk. She's told me about Birmingham and how it's changed and about Mountain Brook and how it hasn't, except for a fire at the Jr. High, and now she's talking about me.

"You look good, Webb. Lost some weight."

"You too."

"You lying sack of shit." She punches me on the arm. "I'm *fat*."

"Never looked better."

"You never should have left."

"New York?"

"Birmingham. *Home*."

"Once."

A while back the highway builders blasted a wedge out of Red Mountain to build an eight lane throughway. Geological flexures eons-old were laid open. Paleontologists from around the world flew in to excavate fossils buried deep in the strata. They found starfish and coral sponges printed on rock and whale bones buried under layers of volcanic ash. When plates of earth floating on the molten mantel collided, layers buckled, shoving up the Appalachians.

Behind us the valley where Birmingham was built was once underwater, a swamp of drowsy dinosaurs, but the city's history doesn't suggest it's evolved since giant reptiles foraged in the

41

shallows. At least a Birmingham *Negro* wouldn't say so, while Mountain Brook Medici maintain The Magic City is Southern Renaissance, a Dixified Florence. It's a question of perspective. You can see whatever you please from a hummock of assets.

Mountain Brook is where Hattie and I are headed. The Claybornes moved there from Richmond fifteen years ago, when the love child was eleven. It's a community goose-fat and feathered with its own importance, *over* Red Mountain, away from the steel mills' croaking smokestacks that money the luxury.

I see drill lines where dynamite was fed deep into the folds. Dynamiting a mountain is Birmingham's style.

"Familiar?" she asks. Hattie interrupts her analysis of Docie's psychodramas and the family constellation.

"Enough."

The Cut reminds me of Brad, our high school fullback. The Mountain Brook team was labelled the *Trojans* by city council, a team mascot that made us the city division laughing stock, and forced us to prove we were tough when crosstown teams called us limp dicks in fourth-quarter pile-ups. We were rich to begin with, so when we played Irondale or Sylacauga or South Gadsden, our bus was stoned by locals, a lot of whose fathers worked for ours. I hardly blamed them. Saturday nights in autumn we pulled up to the creaking, acid eaten stadia and de-bussed in full gear, helmets on, against a rain of rocks and bottles.

Because of Brad we made it to the city championship my junior year, and lost, but we earned some redneck respect, which meant a lot to us, since we knew in our hearts we deserved to get out asses kicked. Brad was a blond block, as fleet as a wingback when he hit the open field. Once during punt return practice I nailed him on the numbers. The punter sliced the ball high off the side of his foot, and when Brad came up under it near the sidelines, I was already a runaway train. The next thing I know Brad is asking me if *I'm* all right. I felt wambly, my head took such a hit, so the coach told me to call it a day. Before I turned in Brad apologized for laying me out.

We all figured Brad was Alabama-bound, to play for The Bear, and then to the pros, but one night when he was drunk up on Red Mountain he fell off the ledge of the Cut and broke his neck. He lived six weeks. I went to see him before he died. What could I say? I felt helpless standing there, hardly able to look him in the eye, knowing he was a goner. I smoothed the sheet. His eyes were shining. He didn't say a word. I knew he wanted me to leave. Soon he didn't want to see anybody. He got psychotic from being paralyzed. The doctors said that's what happened; he'd have been better off dying on the spot.

Brad had been reared Catholic and went to St. Francis' Church like I did. We were altar boys together in sixth grade, my first year here. Right before he died he asked for a priest. He was in an isolation room, because near the end he started screaming every minute he was awake. He kept screaming, The Holy Ghost, The Holy Ghost. I understand he died screaming. Even the priest was spooked. I stood in the hospital lobby holding Teresa, his sister, after my only visit. Brad's father was a devout Catholic with every reason to doubt. He sat on a chair outside the hospital room with his head in his hands, smiling weirdly.

"There's a museum up there," Hattie says.

I see a fenced-in walkway on the highest reach. Over the ledge a model brontosaur leans dumbly.

"Let's go," I say.

"Home?"

"Another hour won't matter."

She takes the first exit and turns back up the steep hill to the Roadcut Museum. It's closed. On the dinosaur's tail someone has scratched a Confederate flag, which someone else turned into a swastika.

"Reptiles," Hattie says. "They deserve each other."

She spins the car around and descends onto the freeway.

"I have to get back to New York," I say.

"I understand."

"I have a job."

"I see. What kind?"

"Professional escort."

"A body guard," she says.

"Exactly. I escort billionaire stockbrokers to leather bars. Make a killing on Thursday and spend Friday night in diapers and chains. Improves morale. Maybe I'll branch out to Mountain Brook."

"One day," she says.

"One day what?"

"You'll need some help." She looks to her left, switches lanes. "Professional help."

"Is there any other kind?"

"Not in your case."

Hattie's a good next-to-oldest sister, always in the thick of the family scrimmage and mediating factions. She wants emotional read-outs and she'll conjure one based on the dirt under your fingernails, if pathos data isn't fessed up. So far Hattie's told me why I'm here and why I left, not just an account of the facts, which she has confused from their source, but the sort of formal analysis mumbo jumbo she offers clients who come in on the insurance dole and spend hours asking intimate advice of a complete stranger. Hattie said I needed to find a human growth potential away from the parental environment. She ought to know. She's a counselor with a private practice. Her main client is Marybelle Randolph, the mother we share, the source of her confusion concerning my five year fugue state in New York City.

"Will you charge me?" I ask.

"Do you have insurance?"

"Or course not."

She turns up the radio, caught off balance by The Grateful Dead, the song, "A Friend of the Devil," a private paean to a dozen acidhead crushes from Mountain Brook High, half of them now diagnosed by crypto-nazi psychiatrists as bi-polar manic depressives. Some never got out of the voluntary nut-houses, they got so depressed by psychiatric succor, soul death, where you become your body, a breathing machine of meat and blood pipes, a bioplast full of dread and methane. You hear your bones groan. You feel your brain function. You watch the lithium gut your liver and swell it like a slug. You scream, but nobody hears, so the mental health sadists commit you forever. You disappear behind the cure, a walking, salted dead.

"Did you know lithium is a highly reactive metallic element used as a heat transfer medium in thermonuclear bombs?"

"Of course."

"Music of the spheres. Are you a Deadhead?"

"Numbskull."

"Runs in the family."

"Or from."

Hattie was a social worker for Jefferson County, but her heart was too large for it. It swelled at the sight of pain and lack. Others' suffering sowed itself and rooted there. Poor families took advantage of her kindnesses. She bought cartloads of groceries and took the kids to Jimmy Morgan Zoo and matinee movies. When she caught a twelve-year-old lifting a twenty from her purse, she said it wasn't his fault. I asked her if she thought it was hers? She got riled and called me a brute. I admit to being flinthearted often enough, but she was a pushover for wily juveniles, whose tricks were familiar to me, and gave them little incentive to fall in line. She'd sweet talk a gang-leader when what he needed was a swift kick. One parroted her talk and said he was *growing*, when the police that morning had hauled him in handcuffed for setting fire to a school bus. He needed to talk, the juvenile corrections officer informed Hattie. That kid had the routine *down*, like a cold-calling real estate swindler, a financial advisor, a poker cheat. I told Hattie if Father hadn't flaxed my ass I'd have wound up in Wetumpka, but she said *that's* why I was fucked-up.

Hattie never stayed mad at me. She's forgiving after she thunders off the cuff, too guilty-feeling to bear a grudge, a good Episcopalian girl who's ashamed of her privilege in the real world, with all the *mea culpa* of a Catholic without benefit of *Confiteors*, since she's a convert to the Unitarian Church.

Soon she wised up about her county clients. Half of them were dealing from the bottom of the deck, fleecing her with pleas and calling her a rich bitch behind her back, even if she dressed like it was the Dust Bowl, to make a point about her sorrowing heart. It was too much. She felt too hurt all the time. And she was losing money instead of making it, so she opened up her own business two years before I left, vaguely billed Professional Services and Psychological Counselling. Now her clients are middle-class depressives, young ambits aglow with uncertainty, purposeful with worry. They eat too much, vomit a lot, exercise to exhaustion. Plastic surgery improves their self-esteem. Their notions of human nature derive from glossy magazines and media mirages about their visionary worth in the world. Hattie says they complain about *astrology*, the dreariness and emptiness of life, sex, art, politics, science. But not astronomy.

We had this discussion in her office. I was there to pick her up. It was Sunday night. We both lived at home. I asked her why more young *men* didn't cashier good sense and pay her a visit. She gave me a meaningful look and said when something's gnawing at a dysfunctional male, he'll self-medicate with alcohol. Hell yeah. I'd been in a sports bar watching football, drinking beer, eating oysters and buffalo wings. I said, most people don't drink because something's bothering them, they drink because it *feels* good. Plain old hedonism. Self-indulgence, a moral dilemma, not an addiction. This wasn't long after I'd gotten looped at a friend's wedding reception and passed out in the street. As I talked to Hattie I remembered arguing with the clerk at the tux shop, who wanted me to cough up ten bucks to get the grease slick off the shirt, and then Mother wanted me to go *see* some cluck about my episode, but I said *no way*. I told her I'd go talk to Father Brennan, who had a crying nose that belied every bottle of Irish whiskey, but she knew we'd sooner get bagged than soul-rap. Then Hattie told me about a bar in Florida. At their grand opening they served four-for-ones and seven guys died from drink. Sounds like bum whiskey, I said. Seven *single* men, she said. Men who wouldn't answer the calls of marriage and family responsibility. Chemically dependent Peter Pans. Repressed men who couldn't have genuine emotions, so they created imaginary ones with alcohol, and shame and remorse haunted them like ghosts.

I told her *I* didn't feel any shame about snoring on the sidewalk, but I regretted having to pay for the ruffled shirt. A *third* of the deaths of men between the ages of 18 and 40 are drink related, she said, repeating, as though I hadn't heard, *one-third*, so don't talk to me about the self-esteem problems of young women, when young men are every day committing alcoholic suicide. It's hard to argue with Hattie when she gets statistical, so I said at least I didn't spend my time blowing chunks because I'd binged on Ho-Ho's.

Anyway, the summer before I saw a heartstopper sitting in Hattie's waiting room. It was closing time. She was thumbing through *Self* and biting her lip, crackling with ill-will, but when I'm hexed I make the mistake of thinking there's universal solution to the female predicament. I made a troubled face, pretending to be a client, and tried to strike up a conversation, but she gave me a look I'll never forget. It wasn't that she thought I was a jerk. I could tell she thought that. It was her eyes. It wasn't that they weren't focused right, either. They weren't. Her eyes weren't *there*. Lights out.

She went in and ten minutes later she exited, grimly smiling. Hattie followed her, white as wax. The office was empty. When the woman left, Hattie beat her palms on the carpet, where she had collapse to her knees.

"No insurance?" I asked.

"That woman," she said, "drew up her chair."

"Is that normal?"

Hattie was out of breath. "She leaned forward and whispered, 'I'm very tired, I need help.'"

"I tried."

"I said, 'Tell me about it.' It's July. Did you notice she was wearing a sweater?" I had. "She took it off."

"Well?"

Hattie pinched her thumb and forefinger together, and then made a swift, slashing motion up and down her blouse.

"She's Catholic?"

"Razors."

"Nooo."

"All over. I almost fainted." So did I. Hattie hugged herself. "The cuts were infected. I asked her, 'Why?' She said,' So I'll feel *something*.'"

"I wonder why she didn't cut her face."

"Not even a question."

"Want my diagnosis?"

"No."

"Demon possession. She needs an exorcist. A lover."

"Cut the Catholic crap."

"You're right. It's lifestyle."

"She's headed for the deep wing of the wards."

"Is masochism a crime?"

"This isn't a crime." She got up off the floor. "I sent her to an M.D. A psychiatrist. I need a drink."

"Imagine."

At a corner bar we toasted the madwoman. There isn't a man in the world modest enough to think he can't save a woman when she's lost her marbles, for whatever reason. But tender-talk never dispossessed a demon.

Like a lot in her profession, Hattie never knew what to do with herself, so she's making a nice living now giving other people in the same predicament advice she never took herself.

She's good at it, because people who pay for advice tend to take it. Hattie said the razor woman was the only client she couldn't help at all. She wound up in an institution. Despite the horse-sense Hattie dispenses, it's the soothsaying swindle that ropes them in. Instead of beads or bird guts, she's got clients' blow-outs to work up, and her astrology-column shoptalk makes sure nobody feels like a wallflower. "Tensions will develop. Know who your friends are. Keep lines of communication open." A dog would play dead to that kind of bull, so I don't know how it helps her clients. I suppose they're just lonely. Besides, I was always told soul-ache put sand in your bones. It's kept my pride-swollen face from closing my eyes. Without it, I'd dance in the street, happy as an idiot, day and night.

I'm relieved to see Hattie hasn't a clue as to why I dogged it to New York, but I'm not surprised. Mother wouldn't admit that big a mistake to her Virginia daughters, even if the eldest has been plowed more times than an Alabama cornfield.

It's hard not to get steamed at Docie, the way she always takes center stage and demands a hundred curtain calls. I'm not good at giving bad news a dead-on look but I ask Hattie to level with me, since all she's said about our eldest sister goes as far back as creation and involves enough psychobabble to turn Freud himself into an apostate.

"This time Docie's not crying wolf. This time she's done it good."

"Done what?"

"It's bad, Webb. Real bad."

"*What's* bad?"

"She's gone off the deep end this time."

"She committed herself?"

"She's in a coma, Webb."

"Mother didn't say anything about a coma. Very ill, she said."

"Mother doesn't believe it. She says Docie's resting."

"A coma?"

* * *

"He was married?" I ask.

"Separated. For years."

"A shrink?"

"Yes."

"Where is this doctor?"

"This time I wouldn't mind."

"Mind what?" In front of us a grey Saab pulls off to the side of the road with a ragged flat.

"If you socked him."

"Where is he?"

"In Atlanta."

"A long distance romance?"

"He's at a conference."

"What about Docie?"

"He *adores* her."

"*Adores* her. What the fuck does that mean?"

A *Silver Bullet* beer truck with a busted muffler passes on the left. Hattie rolls up her window, rolls it back down.

"It's not a medical convention. He went to consult a woman who's a medium. An old friend of his. He took the blouse she was wearing when she wrecked."

"Touching. You said he's a doctor?"

"It's the Southeastern Dawn of Consciousness Metaphysical Society annual meeting, in conjunction with New Order of Terrestrial Healing and Intergalactic Network of Goodness."

"No kidding."

"They're focusing all of the earth's positive energies on Docie's frequency."

"Radio waves?"

"I'm *serious.*"

"An AMA doctor?"

"Docie was addicted to Percodans when she found out she was pregnant."

I look at her. "Pregnant?"

"Six months."

It's typical of Hattie that she's letting out the news piecemeal. She shifts gears, studying what to say.

We pass into Shades Valley. I put both hands on the dash; Hattie changes lanes like it's the last lap of the Firecracker 400.

"They're prepared to do a C-section, to save the babies."

"*Babies?*"

"Twins," she says. "Fraternal twins. They're fine."

Hattie puddles up. I look away. We cross the city limits into Mountain Brook.

"What's this doc's name?"

"Valentine."

Hattie's two years younger than Docie. Like Docie, she's never been married and probably never will be, but her luck with men runs the opposite of her sister's—too few, instead of too many. She's never been much about feminizing herself with powder and warpaint, but she's naturally pretty and big—with a clear, lean face, and sloping grey eyes and a long braid of brown hair. A generation ago in Virginia she'd have been our Old Maid, but she'd punch anybody who said that now. She played field hockey like a nose tackle and was fencing champion at Duke. A hot temper is about all we have in common. Now she's crying.

"How long has she been unconscious?"

"Nearly a week," she says. "She's got a bruise on the side of her head that will make you positively sick." Hattie has slowed down to forty. A pick-up truck, a Japanese wheelbarrow driven by a redneck hippie, honks. Hattie mashes the accelerator, switches lanes, and offers a gesture out the window.

"Last Saturday night she went under for no reason. The x-rays showed there was no fracture. They don't know what to think."

"Was she high?"

"*No.*" She hesitates. "Until we saw the blood tests, we weren't sure either."

"Had she quit?"

"He offered to pay for an abortion."

"At six months?"

"Listen. This isn't a joke."

"No."

So Hattie says Docie thought another abortion would jinx her. She took two weeks off from the pharmacology lab and was beholden on her homeliest younger sister for some R and R away from her usual double trouble—pharmaceutics and sex— holed up pregnant for the detox sweats with the same younger mental-health-counsellor sister who couldn't catch a progenitor with a dragnet. Docie wouldn't go near a hospital. She figured obstetrics would give her enough statistics of deformed and stillborn premature births she'd *have* to terminate the pregnancy. She was addicted again and not far into the first trimester but she wanted the babies. Baby, she thought then. Plus at work she'd been taken off one project and given some mickey-mouse research a graduate student could have handled. Her boss was on to her. So it wasn't just the pregnancy. She had professional risks she was taking. The boss was new, some bigwig down from Massachusetts General who believed in career right down to the kind of hors d'oeuvres your wife serves at dinner parties. A real throwback. Imagine his reaction to Docie. A *woman*, single, wild, stunning, drugged, crazy *and* the best pharmacologist in Alabama. He didn't want anybody on his research team doing personal research, no matter how smart. Docie told Hattie he had petitioned the president for permission to urine test. Half the pharmacologists at UAB would lose their jobs if they pissed in his jar.

* * *

"So I stayed at home and helped her ride it out," Hattie says. "It was awful."

She takes the exit ramp for home and points. Skid marks run off the asphalt and turn into muddied ruts down the grassy embankment.

She points to a pine tree. "That kept her from going all the way down." At the bottom is a rocky creek. In the near dark I see the pine tree is barked where Docie's Audi hit it.

"The twins weren't hurt."

"No."

"Okay. What happened *this* time?"

"She fell in love."

"Docie was his patient."

"At first. Then they went out."

"Another rest home spree?"

"Her insurance won't cover any more retreats," Hattie says.

"A sofa romance."

"Psychiatrists aren't like that anymore. You don't lie down and tell your fantasies to a pervert. It's a conversation. Dynamic. Give and take."

"I see."

"A good health counselor doesn't decipher forbidden wishes."

"He merely acts them out."

"They're not priests, Webb."

"No exorcism?"

"They're people you can trust."

"Or fuck."

"Shut up."

I make a fist. "Or fuck-up."

Hattie, trying not to, laughs, a low fencing-lunge *huh*.

* * *

"One weekend they drove to Pascagoula to meet his parents."
 "If they were ready to nest, why did he *drug* her?"
 "You know Docie."
 "Tell me about Doctor Valentine."
 "He was a conscientious objector."
 "I see."

So Hattie says Valentine joined the Peace Corps and spent five years in Africa. He traveled everywhere. Tibet, Ethiopia, Madagascar. His family's got oil money. When he comes back to the States his parents say train for a profession, or no more trust fund. He goes to medical school to become a country doctor. You know, Hattie says, move to Fayetteville and cure the whooping cough for a bushel of beans, but he studies psychiatry because at the time some doctors thought LSD might be a valuable therapy. He's got grey hair down to his shoulders. He paints and writes poetry. He's at a conference in Atlanta.

"He meditates," Hattie says.
 "You sound like *you're* in love with him."
 "Docie met him through me."

Doctor Valentine is a member of the Southside Unitarian Church. He gives talks on Sufism, Eastern mysticism. He's a real religion scholar, Hattie says. Witchcraft, patristic theology, Manichaeaism. The political origins of heresies. He's published articles on white magic, voodoo, astral projection, the resurgence of Satanism in America. He's at a conference in Atlanta meditating on Docie's blouse.

* * *

"It's hard not to like him. It's funny. He screws up our lives, at the same time he's irresistible."

"He sounds resistible to me."

"He doesn't believe in traditional responsibility, though."

"He's a necrophiliac."

"He's got a lot of girlfriends besides Docie. Do you remember Lisa?"

"The message therapist."

"She liked you."

"Not for long."

"You had hostilities that darkened your aura. She said football was bad for you."

"Football was good for me. It taught me to knock people down when they stand in the way. What about this numbskull."

"Lisa's been one his girlfriends, rotated on a weekend basis. Joints in his hot tub. LSD, or MDA. Massage classes, noncompetitive play."

"O rings, X spots, what gives?"

"Docie's a groupie."

"No way."

"It's not that simple. *He* was in love with her at first. He dumped the other girlfriends for a month, but then he got restless. Docie said he felt too vulnerable. He likes a lot of women. I warned her about him. She accepted the challenge. Then she found out she was pregnant. He assumed the doctor-patient level they never had. He told Docie, a pharmacologist, that because of the drugs she was risking major birth defects. It, he called it *it*. Truth is, he's got two children. Child-support, you know."

"Planned parenthood."

"He admits he's selfish."

"How could Docie be in love with this fraud?"

"He's the one that got away."

* * *

Hattie turns down the road that runs by the golf course. Black caddies stand slump-shouldered in the twilight, their pot-bellied *masz* in stretch pants whacking phosphorescent golf balls up and down the fairways.

"If she wasn't high, how did it happen?"

"Telekinesis."

"Now she's a Sony."

"Nobody knows. Nobody saw. She left the lab at noon. Ab's secretary said Docie came by at 12:30, but he was out for lunch."

"Ab?"

"Abaddon. Formerly Larry. It's his spiritual moniker."

"I see."

"At two-thirty Mother got a phone call from Brookwood Hospital. Docie was geared up for a big fit this time, heading out to Mother's to go through the personality routine, like she hadn't taken a step forward in fifteen years."

"What about Father?"

"He lives on the bluff."

"He found out," I say. I want to tell Hattie he's not my father, and he can sleep on the sidewalk if he wishes.

"What?" Hattie asks.

"Nothing."

"He found God."

We pull up behind a beat-up volksvan whose bumper bears a hundred colorful stickers of global import. The driver, of geo-political purpose, can't navigate down a strip of asphalt deep in the Alabama pine woods. He weaves, tuning his radio. Blue smoke whips out his window.

"No kidding," I say.

"He got religion." Hattie turns on her headlights and flashes the brights.

"Old timey?"

"Somewhat. Not prehistoric. Catholic. Ab said it's a necessity of our paternalistic society that men worship a crucified son. The original divine revelations derived from the worship of nature. Tree sprites, pixies, Mother Earth." The van turns down a street, lights off, and disappears into the dark.

"Joysticks."

"He *is* a scholar of religion."

"Scholar?"

We wind along the narrow road that runs by the Birmingham Country Club. Floodlights come on over the deep lawn, a golf-course turf that slopes up to the mock-Tudor clubhouse. Across the street is a row of Mountain Brook's pseudo Xanadus, with clinging ivories and medieval turrets, or else a Colonial Dame kind of Revolutionary fakery, whiter than the White House, each mansion the owner's custom-made claim to robber barony, where a thousand crosstown servants sweep, mop, wax, buff, shine and scour away all annoying evidence of dusty death and reminders of earthly vanity. Look down in any foyer at the waxed floors and see your smiling face.

The club lot is filled with Cadillacs and convertible Mercedes, with an occasional turbo Porsche a toupeed philanderer wheels around town. In every car trunk is a second set of custom clubs and finely spiked golf shoes. One summer I worked with the *niggers* as a caddy, but quit when golfers gave me thoughts of thrashing monied hicks about the legs with a three wood. Some of them wouldn't walk with anybody but their nigger boy, they were so accustomed to the softshoe. I got stoned once with a caddy named Teak. We worked a foursome and every opportunity he'd wink *watch this*, then he'd lope a slackjawed Sambo. They drank it like water. I'd have kicked them in the pants.

Right now golfers are poolside having backslapping bourbons, saying they *pawed* the front nine this mawning, and the like. When we moved here fifteen years ago Mother put us on the membership waiting list. Later she said the Country Club women were beneath her, anyhow.

It broke my mother's heart to move from Virginia, since Randolphs have lived in the Old Dominion since John Smith made love to Pocahontas. What can you expect when you marry beneath your station, a corporate executive on top of that, a fancy phrase for drummer, whose company plays suburban hopscotch with its faithful? For twenty-two years my putative father persuaded Liberty National Insurance not to transfer him out of Richmond to their Birmingham headquarters, where they count the Alpine stacks of cashflow profit like crack dealers, with machines, only *computers*—he requested to keep his Old Dominion job at my mother's behest—but when they offered him a promotion that would have made him look henpecked had he refused it, The Mayflower vans were loaded up. Mother said we didn't *need* the extra money anyway, since her Randolph patrimony kept us in Virginia's high cotton. She said Father needed more self-respect. She agreed to go. Who knows why? I gave it some thought in New York; under the cold, swaying cables of the midnight Bridge, thoughts came thick as north Atlantic mists, but nothing added up. We moved. The only remaining branch of this Randolph family in Virginia was crazy Clara, tucked away in a musty wing of a mental ward, courtesy of The Commonwealth. Hattie flew up one spring and retrieved her.

Father wanted to live in modest Homewood, or Vestavia, but Mother wanted Mountain Brook, a sad approximation of her notion of First Families. She traveled back and forth between Birmingham and Richmond to sell the most recent ancestral home, originally her grandfather's. It was the same one she'd grown up in, post-bellum, three-story, neo-Georgian brick on a nice stretch of Grace Street, with a white rounded portico and windowpanes so old the sand in them had sagged, making the glass opaque. When I was young I thought they made all the windows that way. Mother factored the sentimental into the market value to make sure no one would buy. She had one offer and raised the price fifteen per cent. Then she rented it to a bourbon flush state senator from Winchester. A few years after we left the house was registered by the Virginia Historical Society as landmark architecture. Now she'd sooner sell her soul than part with that house. I found out later on her trips to Richmond she politicked the Historical Society board members for the honor, and suddenly it didn't seem so prestigious, like she'd taken a chain to a rolltop desk to make it look antique.

Mountain Brook, even though it *claims* to be a city, is just an aimless arrangement of suburbanites, two acre domestic theme parks up and down any given block: English manors, modernist boxes with sawtooth roofs, cotton baron mansions, Spanish villas iced with pink stucco. A Mountain Brook kid has less in common with a retired steelworker across town tending an acre of watermelons than a suburban terrorist of materialism from Bloomfield Hills. Bred in these green pastures, we softboiled our brains with the same TV, received the same toys under the same trees, wore identical duds, given the fashion of the year, and popped wheelies on the same Schwinns on the same configuration of circles, roads, terraces, drives, ways, lanes, courts in stripmined developments with pastoral and elegiac names like Sweetwater Forests. Or Mountain Brook. Where there ain't no *mountain* and the brooks are mostly storm drains, on whose concrete covers domestics at five o'clock line up for their bus rides back to shanty town, if they're not blessed enough to be kept. A suburban Detroit boy and I may not speak alike, but we're cloned right down to the brand names. So when Mountain Brook blows itself up like a paper bag, it's just the sort of puff suburbs like to give themselves. They imagine they're each one different, when they're alike as eggs or Holiday Inns.

We drive down Overton. The oaks overarching the road are in full green; the lighter underbelly of leaves reflects back Hattie's headlights.

She tells me about a shaman in Seattle she's flying out to see for a week's worth of seminars in July. He channels a ten-thousand year-old soul from Jupiter named Friend, who prophesizes the end and regeneration of the earth and the purification of consciousness when showers of love will rain down on receptive psyches, and universal evil will be purged from the earth, the devastated planet rejuvenated, Atlantis restored, bones resurrected, televisions needless. I can't wait. Hattie knows as well as I do it will likely take a volley of hydrogen bombs to do the job, but if she wants to believe some dude from Jupiter is going to give us the Garden of Eden again, she's entitled.

"What about Adam?" I ask.

"Archetypal myth."

"He wants his rib back."

"Let him have it."

"Original sin too."

"Did Methuselah have cataracts?" Hattie asks.

"That was Moses. The burning bush was an optical illusion."

"It wasn't the first."

"Nor the last."

The way her schoolmates picked on her I'm not surprised she thinks of Friend as half a billion miles away, and in her heart of hearts believes Christers are cruel-hearted hypocrites. In Junior High she'd come home from St. Catherine's crying with her blouse torn from a school bus scrap and Mother would say it was *her* fault, for not acting ladylike, so not even the homefront consoled her. Hattie's one of the soberest people I know, a level-headed, no-nonsense, knock-through-the-bull individual, but while her feet are rooted firmly to the earth, she's as gullible as a girl in love. She has glimpses of faith in everything from *Chariots of the Gods* to *I-Ching*. She's likely to believe anything, so she probably doesn't believe in anything at all, but in every other way she's as practical as a plump bob.

My head hurts like I got caught with a ringing right, what with heading home vexed about Docie and Hattie screw-loose over a metaphysical Centaur peddling video visions C.O.D, *one*, she claims, where Friend prophesies that before the Great Purification families will be brought together over the load of a loved one's suffering.

It cheapens Docie's situation to think some alien no-count flicked her into a ditch so he could save the earth. It reminds me of a near bar-brawl I started, when I overheard some guy a few stools down say Docie was a stupid slut. He was the sort of loser Docie wouldn't notice if he were nailed to a tree in her front lawn, so I knew why he was mouthing her. Still I was mad. I got him by the back of the neck and bounced his head off the bar, for emphasis. My—*sister*—I said—she may act like a *whore*—but she's *not*—I said—a *ditz*. By then he was going gumballs, so the bouncer tossed me out, and that put everybody in the mood for a rumble. I didn't hang around. Docie graduated summa cum and fifth in her class, UVA, Charlottesville, under the shadow of her distant ancestor's temple of reason and Deism, Monticello. She may act like a maniac, but she isn't *stupid*.

"It's not a coincidence," Hattie says. "Docie's accident was not an accident."

"What if she dies?"

"She won't."

"I thought you said it didn't look good."

"It doesn't. But she won't die."

"Why?"

"I suddenly just felt it."

With a two-fisted race-driver grip Hattie takes the narrow curve that runs under the bluff. I look up. The tires squeal. In the early dark a crucifix fashioned out of pine sits atop the cliff.

"You're kidding."

"Father's not. He built it himself."

"He ought to drag it around the neighborhood. Beg for alms."

"He did. Mother put a stop to that."

Hattie tells me next to youngest Amelia, a year older than me—is she a love child too?—studies music at Birmingham-Southern

College and lives at home, something, Hattie says, she may well do the rest of her life. I'm too tired to ask why. Eldest-born T.E.—short for Thomas Edison, a nickname he earned when a freshman and fourteen at M.I.T.—is arriving from Budapest Sunday, where he's delivering a paper on origin of the universe. I hope he keeps his findings a secret. Origins are distressing news.

I see the house and I get a case of the fantods. My bowels lurch like freight cars getting started and I wish Docie or no I'd stayed buried like a wharf rat in New York. I have a terrible thought: Docie's accident, and Father's retiring right into the woods, might well deflect attentions from my homecoming. Suddenly I feel lifted from the meathooks, though my conscience aches like a migraine. Who couldn't love Docie, crazy as she is?

We turn down the dead-end and Hattie spins her go-cart through the serpentine gate—Thomas Jefferson design—and up the winding drive. Instead of pulling into the garage, Hattie turns around and points the car back down the hill.

"What are you doing?"

"I don't want to get blocked in," she says. "We've got to go back to the airport tonight."

"What for?"

"Claire," she says.

Behind Hattie I walk to the carport and through the kitchen door. Anna Ruth sits at the table reading a *Birmingham News* propped against an oatmeal box while she absently snaps beans. The kitchen has the loamy, sweet smell of field peas.

"Webb," she says. She stands up, arm strained against the grainy table, and gives me a squeeze around the ribcage.

"My goodness," she says.

I faint.

Hattie puts a wet washcloth on my forehead and Anna Ruth lifts my head to a glass of water.

"What on *earth*," Anna Ruth asks.

"Breakfast. I didn't. I haven't eaten since breakfast."

Hattie gives me a sidelong look. She knows I took a nosedive because of the bomb she dropped about Claire. My knees feel fizzy. I sit at the kitchen table.

"That big town took the tuck out of you," Anna Ruth says.

"Birmingham?"

"New York."

Hattie brings in my duffel bag and canvas case, a bag for an electric cello I bought from a broke rock aspirant who lived in the storefront on Elizabeth Street. On the side is stenciled in indelible ink *The/rapists*, a punk band that couldn't hold Rahway captive.

Anna Ruth puts the colander of beans under running water and stirs the pot of field peas. I put my head between my legs until the seashell roar in my head subsides. Anna Ruth sits down. I sit back and look at her.

"We sorely missed you," she says.

"Really?"

"You ought to hope so."

Anna Ruth's born again, but talks like a farm hand, only without the swearing. At a tent revival one spring Sunday in Goodwater she *saw* it, she said, she *saw* it. Anna Ruth told me this the night I'd gotten bombed at the homecoming dance my junior year and fought a sophomore over a cheerleader named Libby. We'd walloped the Bobcats and I'd scored twice, so I felt like a warrior ripe for spoils. Libby Parker was a dark-skinned Circe with luminous green eyes. Rumor had it she was part Creek. We made out one half-moon night when a group of us hiked back to the Confederate cannonball factory deep in the undeveloped woods of east Mountain Brook. The old factory was a pile of rubble and broken rock against the side of a steep hill. By moonlight it was ghostly. We sat on a rock and kissed.

From time to time a star fell. She dated a linebacker. At the dance, neither of us was going to fight shy of a chance to slip out of the gym for a walk. When he punched me the band stopped; I punched him back. Libby slipped into the crowd. It was a matter of principle, not giving up. The police drove us home. Father stood on the porch for fifteen minutes talking with the elder officer. The officer laughed. The next day Pappy gave me grief in the form of moral instruction; I had to dig a six foot pit for Phillip's new magnolia.

That night while Father spoke with the cop Anna Ruth sobered me with strong coffee. She told me she drank whiskey and it brought her nothing but misery, and moonshine, she said, killed her husband; the sheriffs who beat him up just helped him along the way. Bullshit, I said. Then she told me her son was in the state penitentiary for killing a man. Her son was drunk. Over a *pool* cue, she said. Shot him right through the eye for a pool cue. If I wanted to drive to Rockford, he'd sure as Sunday give me a piece of his mind about drink. I'll pass, I said, but I saw her point. I'd have revenged myself on the pigs if they'd laid their hands on any of *my* relatives, but she said I was too headstrong to understand the meaning of forgiveness. How could you forgive anybody for a beating like that? Her husband? Postmortem mercy maybe. Why isn't your heart full of hate? Anna Ruth acts as often like a Christian soldier marching off to war as a merciful soul who beats swords into ploughshares. The Latin threw her, but she understood what I meant. She put a wrinkly, cool hand on my forearm. It's not *up* to us, she said.

"Where's Mother?" I ask.

"Napping," she says. "Before supper, same as always. Get cleaned up. We eat in half an hour."

I go to the stove and ladle some field peas into a ceramic bowl, a wobbly concavity from Amelia's potting phase.

"Tabasco?" I ask.

"Same place it always is."

I find the pepper sauce in the cabinet over the stove. Anna

64

Ruth unwraps a filet of bluefish and slides it under the broiler.

"How you been?" she asks. Aside from the ribhug she's acted like I never left.

"Better."

"I reckoned as much." She puts the beans in a steamer basket and eases it into a pot of rolling water. She breaks a head of lettuce in the sink. "But in general."

"Lousy."

"You'll get better."

"How?"

"No way out but up. I've been to New York. Twice."

"When?" Several times I thought I saw her, but I was prone to homesick hallucinations.

"War time. I worked in a parachute factory in Newark. My sister got me the job. Took grief for this here *accent*," she says, mocking herself. "But I sparkled like a diamond in a goat's butt. Best worker there. Then Mama got sick and I went back to Tennessee."

"When else?"

"I mean visited. I just visited New York twice when I lived in Newark. Never been back."

"You wouldn't recognize it."

"I expect not. I didn't see that much of it. Tall building or two. Central Park. The second time my date got me so drunk in some dancing club he walked me outside and laid me down in the back seat of his car. He didn't want to leave, so he just left me there. When I woke up we was parked in front of my sister's apartment building. It was four in the morning and he was so stoned he couldn't hardly drive. He forgot where he picked me up the night before. I woke my sister up. That was the end of that romance. You still get boozed up?"

"Me? Never."

* * *

I finish the peas and rinse the bowl and put it in the sink.

"Twenty minutes," she says. She retrieves the broiler pan and bastes the bluefish and slides the pan back under the element.

I head into the hallway.

"Webb."

"Yes."

"Welcome home."

"And."

I turn back. She's sitting at the kitchen table unfolding a section of the paper. She doesn't look up.

"Pray for Docie."

"I have," I say, and know why I haven't.

Anna Ruth's been with us, as they say, since the second year we moved here. After Goodwater she came back to do the Mountain Brook domestic circuit because for a poor white who'd grown up in Appalachia without benefit of education beyond the eighth grade the money was good. She was nearing fifty. Her son was in prison. Her daughter married a student she met at Emory. When they graduated, they stayed in upscale Atlanta, where by Birmingham's poor white measure they were well off. Anna Ruth worked for three families, but after Mother had one of her fainting fits she asked Anna Ruth to work full-time. Within a month she moved into the apartment over the garage, which Mother refurbished. She's lived there ever since. Mother's very attached to Anna Ruth, like the Pharaoh was to Moses.

Friend-of-the-family help is Mountain Brook etiquette, but Father balked when Mother started trying one and the other out, waiting for a *Gone With The Wind* fit. We had help in Virginia—when we left a woman originally from Gum Springs had worked for the Randolphs on and on for fifty years—but in Mountain Brook you were expected to adopt a *Negro* as a show of Christian charity to prove you believed in the equality of the races, even as the thousands of blacks who commuted to Xanadu poured over the mountain into white-meat Mountain Brook in buses with busted windows swirling with diesel exhaust and carried a change of clothes in crinkled old grocery sacks, looking like refugees, which in fact they were, because Birmingham was the slummiest place in the South for a while, and may still be. To be poor and even *white* in heavy industry Birmingham— a colored didn't stand a fighting chance in the demoralizing bog of Birmingham.

Pappy didn't want a live-in of any color. He's from the northeast, Catholic, and middle-class. He'd sooner see the sanctimonious southern gentry pistolwhipped before he'd give in to a Hollywood fantasy about race relations. I admit I admire this quality in my foster-father. But give in he did, for a lot of reasons I suspect, but mostly because my mother reins the purse strings like it was a horse show, with all the right lightness of hoof and grace of leap to start and keep a social standing. At first it didn't turn out as she expected.

Uppercrust or corncake, Mountain Brook's newly arrived had to pay their dues. A backwoods Alabama boy named Jackson made it big as contractor in Birmingham and bought himself a mansion in the Beverly Hills of Alabama. I played football with his son. Just the way the son looked, the side-topped, pennyloafer snots felt bound to pick on him. His nickname was Bubber. His face was as round and soft as a mitt of biscuit dough. His small green eyes folded deep in his face. It wasn't that he was an imbecile. He always looked like somebody was about to yell at him for a reason he'd never understand. During a scrimmage he'd be twenty yards from the scene of action, when a stray guard would blindside him just before the whistle. The hit was legal, but there'd be no purpose in it.

Once I left my playbook in the locker room and came back after practice to get it. The locker room was empty, I thought. I heard a low, choked-up sound. It was Bubber. The poor clod was in the back stall crying his head off. It put a frog in my throat to hear him, knowing he was apologizing to the world for being an ox, when he had no call to apologize for anything;

the world owed *him*. I had an impulse to tell him everything would be all right, but I didn't want to catch him nursing his shame, so I snuck out. And it *wouldn't* be all right; fate had dealt him a hand providence folded before the first raise. After that incident, I watched after him in practice. During the annual black-gold spring game some second string lummox face-masked him on an end-around. The next play I clotheslined the offender flat on his back, and got benched.

I felt sorry for Bubber, but mostly because of his Mama. Rumor was the country-club battle-axes cold-shouldered her, when they weren't but a generation or two removed from being pig-farmers' daughters themselves. She had no friends. She wandered around her huge empty house all day and drank. Her husband ran around on her. Her daughter joined a rich-bitch high school sorority and was ashamed of her. Her son was treated like the village idiot. I'd see the poor woman in the grocery store, pushing an empty cart down the aisle, drunk out of her mind.

Mother paid her dues too, but she was snubbed because she rode around in her dead father's '49 Bentley like Queen Victoria observing the barbarous reaches of the Empire from a clipper deck. After she toned down the Highness act, she made a few connected friends, and with Anna Ruth as first mate, the Garden Club et al. let her play royal fleet, though she never surrendered the notion she was superior, and had travelled to the furthest reach of Bozart as a good will emissary of the Commonwealth of Virginia and Anglican culture. She was put on Arts Councils and elected to library boards and chaperoned fund-raiser court-ships with corporate V-P's, while her eldest daughter's soul was possessed by a cacodemon, which drove her to the thumping and blasphemous adorations of Magis Keith and Mick, twin sisters of Satan, ecstasies of heavy petting, and premium pills from various medicine chests across the spiritual boneyard of the suburbs, where televisions in dens and bedrooms and living-rooms glowed like intergalactic gases, and young siblings, gape-faced, watched the Jetsons Twist to millennial music of the apocalypse. What the grand dames liked about Mother was the odor and ardor of old money.

Anna Ruth helped Mother to adapt to Alabama. She apprehended early on the sort of rich folk she was working for. Mother was the figurehead of the family politic, and from her wing of the house announced decisions of policy it was Anna Ruth's practical duty to execute. If we were to have fish on Friday because an element of Catholicism in the realm so declared it, Anna Ruth decided what kind and how cooked. Baked flounder or broiled crawdads, it didn't matter. There were several traditional Virginia fares—quail and terrapin and Smithfield Ham and Chesapeake crab—requested for formal dinners scheduled well in advance. Beyond that, Anna Ruth was merely to feed us well. Father, she came to understand, was the energetic executive who vanished from seven to seven five days a week—I wonder if *he* had affairs (secretaries? waitresses? sales clerks?)—and the remaining time played an angry judge summoned from his third-floor chambers to arbitrate disputes between rival factions, where he cannonboomed riot acts during the high pitch of civil unrest, enforcing border and property disputes with threat of razor strop. When in session, the court was addressed by all at once. If X destroyed Y's property because Z's thievery of A's money purchased items in question, it was merely because F had been locked in the closet by D before X could rectify his mistake of accidentally melting Y's records in the neighbor's ashcan, when F. had only intended to unwarp them.

Anna Ruth had her own words for us. Once, when I was in the kitchen fixing a coke float, I overheard her on the breakfast phone. It was her second year with us. We were as spoiled as month-old milk, she said. Later I found out she was trying to decide whether or not she would stay on or moved back to Goodwater; I gathered she tolerated the well-heeled and mannered sociopaths peopling this pastoral city with no small sadness and irony. She stayed, which means Mother renegotiated her contract. She grew to like us, though.

I overheard other words that affected me more, and which I remembered. She said the father had a bad temper and took it out on the young boy, treating him like he wasn't his own, making him eat in the garage like a dog if he was five minutes late for supper. I felt a stab of secret grief; so I *hadn't* imagined the special attention I got from Father.

I stood there, still as a white tail seconds before an earthquake. Our family portrait came painfully clear. Here we were, a clan of bellyachers and neurasthenic fainters, and there *she* was, across the universe for all practical purposes, stout as a post, a survivor of genuine hardships only to wind-up a hired hand on a nut ranch, where the wife believed she was an archduchess and the husband, as far as she could tell, was a misanthrope, proud and sharp as a wolf, of fading good looks, burdened with a stunted brood of prehensile children. Compared to us, Anna Ruth was the *salt of the earth*, and happy she'd made unprovisional peace with infinity.

I watched the dollop of vanilla melt in the coke foam; I had no appetite for anything sweet. Doubtless I exaggerated Anna Ruth's state of grace, since nobody who ever lived wasn't granted but a handful of diamond days, and the rest are breaking rocks. But she made me see the coordinates of the class map where I lived unfeelingly.

She hung up and came into the kitchen. She stopped in the doorway. It was the first time I saw grown-up blush. I wanted her to leave. She was a cloud of conscience. She saw my adversary situation with the misanthrope, though, so I sidled up to her and helped around the kitchen.

On game days in the fall she fixed what ever I liked for dinner, and sent me off with a knock on the arm. When we played for the city championship, she was the only one from the house who came to the game. My family was embarrassed by football; in fourth grade Mother forced me to take a ballet class to discourage my enthusiasm for pigskin, but I turned it into a collision sport, so I didn't last too long in tights. Family acted like my love of the game was an unfortunate club-foot deformity it was best to ignore. It was. No Randolph of Virginia born would have been caught dead at Legion Field for the Auburn Alabama showdown in the company of eighty-five thousand trash-drunk whites rooting for the most stubborn pack of plow boys, much less be seen at a high school championship. As for the Yankee Clayborne, Father had no use for Dixie's gridiron religion, where glossy publicity pics of The Bear walking on water were sold like Catholic icons in hardware stores or given away with fill-ups of hi-test.

We lost the game. I punched a locker and broke my hand. Anna Ruth drove me to the emergency room.

"Hothead," she said as we left the hospital.

"You bet."

My hand throbbed in the fresh cast.

"How long you expect to live?"

"Forever."

"Snares and delusions, Webb. Nothing but."

Ever since I left for New York I've thought about what she told me once when I'd come back for Christmas my sophomore year at C.U. Hattie and Docie and Mother and Amelia are in the den scraping like cats, so no one even notices when I come in. I go to the kitchen and pop a beer and say to Anna Ruth, Business as usual, I guess. She presses her broad mouth into a frown, and her icey blue eyes lighten as she draws down her brows. I don't know where you come from, but you *ain't* one of them. At the time I thought she meant I wasn't a lunatic, but on the sidewalks of New York, worn slabs scuffed by a billion shoes, the moment resurfaced in a different light.

The house Mother bought in Mountain Brook is as Richmond replica as she could find. It's three-story neo-colonial brick, white-trimmed and ivied, with a back yard that's a *House Beautiful* affair. She fancied you couldn't tell it from a plantation on the James, except that it's smaller, and there's no river running along the slope of our front yard, but a road that cul-de-sacs into a circle, and the back yard isn't cedar fenced and kept trim with grazing thoroughbreds, but sloped after fifty yards to a bluff steep that overlooks the links, where I used to lean out of an overhanging three and shout at the putters on the green below, to break their concentration.

One time they got fed up and four of the old dudes lined up off a bunker and started blasting golf balls in mortar arcs right up to where I was hanging. I beat a retreat before they beaned me, but I came back with a handful of green stinging pine cones and let fly. I lost my branch grip and fell down the bluff.

I came to in a hospital room, a thigh-bone broken, branch and briar scratched, with knots on my head, and bruises the color of aged steak all over. I was lucky to be alive, they said. Hattie asked if I'd scored at hit.

Mutt is buried on the bluff. He was an S.P.C.A. stray I saw advertised on the local news. I was twelve. I called him Mutt because that's what he was, mostly black lab, with some English Terrier thrown for smarts, and just the right ratio of meanness to fidelity. He was skittish, though, like he hadn't been raised right. When the sun went down some nights he bayed as if the Prince of Darkness himself were trotting by, back deep in the woods. The next-door-neighbor Jimsons complained.

Mr. Jimson was a fat slob who drove his purple Cadillac to the bottom of his drive every morning in his bathrobe, an ashy cigarette dangling from his hungover face, eyes squinting into the smoke, just to pick up his *Post-Herald*. Then he'd weave back up the drive, leaving tire tracks in the monkey grass. His wife looked like an eastern bloc powerlifter gone to coffee-cake pot; she watered her backyard flowerbeds in a full-bodied girdle that packed in her butt as taut as a Superball. The Jimsons complained and complained. There were obese-jokes about why the Jimsons were childless. They resented the stampede of the wild folks next door, and Mutt didn't make them any kinder.

They called the cops twice. What could I do? Poor Mutt was jumpy about something. Every night I calmed him down as best I could.

One night I woke with a start. I jumped out of bed and ran down to the back yard. Mutt lay near the Jimson property line, stiff as a poker. The vet said he'd eaten a pound of poisoned hamburger.

With some rubber tubing from my chemistry set I siphoned a quart of gasoline from the riding mower and set the Jimson's toolshed on fire.

What had the dog done? If Mutt was nervous, it was hardly a reason to kill him. You'd have to dust every insomniac on the planet if *nervous* be just cause. When Father did his strop routine, I swore I'd never show pain in front of him as long as I lived.

The Jimsons wanted me locked up in a home, or else sent to an *psychiatrist*, but Father said No deal. He sent me an hour every week to talk with a priest at the downtown rectory of St. Christopher's. This lasted a month. I told the priest what I told Father. Next time I'd burn down his house. Father Thomas recommended counseling.

Mother was never so disgraced, but she's never so disgraced once a month, so she settled up and it blew over. Every time I thought of Mutt I wanted to see that fat slob in his bathrobe, running in circles, a dancing fireball. I prayed there was a place in hell where'd he'd eat Alpo for eternity.

When I formally confessed the sin in the dark booth of St. Francis Church, I asked the priest if God punished people for poisoning dogs. He said that the state of my soul was more important to God than a helpless animal. I was proud and vindictive, he said; he asked me to beg for the mercy of the Blessed Virgin for the sin of pride.

I felt evil kneeling in the dark booth, smiling to myself as he spoke, glad I'd torched the toolshed, imagining the Jimson house lighting up the night sky like the gasoline tanker that blew a crater across two lanes of I-20.

* * *

Before washing up for supper I walk through the house. From the basement dark to the heirloom living room, everything is the same. Half of the bedrooms on the second floor are catacombed with stacks of National Geographics and slide-top desks piled with old books. Replicas of Revolutionary pistols and sextants aside blue-patterned stone china of Williamsburg tour shops line the mahogany wall shelves. Above maple-cased barometers and silver gyroscopes, opera glasses and bird-watcher binoculars, maps of Revolutionary America are pinned, illustrating the battle strategies of Washington and Lafayette, suggesting that victory in war is not mostly luck drunk with one side's higher purpose, but divine will.

Mother claims the Randolphs fought only in the Revolution. In every war since they tucked tail and *rand off*, as Anna Ruth phrased it. They served as humanitarians, nurse volunteers, doctors, and minsters to the dead, as if the last war noble enough for them to shed their blood was a tea party in the Trenton snow, where periwigs glinted in the silver of starlight, and flintlocks popped with the politeness of a well-turned phrase, and the conversation called war ended on a decorous note of regret for the dead, who made sporting bows into the snow. My mother is a Colonial *Dame*, none of this second rate D.A.R. stuff. If you say you met Ed Pickett the fifth or a scion of Jeb Stuart, she'll glower like you're a sharecropper tracking mud on her rug, all to remind you the war between the states was a mercenary, white-trash sort of affair, and Abe Lincoln nothing but a rail-splitter. I have a thrice-great uncle who was conscripted to tend the Confederate wounded, who himself was hit in the knee by a shattered cannonball during the second Battle of Manassas. Why he was there no one knows; he was supposed to be south of the battle patching Rebels back together. His leg swung loosely at the knee. He enlisted a poor corporal to finish the amputation. Uncle Randolph survived, and was awarded the

Confederate version of the Purple Heart. He died in '85, full to the gunwales with laudanum, complaining his missing shin was killing him. Beyond that, the Civil War is declasse, WWI the beginning of the end, and the second World War Armageddon trumpet blasts, when the wolf that suckles Romulus and Remus licks her chops and devours the founders of Western Civilization. The second World War took the best and the brightest, she said, and bootlegger's sons rushed in to fill the void. I know Mother generalized from heartbreak; she lost boyfriends and fiancés. My alleged father never much appreciated her assessment that only the second-rate survived, even if a future President was a womanizing coward who made public shows of courage aboard a dinky boat. Father was a demolition frogman and a decorated fighter.

The rest of the bedrooms are set up for guests, baby breath white or pale blue, with canopy beds and lacy nightstand covers and porcelain lamps with silky shades, and polished walnut chests of drawers with mirrors that make you look better than you really do. The hardwood floors have a seasoned squeak, and the high-ceiling rooms a settled air. A crib is bedside in each.

The bathrooms are bright-white, small-tiled, with claw-footed tubs and chained stoppers dangling from the spouts, and large ceramic basins, where the water doesn't splash, but gurgles politely. After fleabag johns down dark hallways, warehouse shitholes jackhammered into concrete floors, and jail, I'd forgotten how fast a bathroom registers where you stand in the world. Anna Ruth's scented the splendors with Pear's soap and lavender.

On the third floor are two large rooms, one of them converted to an office where my alleged father worked, and later slept, now bare and swept clean, and the other down the hall my old bedroom, where I drop my duffel bag on a battered club chair.

Someone's taken down the pro-ball pennants and team photographs and high school and college letters. There's a white square on the wall where a boxing photograph was hung. I find it in the closet where the other tags of my sporting life are stored. I wipe the glass clean with my sleeve.

In the photograph I'm throwing a hook in the Golden Gloves state championship. It knocked the guy down and put me in the quarterfinals, where twenty seconds to go I was clocked by a guy from Dothan. The first two rounds he nearly low-blowed me into the boys' choir. When I backpedalled in the third and pivoted right, my gloves lowered for fear of injured jewels, he caught me with a hook that put me halfway through the ropes. It took me ten minutes to remember my name.

Later I found out the guy's father was the man who ran against the Wallace machinery every four years for the Democratic nomination for governor. He'd been a bombardier in the second World War. On a night mission over Germany flac ruptured a fuel line and set the plane on fire. A bomb on the rack beside the open hatch caught fire. He picked it up and dropped it out the hatch, saving the plane and the crew, but he was disfigured horribly.

He returned to Alabama a state hero; he made a handsome killing off soybean futures and farm machinery and built a tire plant in Dothan. He bought a local television station. Every election year he'd buy statewide time and air himself without his wig, eyebrows, lips, nose, or ears, as featureless as candle wax, and make a plea for governmental honesty. He likened his workday prosthetics to duplicity in certain politicians; he came before the public undisguised, exactly what he was. Every election fall Alabamians watched his half-hour pitch with appalled fascination. His head looked like a big toe with the nail torn off. The night I boxed his son he was ringside with his face on. He must have been proud of his kid. I figured Troy learned how to fight challenging wisecracks about his daddy.

On a low table against the wall sits a potbellied Buddha fatly smiling. A meditation mat lies on the floor before it. On the opposite wall are tacked posters for an art gallery opening. In one of them two nudes sit on a sofa in the dark watching a TV, dumbly agog, their faces spooky from the blue moon light of the screen. The other poster is a black-and-white photograph of a row of urinals snapped at pee-level. In the corner stands a woman who looks at the viewer like she's clever because she's strung with hubcaps and therefore knows some secret about the world you're too stupid to understand.

Now that I understand the emperors have no clothes and the cosmos is a tirebitten nightmare lined with pisspots, I can sit down to supper with a clean conscience.

In the bathroom washing up I look out over the floodlit yard and see a white-bearded man with a wild shock of white hair walk out of the woods and pick up a tray off the back steps and carry it into the woods.

Mother appears out of the dark hallway that leads to her wing of the house.

Her hair, instead of beauty-parloured like a rising crown, falls behind her ears in gray cords. The long blue regal bedroom robe is gone; instead, she's wearing a beige blouse and summery shoes. She's lost weight. Her face is more deeply lined, cross stitched with wrinkles where it's thinned, making her look more firmly focused.

"Mother?" I ask.

"Aerobic dancing," Hattie says.

"You look great," I say.

She looks ghostly. "My blood pressure is down nearly thirty points," she says. "Welcome home."

We embrace, lightly.

"We will be seated soon."

I move into the dining room, addled by the calm. I fix a bourbon out of the sideboard.

I was prepared for a spiel all the way down the genealogical line, how Randolph boys all the way back to the first Webb from Londowntown 1607 washed ashore with Captain John

Smith, all of them late bloomers who married hothouse flowers, or tobacco speculators the wheel of fortune turned into Indian givers, the same wheel that won and lost fortunes a dozen times before they abandoned gambling, drink, and brothels to stand fast for their families' futures, their sons and their sons' sons not turning the corner on maturity until they were well into their thirties, all the way up the long, lonesome family road haunted with ghosts and nervous doom across two centuries of Virginia prestige to Edmund Wilder Webb of Birmingham, Alabama, who ran off sans his banjo to make his own exploratory blunders in New York, where two of his ancestors were laid to rest in the graveyard of Trinity Church in the heart of Wall Street, Randolphs who fled Virginia and farmed the south end of Manhattan isle in the 1750s and were never heard of again until their great grandsons sold what was left of the land in single commercial tracts for a hundred thousand times what the original brothers paid for the whole southeasterly tip, returned to Virginia with a fortune that launched the Randolphs into tobacco trade that finally proved more lucrative than slaves or flour mills. Or farms.

I expected this *not* because I hadn't had my ear bent to the lore on a hundred previous occasions of captivity, when Mother held forth, and nothing, and no one, stirred—whatever the subject of conversation, Mother is able to seize its smallest thread and weave it back to the imperial tapestry of First Family, but more because I knew whatever bluff it took to put off showing her hand, my mother had already anticipated and memorized and rehearsed—probably the same evening of the day I bolted—her genetic explanation, which would put down my cat flight to inherited disposition. A curious interpretation, I figured, if only because it disavowed still, even to my genes, any influence of a father. And I expected her version of events, even if—particularly if—a deliberate lie, to reflect her faith that fortune, over the longer haul, always favors Randolphs.

Instead, she gives me a straight look that telegraphs one of two things. Either I was touched in the head to imagine what I did five years ago, or it's a secret best kept under wraps until this Docie-crisis blows over. Either way, her look said *shut-up*. I fired back a tacit *yes*, appended with a humble request for an itemized bill of goods I'll wait the rest of my life to see, but one no Randolph hush money will gainsay.

Whether it's her thinning features, or her casual appearance, nearly unkempt, or the way her eyes have moved farther apart and deeper into her face, as if sunk there by a sorrow, I can't say, but looking at her I felt her whole attention transfixed, as if anticipating what in her mind is already a *fait accompli*.

Hattie pours a sherry out of the crystal decanter on the sideboard and sets it at Mother's place at the end of the table.

Anna Ruth and I bring in from the kitchen Blue Willow serving dishes of fish and field peas, a cold glass bowl of salad, and a basket of yeasty rolls and cornbread.

I note fish on Friday is still observed, though the Montgomery governor's mansion entertains more Catholics tonight than the Claybornes.

"Where's Father?"

"Preoccupied. You would please say grace, Webb."

Mother has not looked at Hattie since they sat. We always had the prayer ring at meals, though it served more to embarrass than bless. We're sitting too far apart now.

"*Deus absconditicus. Gloria Patri, et Filio, et Spiritui Sancto.*"

"Is that it?" asks Mother. "A few words of meaningless Latin?"

"For now," I say.

"Think about Eudora," she says.

The long dark table is set with shiny silver and china. The crystal goblets sparkle. We pass the platters of food left to right.

Once a day we went full formal with Virginia wares, even if neighbors were grilling hot dogs next door, while their guests grazed the fairway lawns with paper cup cocktails. Mother wanted us to remember generations of Virginians ate off the same china with the same bent, tarnished forks. The crystal decanter Hattie poured sherry from supposedly sat on the Presidential desk when Madison managed the War of 1812. But if it was Madison's, how did the Randolphs get their hands on it?

Mother has up a tiny silver bell next to her setting. We stare at our plates until the tiny crisp tinkling sets us lowering.

"*Accipite et manducate ex hoc omnes,*" I say.

"What?" Hattie asks.

"Let's eat."

"Mother," Hattie says, "Webb asked where Father is."

"He's living in the woods," says Anna Ruth.

"I saw him. Something."

"He keeps to himself," Mother says.

"So," I say.

"He comes up for Sunday dinner sometimes. And not another word of Roman rubbish. If you wish to pray outloud, *The Book of Common Prayer* has stood the Randolphs in good stead for well-nigh five hundred years."

"No he doesn't," Hattie says. She breaks off a wedge of cornbread and butters it.

"We never camped out," I say. "What gives?"

"He built a retirement house in the woods, half way to the bluff," Mother says. "A cabin, I mean. As a hobby. A shack, actually."

"But you've never seen it," Hattie says. She cuts me a conspiratorial look.

"I have no intention of seeing it. When my last breath is drawn it shall be standing there still, unseen by me."

"Well," I say.

"Well what?" Hattie asks.

"What went wrong?"

"Nothing," Mother says. "He has merely lost his mind."

I pass the field peas to Anna Ruth.

"He was struck by God," Anna Ruth says.

"Sort of like *lightning*," Hattie says.

"Preachers," Anna Ruth says, "call it the glory of the light."

Mother stares at her sherry.

"He came downstairs one morning and asked for a box of matches," Anna Ruth says. "Later I'm fixing to go the grocer and he's in the back yard standing beside a heap of clothes and boxes of old insurance papers and murder mystery books. He's wearing the oldest, rattiest, Clorox-rotted rags he owns. I don't pay him any mind. He's blue because he's retired, I reckon. He's just clearing things out, assessing the situation, making up his mind about what to keep and what to throw out. But when I come home that whole stack is blazing, smoking up the sky, a fire truck pulling up right after I do, and he's standing on the edge of the woods dancing and singing and jumping round."

I get up and fix another drink.

With a pale linen napkin Anna Ruth wipes her mouth.

"The fireman hose down the bonfire, Phillip is cussing like a devil because they trampled his flowerbed, even though it's January, and your father climbs up a tree on the bluff and won't come down. He's singing and praising the Almighty like nobody's business."

"It *isn't* anyone's business," Mother says, "especially not the neighbor's. I stood under that tree and told him if he had a mind to act like a lunatic he better do it where nobody can bear witness. He came down when got hungry. All that joyful noise gave him the appetite of a pack horse."

"He burned the rest of his suits in the barbecue grill," Anna Ruth says, "so the firemen wouldn't put him in jail. One by one, every one. He was the happiest man alive." She takes a drink of icewater. "Then he ordered wood from a lumber yard and tools from the hardware and hammered up a cabin in the woods. He hasn't shaved or cut his hair since, and bathes just about as much."

"Does he sleep in a coffin?" I ask. "I mean, some monks do. Did."

"Not yet," Mother says.

"So do vampires," Hattie says.

"So what is he doing?"

"Praying," Anna Ruth says.

"For what?"

"I have no earthly idea," Mother says.

"At my five year reunion at Duke," Hattie says, "I spoke with my former professor of clinical psychiatry about anti-social behavior, particularly in the field of geriatric behavior management. Trigeminal neuralgia, senile dementia, accidental falls, incontinence."

"One need not be elderly to be demented," Mother says.

"A case in point," Hattie says.

"I asked him, 'What does it mean when a grown man, passing through the final stage of adulthood, with his parenting responsibilities behind him, and his occupation and purpose in the social realm taken away because of forced retirement—'"

"A released resource as a result of permanent downsizing," Mother says. "In other words, *fired*."

"'What does it mean when he burns all of his clothes and wearing nothing but tatters retreats into the woods, proclaiming the Kingdom of God and the end are near?'"

"Is that what he says?" I ask.

"In a nutshell."

"So, what did the shrink say?"

"He's not a shrink."

"Keeper of the damned," I say.

"What?"

"The mental health Nazi."

"He's merely trying to punish us for his sins," Mother says.

"Who?" I say.

I put down my knife and fork.

"Your father."

"What sins?"

"We all sin, don't we?"

82

"Sooner or later," I say, "you will tell me."

Hattie, ignoring us, continues.

"The professor said religious mania is the result of a childhood overvaluation of the father figure. He can't deal with his father's death or the aging process or retirement, so he exalts the father figure into a god and asks forgiveness for killing him."

"He's been touched," Anna Ruth says. "I've seen it before. He may *look* crazy, but no ma'am, he sure enough isn't."

"He's a selfish baby," Mother says. "Religion is about charity, decency. What's decent and charitable about living alone in the woods like a savage?"

"In CCD," I say, spooning the last of the field peas, "we learned in the Dark Ages monks prayed continuously, to take up the slack for the millions whooping it up, fornicating and drinking, having a high old time before they bite the dust. Prayer sustained divine will and kept the world from flying to pieces."

"CC what?" Anna Ruth asks.

"Confraternity of Christian Doctrine," I say. "My catechism class. Every Wednesday afternoon at St. Francis'. After school."

"You fought it like the devil," Mother says. "I told your father if you didn't want to go I couldn't make you."

"So rosary beads," Hattie says, "are going to keep nuclear warheads from turning us into cosmic dust? Shield us from ultraviolet rays? Keep an asteroid from smashing into Siberia?"

"Why not?"

"I should have never allowed him to raise you with such superstitions," Mother says. "Or Edison either."

The nickname T.E. for her genius son never caught on with Mother.

"T.E.'s a physicist," I say.

"And you?"

"A bastard," I say.

"No you're not," Hattie says. She's too far away to punch me on the arm.

"In any case," Mother says, "if you see a bearded beragged

specter drifting through the woods singing nursery rhymes to the pine trees, do not be alarmed. You know now who it is."

"No, I don't."

"And he won't come into the house even if Docie is gravely ill, much less trouble himself with a visit to Intensive Care." She sips her sherry twice, then a third time for good measure. "The way he looks, they'd lock him away before he made it through the lobby. You'd think he was Moses seeing a burning bush, his eyes are so lit up. He's gone pure lunatic, I tell you. Even the pope has sense enough to shave."

"Where is Docie?" I ask.

"St. Luke's." The table falls silent.

"I've never heard of it. Is it new?"

"Brand new," Mother says. "The best care money can buy. And it's a beautiful building, as nice as any old Catholic hospital."

"Last year Mrs. Jimson nearly died of fright," Mother says.

"About time," I say.

"She saw your father wandering around their property line in the woods like he'd escaped from the state asylum."

"The Randolphs is a private facility," Hattie says.

Mother takes a deliberate drink.

"I told Mrs. Jimson it was our new yardman."

Mother spoke before she finished swallowing. She coughs. With her tarnished fork she idly tinks food around her plate.

Hattie leans forward, wincing.

"Are you sick again?" Mother asks.

"Yes," she says. Hattie leans forward for a fencing lunge at Mother, tickling her catastrophe, she calls it. "First, we have a gardener; his name is Phillip. We don't need a yardman. Second, the only relative I have in an insane asylum is Aunt Clara."

I stare a stone-lipped *don't*. She sits back and rubs her stomach, considering another angle.

"My sister is *not* in a state institution," Mother says.

"No one said she was," I say.

"She has been," Hattie says.

"Her unfortunate condition," Mother says, "is tended to by the best doctors and nurses money will provide. It so happened The Commonwealth of Virginia's public institutions provided excellent care. The charitable institutions of Alabama aren't fit for livestock."

"What she means," Hattie says, looking to me, "is that Medicare now pays for private care, but in Virginia fifteen years ago not even the best insurance would cover all the costs. *And* Aunt Clara didn't have any insurance."

"Why not?"

"Accost the next unfortunate living on the street," Mother says, "and ask him if he has paid his quarterly premium, major medical, life, dental, what have you, and if he has not, ask this person why he has failed to arm himself against the merciless blows of fortune."

"It's a promise," I say.

I drink. The room takes on a bourbon glow.

"So you had her declared incompetent."

"She became a ward of the state," Hattie says.

"Ye gods," Mother says, "she didn't even know her own name."

"She got so bombed in Byrd Park," Hattie says, "with the parents at T.E.'s twelfth birthday she fell in the boating pond. She nearly drowned."

"How do you know all this?" I ask.

"*Hattie*," Mother says.

"Three years ago the state of Virginia passed a law making any ward of the state the responsibility of surviving relatives. A clean-the-nut-house bill. Most weren't as lucky as Aunt Clara. A few were forced on poor relatives. Others were sent to halfway houses, or returned to the state institutions like undeliverable mail, when relatives consulted their lawyers and were told the law wasn't legally binding. When I was in Richmond making arrangements to fly Aunt Clara to Birmingham, I looked into the competency proceedings. At that point she was a goner. No speech, no real reactions, the saddest, quietest thing you ever saw. A testifying psychiatrist said prescription amphetamines and barbiturates and narcotic pain killers combined with binge drinking aggravated an organic personality disorder."

"You mean just living, don't you, Hattie?" Mother asks.

"No."

"Also," Hattie says, "I discovered an interesting detail about our aunt."

"Hattie," Mother says.

"In 1948 Aunt Clara was delivered of a baby she put up for adoption. I contacted the agency, which went out of business in 1963. Suspicious practices. Infants missing, swapped, exchanged. Very nebulous, disturbing aura from the reports I read. The state appropriated the records."

"Well?" I ask.

"They refused to give any details about the adoptive parents, or even the sex of the child."

"It was a girl," Mother says. Her face is pale and red. She stares at her plate.

"Who was the father?"

"You'll have to ask her that yourself," Mother says.

"Where is she?"

"In Bellewood, east of Irondale."

"Your Aunt Clara paid for her mistakes." Mother's voice is a whisper up a notch. "I know more than you *ever* will how much. For God's sake, have pity on her."

"Me?"

"You."

"So it's all true," I ask.

"Story changes every time I hear it," Anna Ruth says.

"Stories do," Mother says. "But it's true, even if the story changes."

I pour another bourbon out of the sideboard. Hattie brings in a pot of coffee.

"So father knows, is *aware* of, Docie," I ask.

"I suppose so," Mother says.

"Dr. Carnell, my professor, said religious delusions often involve a chemical imbalance that causes sexual dysfunction." Hattie has found her angle. She sits up. "For my part, I think that sort of view is too limiting. On the astral plane, he's coming to terms with former lives. Sometimes souls who can't resolve a path out of this plane of existence hang around to haunt the living. Friend said alcoholics, for instance, have mischievous spirits raising a ruckus all around them, egging them on, so they can vicariously enjoy the intoxication of the dysfunctional person still in this dimension." She cuts me an touche look.

"Phillip could grow an acre of corn in that talk," Anna Ruth says.

"Looks like he has," I say.

"Your father never had a dysfunction in his life," Mother says. "If anything he feels like he wasted his life for *not* having constraints. The vice of anger, to name one. Remember people used to have children out of wedlock, but they were never for a moment proud of it. Now nobody gives a damn."

"I don't follow."

"Ask Hattie."

"Hattie?"

"A daughter of a friend of Mother's is pregnant," she says.

"So?"

"The father won't marry her," Mother says.

"Not true," Hattie says. "She won't marry him."

"Who? Why not?"

"Katie, Caroline Simpson's daughter."

"Without the Simpson trust," Mother says, "she'd marry a bricklayer if he went to his bended knee. On her twenty-fifth birthday she received the same trust arrangement Edgar and Rebecca did, only she lost her head. She dresses like a call-girl and she wears more crucifixes than a nun. She's turned into a little nut, I tell you."

"The guy's a jerk," Hattie says. "She wants a baby, not a

husband."

Mother's neck flushes red.

"And *you*. What does this princess want? Two husbands? Five? None at all is what you've got. Are you above the bonds of matrimony?"

"I know *what* I want. No bondage for me."

"A slave to vanity is what you are. Which is worse?"

"Marriage."

It doesn't surprise me Katie got hooked up with a no-count she won't marry. She had sonar for sounding the wrong men. My sophomore year we had a spring break fling that left me a heap of crepuscular longings, despair, and a body that could barely walk without tottering. Kirstin's parents—trustees better describes—were vacationing in Egypt; her mother, at the time, was an amateur Egyptologist, mystic, sorceress, and congenital millionaire. Her mascara'd eyes look like serious shiners. Katie had intimate knowledge of Eros, and when she cried out with incantatory signs of pleasure, she nearly drove me clear out of my mind. There wasn't a branch unexplored on the Tree of Knowledge. Nothing happened but endless pleasure, which is boring, after a while; after seven days, it's downright depressing. Nevertheless, one afternoon we were lying on her wide, third-floor bed. She could tell I was falling hard, so she showed me a picture and let me know where I stood. She was in love with her Greek professor at Vanderbilt. I got up and leaned in front of the dresser mirror. How could I have imagined we'd sail past spring break? Shame at how stupid I looked burned my ears. She expected him to divorce and remarry, but later she found out he free-lanced with students with no intention of surrendering the comforts of home for a new one. When I saw her the summer after graduation, she looked like he'd feasted on some tender part of her heart.

"How's the magazine?" I ask.

"It's not a magazine," Mother says. "It's a scholarly quarterly devoted to publishing serious historical essays concerning regional lore."

"'Lurleen Wallace: Saint or Satan's Whore?'" Hattie says.

"Are you *drunk?*"

"Of course not," Hattie says.

"Caroline joined our advisory board last week," Mother says.

Vulcan Quarterly is a bozart production; the Simpson stamp is more than approval. It's intaglio on gold leaf.

"She bought a seat on the board," Hattie says.

"Volunteer work takes her mind off her daughter's problems," Mother says.

"You should try it, Mother," Hattie says.

"The great granddaughter of the man who came from Fall Creek with nothing more than a mule and a feedbag and twenty freed slaves and started Birmingham Steel and helped found the town after the war when there was nothing here but mining camps and abandoned sharecropper farms doesn't *need* to buy a seat on any board. She already owns the entire building."

"She doesn't own Katie."

"She may surely *dis*own her." Mother looks at Hattie, then me. She couldn't have known Katie was in possession of enough sexual paraphernalia to demoralize half of Christendom. "Living in New York and due next month without a husband and unwilling to tell her mother *who* on earth the father is, if she even knows, high on the hog off Simpson money like it'd grown on trees she'd planted a hundred years ago and wasn't a gift that bore obligations along with benefits she takes for granted. But that's the way women are these days, all glands, like baboons, and predictable as the moon to forget their family's reputation."

Hattie and Anna Ruth exchange glances.

I wonder if Mother thinks I got Katie pregnant in New York. I don't know how Katie got pregnant. She had double redundancy birth control—lambskin condoms, diaphragms, D-con spermicides—in case in the all-purpose Pill failed. That baby wanted its way into this dizzy world.

Hattie doesn't eat, she *feeds,* and this bothers Mother to no end. While we dine again in silence I can hear the ice clicking in the water glasses and the wet sound of Hattie munching. Mother has a blank, glaring expression, a look like, Well, it's too damn late for me to do anything about *you.*

"Perhaps," Mother says, "you have to eat for three as well, Henrietta."

"Maybe four," Hattie says.

Mother looks melted down and pale.

She politely crosses her knife and fork on her plate and rises out of her lute-backed chair and puts her napkin to her mouth. She's already crying when she turns out of the room and floats to her wing of her house.

I look at Anna Ruth, but she's looking at Hattie, who stares at me like she's about to say something mean about Mother.

I wonder why I had to be born dumb, because suddenly the supper's conversational Stratego comes clear. Henrietta's pregnant, by damn, as far as I can tell, three months.

Hattie smiles up at me.

"Is it true?"

"Yes," she says.

"Boy or girl?"

"I haven't decided yet."

We clear the table and wash up. Dinner's not sitting well, and Hattie's stockcar driving won't help, so I ask her if I can drive to the airport.

"Alone?" She gives me a you're-past-the-legal-limit look.

"No."

Mother believes Hattie tossed her diaphragm out the window like a frisbee and got with child out of spite, pulling a final Aunt Clara on the family name. There's truth to that. A blood tie makes love obligatory, if ambivalent, but they've so knotted up that painful obligation with every conceivable weave and hatch they're like the same cut of cloth.

But in public they act more like *Spy vs Spy* than mother-daughter. They pack off grievances like pipe-bombs and accuse one another of treachery even as they blow one another to bits.

Here's how it went down: Mother asked Hattie to give the baby up for adoption, Hattie declined, as much out of umbilical ties as a will to resist Mother's imperial designs. After all the fits were thrown and the scenes turned pastoral in the aftermath of stormy confrontations, Mother asked Hattie to move in for the duration. Hattie agreed, anticipating treaties, but she knew in the cockles of her heart she was powerless to turn away from the parent who caressed her with so much critical attention growing up. Hattie has never lived long outside the ten-mile radius of Mother's domain.

Neither has Amelia.

Nor Docie, either.

"Faster," Hattie commands the Audi in front of us. She flicks her lights bright. The driver's head and his spiky hair with white patches of scalp look searchlit, as if we're seeing more than is legal or polite. "We're going to be late."

"Good."

"He reminds me of you," she says, dimming her lights.

"That guy?"

"The father."

"Whose?"

She pats her stomach. "Are you embarrassed?"

"I'd marry you."

"He's self-educated. He used a word for it. Autodidact."

"What does he do?" I ask. We blast through the Roadcut in Hattie's module.

"He's a correction's officer. He works nights. Reads two or

three books a shift."

"He's a prison guard?" I sound like Mother.

"Minimum security."

"That reminds you of me?"

"Looks. The way he looks."

"Why won't he marry you?"

"He's already married."

"Does Mother know?" Hattie honks and passes the drifting Audi. The driver, a ring in his nose, flips us the bird.

"No. She thinks he's divorced. He *is* separated. His wife is thirty years his senior."

"How old is he?"

"A few years older than me. Thirty-five."

"Maybe she'll kick off."

"He'll marry his mother then."

Vulcan in the dusky light stands atop Red Mountain. He leans towards downtown in benediction of the Bessemer mills, the derivative scale-model skyline—a grey smile with missing teeth—the easterly shacks and warehouses and shanty towns in their shadow, blesses the gritty public pools and the soot-gouged, pebbly benches of the parks, the lifeless beslimed lily-ponds of the public library, the adult book stores and pool halls and bus stations and federal projects and fast food chains, blesses the northerly developments that ramify clear to Huntsville and the sprawl of westerly pine woods stretching into the twilight distance, where legions of dead Chevies sit deep in the woods on cinder blocks like memorials to the lost war of the modern confederacy and its infantry of rednecks, and with his raised arm wards away all mediocre folk from southern passage to the Elysian fields of Mountain Brook, except domestic help, Negroes only need apply. The traffic indicator on his torch is red; another citizen has died in a heap of twisted metal and exploded tires.

* * *

"At first, that I didn't want to marry him. That nearly put her in the hospital. Chest pains, the dizzies. She was in bed for days. Then I told her the truth; he won't marry *me*. She practically leapt up, and asked me to move in."

"Sounds best, for the time being."

"Mother needs me there."

"Does he come around?"

"Not on your life. She called the cops when I said he was coming by. She won't have any *prison* guard on the Randolph estate. She's superstitious."

"Sounds psychic."

"He visits me at work."

"He's not a *patient* I hope."

"No."

Hattie downshifts and changes lanes. We pass an abandoned warehouse. Inside bums stand around a barrel fire beneath a clerestory of busted windows.

"He's happy about the pregnancy, but I don't expect much parenting from him. He's still looking for the right life-companion."

"His life is half-over. What's wrong with you?"

We pass a Confederate Angel riding a spidery chopper. He wears a spiked helmet, German, WWI, and a blue-jean jacket with cut away sleeves. On the back of his jacket is embroidered a faded Stars and Bars. His earring is a large caliber rifle casing. A heartshaped *bitch* is tattooed on his flabby deltoid.

"Our auras don't mesh," Hattie says. "It *is* my fault. I'm much too possessive. He needs more growth experience with other people. In terms of reincarnation, he's still very young."

"I never thought of using metaphysical one-liners to get laid. How can you talk so reasonably about this guy?"

"I'll have the baby. I won't need him. If he wants to come around, it will be on my terms. If not, fuck him."

"I'll help. I won't be much. Teach her how to knock people down. You can teach her how to fence. She'll need to know, soon. Satanism is on the rise."

"It's a girl?"

"My guess."

"Why so violent?"

"Why not? There are three shades of family: the militant, the suffering, the glorious. We had enough unhappiness; glory is out of the question, for now. Militant is due."

"Okay."

We race under the pink vapor lights along the elevated freeway, through downtown, the twilight ruin of smelting and choking smoke. Oddly, tonight the air is clear.

"I met him at a spiritual encounter group."

"The Unitarian Church?"

"Yes. He doesn't have a formal education, but he's real smart."

"Again," I ask, "why won't he marry you?"

"Hell, Webb, he's not even divorced yet, so lay off the Judeo-Christian horseshit. I haven't seen you walking up any aisle."

"Claire wasn't pregnant."

"How do you know?"

"Has Mother met him?"

"No, but he already doesn't like her. He says when the Revolution begins people like her are going to the wall."

"What revolution?" She's echoing the rodomontades he probably trowelled on bedside between sexual favors.

"When the impure will be purged from the earth."

"Cosmological enemas."

"For*get* it, Webb."

She accelerates and whips past a natural gas truck. On the back of the tire flaps is stamped "Heil."

"What's his name?"

"Never mind."

"Good family."

"He doesn't believe in surnames. It's patrimony."

"Nor in matrimony neither."

"Who bolted before the invitations were engraved?"

"I did. I'm a bastard."

"Son of a gun." I look for any clue of a secret shared. I see none. Her euphemism was aimed at Mother.

"How will child support services serve a him subpoena if he doesn't have a last name?"

"They won't. I'm not suing him."

"Is Claire pregnant?"

"Not by you."

Stopped at the red light beside us two deaf women in an Accord argue with their hands.

Hattie's downturn luck with men has taken a longer run than anyone had reason to expect. When she was fourteen she wanted to run away and work in a glove factory in Kentucky with an underground d.j. reincarnated in microdot and *Jesus*. Now she's pregnant by a metaphysical prison-guard who wants to haul her mother in front of a firing squad. That's his appeal.

No, it's simpler than that; Hattie went way out of her way to select a progenitor who would never pass Randolph, FFV muster. She needn't have gone half so far. No one ever would.

The church where she met him is not so much a congregation as a cross between a swinger's club and a philosophical society, with summer retreats that address the Big Question, like how many affairs are possible in a ten day stretch? When I was home my senior year at C.U., Hattie invited me to one of their free-for-all Sunday services, with the promise of brunch. I never saw such a group of goofballs in all my life—porcupine acupuncturists, myopic aura-readers, logorrheic channelers, acidheads fried to speechless wisps, their eyes as dull as old marbles, phrenologists, astrologers, fortune tellers, all of them trembling so with gossamer sensitivities I wanted to blow them over with a huff and a puff. Members of the congregation took turns at the pulpit and made a racket about reincarnation and plants having souls. One young woman with a sweet face and tiny voice discussed how dimensions are malleable and how we create our own reality because the physical world is just an extension of our psyche, but I would have laid anyone in the room a hundred-to-one she'd never been slammed in the face with Everlast, or bodypunched so hard her rib cage felt like a Japanese lantern. Another woman who practiced white magic said Jesus was a warlock who pulled rabbits out of his hat, so to speak, but *she* was denounced by a man who said Christ was an invention of St. Paul, who used the Resurrection as bait-and- switch to swindle the underclass.

I was still a reflex Catholic, so it sounded like Tower of Babel talk to me. I've since relaxed the grip medieval dogma has on my soul, with more vertigo to show for it, but at the time they all sounded damned.

Expecting to take Communion I silently confessed to the sin of pride—after all, imagining fellow Americans cast into the brick-kilns of hell does not constitute charity—but instead of transub-stantiated wafers and wine they served Wheat Thins and wine spritzers. At a reception afterwards Lisa, the massage therapist, who was legally blind, judging from her glasses, told me my aura was dark blue. I was a violent, sad sort. I told her I was Holy Roman down to my bones. She said that was my appointed burden to bear in this life. I asked her if she was too? We all laughed. I gulped the effervescent wine, took Hattie by the elbow, and headed for brunch, but not before she invited the whole flock.

In the car I told Hattie all that mumbo-jumbo was a window into a dark world, where Satan waited for the first sign of weakness to make a play for your soul, and that every documented case of possession in the U.S. involved an adolescent whose parents fiddled with witchcraft. We yelled about evil the whole way over. At the theme restaurant I ordered prime rib and Wild

Turkey, while the crowd drank diet wine and dined on salad.
Halfway through my primal cut a vegetarian miser so pale he
looked like he'd been leeched by a medieval barber glared at me
with horror as I sliced the delicious roast. He was eating what
looked like sweet feed. *Plants* have souls too, I said. He stared
at me like I was a cannibal. In an earlier incarnation he must
have been a cow. Perhaps I was dining on a near relation.

Hattie always wanted to fit in, regardless of the adopted
group, and changed world-views like skirts. Her stubborn, Dark
Age brother embarrassed her. Her friends were well-heeled,
visionary hippies; I was Catholic ape up from the catacombs.
Hattie never asked me back.

Lisa, though, took hopeful note of my ignorance. She offered
me a free message. Later that week, during the rubdown at her
office mellowed with sitar music, she said football would make
me a cripple; my chakras were full of knots. At the time my
knee was in a cast, and I was sadder than I ought to have been,
knowing I'd never flatten another linebacker.

"Do you have a girlfriend in New York?" Hattie asks.

"No," I say. Like a tired boxer, Hattie is telegraphing her
punches; she wants to talk about Claire.

"Does she have a name?"

"She doesn't believe in them. Isn't this the airport turn?"

"No."

"What's her name?"

"Ashley. Laura."

An ice-cream truck slumps to the side of the road with a flat.
An old man in a white shirt and black bow tie swears and kicks
gravel at the Bozo painted on the panel. Clown music passes.

"That's her stage name."

"She's an actress?"

"Off Broadway."

"Really?"

"Times Square."

"How did you meet?"

"I was a bouncer for the club."

"Club?"

"She's a live sex-performer."

"Not a dead sex-performer?"

"Most everybody who ever lived. Honestly. She specializes in the educational exhibition of Sapphic love. It's the only humane way to behave these days. In the week I worked there I learned a lot."

"Claire's a reporter."

"To whom does she report?"

"The Science Section of the *Post-Herald*."

"Is she still a lesbian?"

"Never was."

"I regret to hear that. I was looking forward to a reunion."

"She's getting divorced."

"Excellent."

"Her mother's dead."

"I know."

"She doesn't have any brothers or sisters."

"True."

"We sort of adopted her. We're her family now, Webb."

"Is she pregnant?"

"Was."

"I know. She had a miscarriage."

"Several."

"Did she have a baby?"

"Not by you."

A tiny triangulation of blinking lights descends in the distance.

"What's she doing in Columbia?"

I motion for Hattie to pull into a 7-11. I buy a quart of milk. Hattie backs up demolition-derby onto the airport road.

"It's been a nasty battle, Webb, so be considerate."

"I will."

I drink the milk.

"So why is she getting divorced?"

"Adultery."

"Did she cheat on him?"

"She's got this loyalty complex. Like this prick has a god-damned *right* to run around on her."

I turn down the radio. A man imitating a chicken is advertising fried nuggets, with two new sauces, an exclusive Magic City extravaganza. Then d.j. makes a farmer's daughter joke. It is so frankly obscene I laugh from disbelief.

"Shut up," Hattie says.

We ride. A jet screams overhead.

"I'm glad you have Laura, or Ashley, or whomever."

"Claire has been under a great deal of stress and spiritual disharmony lately. She doesn't need any guilt trips laid on her."

"I won't lay a hand on her, I swear."

"That's not what I mean. Guilt traps either."

"She's not my mother."

"What's that supposed to mean?" Hattie asks.

"You don't think I loved her?"

"No."

We park in the short-term lot and walk to the terminal.

Hattie is imitating Mother. "And my *own* children treating me like the hireds, and only Claire taking any interest in what I'm doing, while the rest of you say I'm afraid to leave my own house, when you know I don't care for cars and never learned to drive properly and can have anything I need or want delivered to my front door."

"She doesn't go out?"

"No."

"The last time this happened."

"I know."

"Amelia tried to hang herself with a pair of *L'eggs*."

* * *

"Claire saw this coming."
  "Saw what?"
  "Docie's accident. They're close."
  "Docie and Claire?"
  "Yes."
  "How?"
  "Claire has low-grade psychic ability. For instance, you'll be thinking of someone, and out of the blue she'll ask you how they are. She isn't aware she's doing it. The day of the wreck she was anxious about Docie and called me at the office. I was counseling a recovering suicide."
  "Post-mortem?"
  "She failed."
  "Claire majored in physics. She doesn't believe in ghosts. Spooky action, but no ghosts."
  "Do you?"
  "Which?"

Nuke the Gay Whales for Jesus.

We pass a battered van with skull and crossbones stenciled on its side.
  "Baptists," I say.
  The bumper reads, *Visualize World Peace.* On the bumper of an old Nova, *This Car is Covered with the Blood of Jesus.*
  "Who *is* this *Jesus* guy, anyway?"

"When are you due?" I ask. Hattie maneuvers between two cars.
  "October 31st."
  "Halloween?"

She laughs.

"Maybe."

I was born on All Saint's Day, the eve of warlocks, traitors, breakers of their solemn word. Growing up I was variously razzed as Frankenstein, Lurch, Blob, Thing, Boris, Quasimodo, Baby Huey, Sad Sack. Turn us again, O God, and cause thy face to shine; and we shall be saved. Gloria Pappy. I lived up to my monster rep with the help of Zadoq, a slow-witted hyperactive whose parents let him graze the suburban hillsides like an untended goat. Herr Doktors put him on stimulants to calm him down. One night I got arrested by the cops when Zadoq tossed an egg at the passing patrol car. A wet thump, a direct hit. Zadoq skedaddled. I heard him howling like the village idiot as he ran through the dark woods, when the police beam blinded me. I could have squealed, but Zadoq was a simpleton, and other than me the only other neighborhood scapegoat. We had to stick together; besides, no one would have believed me; my army jacket was weighted with Grade A Extra Large.

That night Pappy whipped me good, until I couldn't breathe, since he thought I'd egged the patrol car. Why not? I didn't inform him otherwise, since he would have added fifty lashes for lying.

If Want You My Gun, Try It

We walk through the electric-eye doors. They *shss* open. In the main terminal Arrival and Departure screens nose down from the ceilings like the alien eyeballs of *War of the Worlds*. When the laser-eye zapped the pleading priest, part of my faith went with him. Later *2001* vaporized the Roman Missal, ground zero.

I feel Rosa over my shoulder.

Claire's flight is delayed, so we sit down and wait. Video games lining a wall of the terminal are manned by kinetic adolescents.

Screens sparkle, bang, and whir; kids gape into the blinking screens, their hands blindly dexterous on the knobs and sticks, their mesmerized faces pulsing with the phosphorescent lights. A retiree in a golf cap drowses in front of a M*A*S*H rerun. Another T.V. is tuned to snow; it looks like what a foot feels like asleep. A businessman rustles his *Journal* and impatiently hikes his pants, crossing and uncrossing his legs.

The terminal building has the grimy feel of a pay phone palm-oiled by a billion hands.

"Let's wait at the bar," I tell Hattie.

"Order me a glass of whole milk," Hattie says. She heads to the woman's room.

I sit at the bar.

"Whole milk," I tell the bartendress. She turns away. "Make it two."

She totes the drinks.

"Got it that bad," she says.

"What?"

"I ain't afeared of flying."

"Nor I. I'm afraid of falling."

"I hear ye."

She lights up. She wears a copper-colored wig and peach-brown lipstick. Her brown neck is cross-stitched with nicotine wrinkles.

"Where you headed?"

"I don't know yet."

Her teeth are very white. She taps a long ash into an empty beer can.

"Best quit."

"Drinking milk?"

Hattie slides onto a barstool and holds her stomach.

"Christ I'm fat," she says. "What are you smiling about?"

"Your bastard baby," I say.

* * *

"She missed her flight," I say to Hattie. We're waiting by the metal detectors. Passengers file by.

"There she is," Hattie says.

At the back of the pastel crowd Claire rounds the corner, as aristocratic and blue-white as sculpted ice. In a purple jacket white T-shirt and jeans, she leans to one side, lugging carry-on baggage, but when the crowd parts around us I see her crooked gait is the result of a kid riding her hip, a blond Fauntleroy in bib shorts with wet combed hair looking as pleased with himself as Hannibal crossing the Alps.

"She crotch kicked that jerk in court. She *won*," Hattie says. "I can tell."

Claire sees us and smiles. I smile back. My lip twitches like an idiot's.

"Meet me in the bar."

Hattie grabs my arm. "No."

Claire lowers the chump and lets him walk. He tottles and plops on his diaper pad. Claire stands him up. He falls down again. He unties her sneaker.

"Take her bag, Webb."

Claire hands me a half-open canvas travel bag overflowing with bottles, paper diapers, baby wipes.

Claire and Hattie hug. They hug again. Rug-rat hugs their legs. Hattie lifts him up. She hugs the rug-rat, Claire hugs Hattie, and the rug-rat hugs Claire. Claire kneels and ties her shoe.

"Excuse me," I say, holding up the diaper bag, "where do you want this?"

"Hold it," Hattie says.

"It smells like poop," I say.

Hattie cuts me a look.

"Give it to me," she says.

I hand her the bag. Hattie hands the baby back.

"Hello, Webb," Claire says.

"Howdy," I say, going sodbuster. I don't know why.

"This is Brett." I step up and lean in for the hug dance, but Claire puts out a friendly hand, throwing me off balance. My bad knee buckles.

Pain like the fury of a bad tooth shoots through my knee. I twist to the good one and fall to the floor.

I get up. The only hope is to play bellhop.

"Claim check."

Claire tears it off her ticket. "Beige, with a *Catholic University* sticker on the side."

"Go Cardinals."

"It's good to see you again."

"Likewise."

Her eyes focus inwardly, like a blind girl's reading Braille.

"You look good," she says, as if she's surprised to see me alive.

"I don't feel so hot."

"Me neither."

She looks away. Irritation plays about the corner of her eye, where a mole like the crown of creation sits. I kneel down and tie my shoe.

"Get her luggage," Hattie says.

"It smells like poop!" Brett says.

I walk to the baggage carousel. I feel like I'm standing on a trampoline, then I realize my knee is going out again.

Hattie and Claire sit in the front seat of the hatchback. Claire holds Brett. I feel like the back half of pantomime horse.

"New York?" Claire wheels around holding Brett like a blocking dummy. He whines and pulls her lips.

"I want a son," I say.

"Really?" Claire says.

"So I can kick his butt up and down the block, make a *man* out of him. Humiliate the peckerwood into full stature."

"I'm too tired for this," Claire says, looking at Hattie.

"I'm not," I say.

"I want to hear about New York."

"There's nothing to hear."

"What did you do?"

"Slept in the gutter."

"Seriously."

"Most seriously."

"Anything else."

"I courted hookers in Times Square with bongos and plastic roses, where space-time is especially warped, due to the incredible energy that eroticized malice generates, like dying stars ready to go *boom*."

"Wow," Hattie says.

"I know you worked," Claire said.

Hattie turns on the radio. A thumping cacophony accompanies the warbling of a pop star, who wants to eat his girlfriend, he says.

"I worked," I say. "I was President elect of the Wobblies when I got a telegraphic summons to hellhole B'ham. The Wise Men of Gotham will have to make do without my illustrious street smarts."

The D.J. says Birmingham is heating *up*. The Magic City is *hot*. His voice is gravelly, smoked. Birmingham is *hot hot. Hot*.

The city is on fire. Flames devour the downtown area, move towards Mountain Brook. Skyscrapers totter and collapse. Vulcan fashions Pandora out of Alabama mud.

In her dorm room one night Claire was equating velocities and orbital rates when I opened her robe and kissed the unsunned white of her breasts. She closed her textbook.

"Can you account for the universe?"
"No."
"*Ex nihilo,*" she said.

The first time I spied Claire on campus she looked lean as a compass needle. She ran track. Too thin, I thought, a sylph.

When I saw her for the first time in full nakedness I realized she wore clothes as a disguise. Her contours were as full of symmetries as gravitational forces. Densely bodied and sinewed, she was full of fine sand, more hourglass than compass needle.

I realize now my graduation night tackle was *Wild Kingdom* mating play. With my bad wheel, I couldn't have caught her in a ten-yard dash; I'd have gotten cleat-divots flung in my face.

Skyey-eyed, brainy Claire. She let me catch her.

Homunculus Brett serenades his mother thorough mucoused reeds. He coughs and laughs. Hattie coos. Claire musses his hair.

"You found him in the bull rushes."
"His Daddy's a judge."
Hattie and Claire talk.
I read somewhere that bird songs are territorial. They all signal the same thing: "Go away."

Claire gives me an obligatory look to the back seat, so I won't feel left out, which excludes me all the more. I'm trying to look like what they're talking about has me hitched up with interest, when I'm taken by Claire's face, which I had not realized I had forgotten. Her words go by me like a breeze.

"What?" Claire asks.
"It's spring," I say.

* * *

Hattie and Claire discuss baby formulas.

How to face up to Claire's marriage to a vampire? Fly to Charleston: silver bullets, stakes, vespers.

Sursum corda.

A car with a plastic cockroach on its roof passes on the left.

Instead of saying I bounced a sex circus, I'll tell Claire I worked off-Broadway; instead of hanging sheetrock, branch-managed a division of HUD; instead of shuffling papers, raised funds for a major foundation. Then I'll tell her played poker and puffed cigars with Gracie Mansion politicos, and drank mineral water with famous New Yorkers at literary parties, leaving out the part about the cardshark kitchen help, who beat me at Go Fishing, and the fact that the only people I met were domestics, maids and busboy cocktail butlers. I'll repeat some of the mayor's jokes, leaving out the fact that everyone within earshot of the Democratic luncheon I worked was obliged to offer up a laugh. I'll tell her I was on New York television, omitting the fact that I was an unfocused shoulder bussing the mayor's table, while the news camera's hot lights made his forehead glisten like a warmed-up boxer's before a bout, or a drunk's the day after. Then I'll tell her about the champagne gala affairs at Lincoln Center (I uncorked in the service kitchen, and after work hefted a case to the curb and hailed a taxi, tipping the driver a bottle) and the thundering applause and standing ovations Pavorati got at the Met, the film parties I crashed, and the rock stars I brushed up against, and make up a bathroom encounter with a famous actress at a Forbes balloon party in the Hamptons. And

I'm going back when Docie recovers, for an important reason why.

We pass a billboard, brightly lit. A woman wearing a Danskin holds a towel around her neck like a winded welterweight. She sweats. Above her head, in large letters: "Live Forever." Below: "The First Baptist Church of Birmingham."

"So who gets fed to the lions?" Claire asks.

"Southern Baptists *are* the lions," Hattie says.

"I'm king of the bums," I say.

"Bumptious," Claire says. A laugh all around, Brett the loudest.

By the time we wind up the drive I'm glum. Of the four humors my mix is tending to a predominance of bile. Melancholic, In-Darkness-Let-Me-Dwell stuff. Even simple untruths guarantee finger-cramps when you untangle the lies from the credible threads you weave them from. With tall tales, you can count on knuckle aches no aspirin will numb. It's wearying to think of the ways I could fig my life to give it a glint of glamour, *only* to impress my ex, now procreant with Vampire, guiltiest judge south of the Mason-Dixon, but it's now disheartening to think Claire wouldn't care if I was a board member forty floors high, or a Bowery bum rummaging a corner trash can.

I unload the car and put Claire's bags at the foot of the stairs. Mother floats out of her wing of the house fully composed, Anna Ruth follows Claire through the kitchen into the living room and baby-talks Lord Brett peering over Claire's shoulder, Mother hugs Claire and His Eminent Kinglet Brett breaks wind and Anna Ruth hugs Claire and Mother hugs Plentipotentate Grand Vizard Brett, who hiccups, and everybody hugs everybody and all of a sudden we're at a goddamn *funeral*.

I pour a glass of whiskey out of the sideboard.

"Webb," Mother says, "why do you stand there drinking when you can see Claire's bags have to be taken upstairs?"

"I'll do it," Hattie says.

"Not in your condition," Mother says.

"Watch me."

Hattie locks horns with Mother in order to hog the late-night girl-talk with Claire. I offer drinks all around. There are no takers.

"You look tired," Anna Ruth says.

"No problem," I say. Anna Ruth glares at the glass like I'm drinking Drano.

"Cheers," I say.

Hattie with the bags and Claire with Dalai Lama ascend the stairs. Overhead squeaks suggest Claire's staying in the middle room facing the front yard, but Anna Ruth's Mental Hygiene Pogrom—a litany of signs, symptoms—keeps me from concentrating on the ceiling noise.

"Think of how you'll feel tomorrow," she says.

"It'll help me sleep," I say. "I've got jet lag."

"A lot lags in you."

"You know."

"Sure enough I do."

I slide into the den. I drink; I float around the room, disembodied, happy as a dead man when he realizes the light at the end of the tunnel is an oncoming train.

A forty inch Hatachi, the screen as blank as a bank of fog, sits in the pine cabinets aside Mother's leather-bound edition of Gibbon's *The Decline and Fall of the Roman Empire*, and hardback editions of *The Federalist Papers* and *Notes on the State of Virginia* and John Marshall entire. A college anthology of historical essays sits beside a well-thumbed female fable about sex-romps in jumbo jets.

I turn on the television. A blond dominitrix in leather g-string, wearing a rubbery bra studded with silver spikes, with a guitar and a whip, lashes the hysterical audience of teen-agers, who undulate as if disoriented by the psycho frenzies of bum acid. She screams and strokes her guitar. Her tongue darts in and out.

I switch to the Christian channel. A carnaged weightlifter, his body kneaded knots of muscle, orates to a gymnasium of Christers. Musclebag pauses, flashes, as if by magic, a number for pledges for the ministry of God. On his t-shirt is emblazoned in blue lightning POWER.

I spin from station to station. I spill bourbon on the armrest, sop my sleeve.

A wrestler draped in a Rebel flag punches his opponent's gut, knees him in the face.

The Giants finish off the Braves in the top of the eight with a one-out grand slam.

An aerobics instructor in black Spandex bounces to soft rock as she recites the 23rd Psalm.

A Kung Fu stooge kicks and flips and chops a horde of attackers armed with Arabian sabers.

A talk show ad spot flashes. Next week's guests will include recovering lesbian alcoholics looking for suitable sperm donations—high I.Q.'s, blue eyes—Nobel Laureates, indecisive hermaphrodites, a Calvin-country tandem of ball-cutting feminist bushwhackers out to sack the empire of art and porn with legal sanctions.

I shall not want.

I call Becky in New York.

A voice I don't recognize answers the phone.

"Who's this?"

"Tom."

"Tom Thumb?"

"Are you the collegiate butthole from the CBGB's? Mr. Southern honor button-down Oxford?"

"You got it. I gave you a whack or two, fuckface."

"Speak of the devil. I fuck with my face every chance I get. In fact, I'm about to lick some very fine pussy right this minute."

"Grunt on. I'll gut you like a bloody pig soon enough."

"I'm shaking." I hear Becky say, "Tom, hang *up*."

"You know what Becky likes? A little pain with her pleasure, Catholic boy. A good whipping with the licking."

"You know how Marlowe died."

"Who's fucking *Mar*lowe."

"A dead man. Dagger in his skull. He died cursing *God*. You won't have so much luck. First I'll roast your hands. Pull a Pinocchio on your flippers. Shish kabob ear and eye and rip your heart out with tweezers. And that *pin* in your tongue. Wire it to an electrical socket. Start a new dance craze. Princess Tiny Meat's 120 volt terpsichore. For starters."

"You're one sick fuck."

"*Dominus vobiscum.*"

"Fuck you."

He hangs up.

I imagine Becky on her knees leashed like a dog in black studded leather, silver-chained, nipple-pincered, feigning fear and begging for sex and mercy, doing lines from a mirror on the floor, laughing and moaning while Tom Thumb palmsmacks her rump and works her up with a ridiculous footlong dildo. Sarah Lawrence my ass. Then I imagine Becky leatherstrapping the priapus to her bountiful mons veneris and reaming Tommy with a look of supercharged triumph, masturbating herself into orgasmic arias while Tommy groans for clemency.

I call the loft. Bill answers.

"Dominoes."

"Is Becky there?"

"Who's this?"

"Tom."

"Mr. S and M. I thought she told you to buzz off."

"No kidding."

"What?"

"This is Webb."

"I know."

"You have any work?"

"More than you can handle. How's your sister?"

"Fine."

"Becky practically moved in today. Better hurry back. Skinhead's dogging her like crazy. Won't let go. Snapping at her lovely hocks day and night."

"Tactfully put. Don't tell her I called. No, tell her. Nevermind. Don't tell her."

"No can do."

"Which?"

"You tell me." I realize Bill is smashed. Someone says, "Time is money, asshole." Bill says, "Understand, I have no foreknowledge of whether she will know whether you called or not, we're recording *all* phone calls. Soundtrack for kinetic mobile installation. Some meaningless afternoon touring an abominable MOMA biennial Becky will hear your pining voice digitized from Alabama wondering where she is and who she's with, while lifesize neon Kens, their heads in guillotines, cunnilingal bubble-brain Ivy League Barbies, who watch MTV and read Foucault and eat Orville Redenbacher popcorn, artificially flavored with artificial butter flavor. Did you see *Last Tango in Paris?* 'Butter.' She knew what *that* meant. Got a friend waiting. Parkay. Plenty of work. Hurry home." He hangs up.

I mix a godspeed drink for Becky.

Claire wants me to say goodnight. She summons me up the squeaky stairs, down the dark hall.

From under Claire's door low voices sound, one minute as solemn as foghorns, the next as silly as schoolgirls.

I go downstairs and find the bottle and head into the den. I punch the television on.

I drink by the neck, while Hattie and Claire play me for a dumbsock.

I turn off the T.V. Muffled voices through the floorboards,

then doors opening closing and hallway creaks. I stand at the bottom of the stairs. The upstairs lights go out. I bump into the front hall table. My whiskey glass falls to the floor and bounces. It was a very stupid glass, a doltish flagon for my gluttonies.

In the den I take pop after pop off the bottle. Claire lies abed upstairs waiting for me to kiss her into dreamy consciousness. A sleepy heat rises from the sheets.

The stairs move like a down escalator. I fall up to where the stairwell turns. A small window looks out over the backyard, now dark and lighted only by dim stars. A faint flame moves in the woods.

The dark is black and thick as flesh and swirls with colors and popping dots. The silence roars like there's a hole in my head where the wind rushes through.

I open Claire's door and creep inside. I kneel by the bed and prepare a speech, but words swarm in my head, a hive of startled bees.

I flop forward, hug the sleeping mound. Before I hear a scream I notice Claire feels plumper than I remember.

She kicks me away, onto the floor, where I sit on my rear end, legs straight out, like a kid plopped on his diapers.

The bedside light blinks on.

"What in the *hell* are you doing?"

Hattie sits up.

"Claire's room is down the hall," I say.

"Are you asking?"

"No."

"Don't bother her. She's very tired. So am I."

"Me three. Do you mind if I sleep here?"

I stretch out on the hardwood floor.

"Out, Webb."

"Leave me alone."

"Leave *you* alone? You're *bombed*."

"A bombardier."

She doesn't laugh.

Hattie stands over me and pulls my arm.

"All right."

I get up.

"Night."

"Webb."

"Yes."

"For chrissake, go to bed."

I hiccup.

"Yup."

I stand at the head of the stairs and sway like I'm standing on one leg. A drunk body is divided into two parts, right at the waist, and connected by a ball-and-socket joint that swivels the more you swill.

I splash my face over the bathroom basin. I lean my forehead against the mirror and breath, eyes closed, trying not to vomit. The room levels, lands.

I try the door down from Hattie's. Claire's scent's as distinctive as honeysuckle, not cloudy like perfume, but a mesospheric clearness. In New York I might be taking an autumn afternoon walk in Central Park, feeling bittersweet and sad about my suffering, when a stunning model would stroll by drawn chariot-like by majestic leashed Afghan hounds and with one whiff of that rain-rinsed scent I'd fall through the asphalt. And that notion of myself walking through spring rain grieving, or on windswept roads in wet autumns, as replete in my wonderful pain as an actor in a movie, or daydreams of Claire I'd have about Claire dying in childbirth and me showing the wide world what a long-suffering genius of pain I was, raising the baby on my own, self-sacrificial and godlike, with my picture on the cover of *People*—St. Webb, love-artist and martyr, slays the dragon of loss—and everybody would see what a soul of suffering I was, and then of course there'd be a thousand more adoring women who thought I was God's gift, and they'd all have to die too, just to prove what an saint of a suffering I was, well, all this puffery would collapse to a pancake with one brush against reality. All I wanted was Claire, and I'd turned tail and run like a scalded dog.

I kneel by the bed and nudge her awake. Her sleepy heat makes me sober and drunk all at once.

"Claire."

"What are you doing?"

"Forgot. Goodnight."

"What?"

"I forgot to say goodnight."

"It's one o'clock," she says.

I lean over to kiss her, but I can't find her face.

"You haven't been drinking all this time, have you?"

"Of course not." I hover over her, bob down to the sound of her voice. My nose hits her shoulder.

"Webb, please, go to bed."

"Can I stay here?"

"No."

I lie down next to her.

"Webb."

"Yes."

"Please go."

"I can't sleep."

"We're *all* half-crazy because of Docie."

"She's never as bad off as she acts."

"People don't *act* unconscious. Most people, anyway."

"You don't know Docie."

"Have you seen her?"

"Not yet.

"Then shut-up."

"I hear you."

I put my arm around her. She rolls away, her breathing rhythms gone to snoozing.

The bed spins. I kneel on the floor.

"Didn't anybody tell you I'm a bastard. How am I supposed to feel? I'm a bastard, Claire."

"You could act nicer." Her sentence trails off, like she's

drugged.

"Honest to God, I'm a real live bastard."

She rolls down a little more, like she's put her brain in park.

"Goodnight," she says.

I nudge her again.

"I'm crazy about you," I say. "I don't care if you've been married before, and I don't care about Bubba, either."

"I guess not," she says, sleepily. "You can't even remember his name."

"Flapper, Bubber, what's the difference?"

I feel a whitehot flash in my brain, like somebody popped a flashbulb in my face.

I remember the Caliph Plenipotentiary's Christian Given.

"What kind of name is *Brett*?"

"His name, his father's name, his father's father's name."

"What's his father," I ask. "A textile worker?"

"A federal *judge*, Webb." She raises her head. "Now get the fuck *out*."

"Are you trying to seduce me?"

"I will *traduce* you with a goddamn baseball bat, if you don't let me sleep. I'm *exhausted*."

"Desdemona," I say. She remembers Othello's final plaintive, piteous speech, after he's smothered his beloved with a down pillow.

"Was his circumscribed?" I ask.

"I divorced the prick," she says.

"You're mouth has gotten a lot awfully *foul* since I saw you last."

"It happens. Your breath could stop a bus."

I stand up.

"*The Tragedie of Edmund Webb Clayborne, Bum of Alabam.* Wherein Halitosis Humbles A Great Warrior, Brings Him to His Knees, Killing His Brag Countenance With Mouthe Washe." I fall back on the bed.

"Maybe you wouldn't be a degenerate gasbag if you *did*

something."

"Doubtful."

"Give yourself something to do."

"'I'm come from Alabamie with an Uzi on my knee.'"

"You're full of it."

"Blackface. The audience is white. With my assault rifle I take them out. At the coroner's office the corpses are draped in white sheets woven from North Carolinian cotton, picked by black itinerants and sold in outlets up and down I-95, by the Bratts, a pack of homewhite bonewhite walking dead men."

"Give it *up*, Webb."

"Now what does this voluptuary do to shelter, feed, and clothe his corpus?"

"I said he's a federal *judge*, Webb."

"He thinks he can *judge* people? Me O My. I stand accused. But this deluded fellow must die very soon."

"*Please.*"

"I'll kick his big butt."

"Christ."

"Yes, I will. I can see the dogface now. Paunchy, spreading cheeks and piles from sitting on his fat ass all day. Ulcers, turkey waddles. A tic in his left eyelid, his body sack full of half-digested shit comprised of steak and scotch and 20,000 Btu's of B.O. A legal windmill."

"All right already."

"I'll be in Charleston by sunup."

Claire springs up, like I pulled a lever. She speaks her level best.

"Docie's is at death's door, and you have no more sense or empathy or human concern than to get so drunk you can't even stand up." I reach out. She recoils like I'm a rattler. "Keep your hands *off* me."

I fall back on the floor.

"Get up." Claire leans over me and tugs my shirt. The lights are on. Claire is wearing pink p.j.s.

"I love you."

"Right."

Brett wakes up, whimpers.

"*Damn* you."

I stand up and fall down.

Brett laughs. "Bumptious!"

"Please get up," Claire says. She bends over. Her pajama top falls open.

"Honeysuckle," I say.

She swats my forearm.

Brett says, "Mary ate a little lamb."

Claire splashes cold water on my face.

"I need asleep," I say.

"So do we all."

Though numb as a block, I am suddenly ashamed.

"Of course."

I pull myself up by the bedpost.

Brett says, "She lived in a shoe."

"Goodnight," Claire says, with a we'll-see-about-forgiving-your-drunk-ass-tomorrow look.

She climbs in bed.

"Good night."

When you don't have a prayer of a trump card, you've got to bluff love into belief, and I haven't acted like your stand desirable-male, chain-link gold and imported sports car, with a body from the Medieval racks of health clubs, but more like a half-wit on amphetamines, blowing it to the four corners, with no subtlety.

I gauge the depth of the drunk, and how that small flame that whispers worthlessness is turned into a bonfire with booze. I *know* Claire liked me once, and I never was a mink-mustache, after-shave short, or the kind of guy who reads *Playboy* for the articles, but a jughead with a screwed-up heart.

In my room I sleep on the floor, because the bed is spinning like a wing nut about to fly off the bolt.

III

"Praying?"

Claire stands over me.

"*Mea culpa Bibite saecula saeculorum.*"

"English please."

"I'd rather have a frontal lobotomy."

"Too late." She kneels down.

My head feels like a jammed thumb.

"Come to breakfast."

"What time is it?"

"You needn't be embarrassed."

"No?"

"Mortified, ashamed, absolutely. Embarrassed? Don't do yourself the favor." Claire, for the moment forgiving, gives me a rosy, well-rested smile filled with the dewy expectation of a new day. I feel like a pelt on the interstate that used to be a dog.

She closes the door.

I turn over on the hardwood floor. The left hemisphere of my corpse is without proper sanguinity to embrace so splendid a Saturday morn.

Docie.

I hear a lawn mower buzz in the backyard like the drone of a plane.

I dreamt I was on a vintage bomber, WW II flak footage threaded with scratches, when I got sucked by my shirttail out the bomb hatch. Bombardier. I woke when I hit Birmingham, and the first time I slept with Claire.

We were watching a late-nite 40's propaganda film in her dorm room about a Flying Fortress; the movie turned sound-track as we slid off the sofa. Outside it stormed, then rained. At dawn the national anthem cleared the skies. Old Glory flapped over Annapolis.

A wave of nausea washes up my bedside confession of bas-tardy. A dead sting ray, a gull with gunked feet. A beachhead of regret. Mobile Bay is three hours away. I'll walk south, slide in, swim to Cyprus.

I pack my duffle bag and climb out the window and glide down the drain pipe.

My weight yanks the mortar nails from between the bricks and as I fall past the bay window I see Hattie and Anna Ruth and Claire in the yellow breakfast room sharing sections of the morning paper.

"Rosa," I say.

I land in the boxwoods.

Phillip shuts off the lawn mower. He pushes aside a tangle of branches and looks inside the bush.

"Tossed your ass off the plane."

"I'm fine."

I taste blood in my mouth.

Phillip offers me his hand and pulls me out and retrieves my duffle bag.

"Bag broke the fall," he says. "What the hell does that say?"

"Christ."

"Goddamn bush is ruined."

"Sorry."

"Drain pipe too."

"My apologies."

"Ain't mine."

"This helps," he says. He hands me a silver flask. The taste in my mouth is not blood but the metal taste of fright.

121

"No thanks. That's it. Finished." I hand it back.

"Say what?"

"I was just leaving."

"Suit yourself."

"Come here," he says. He pours bourbon on a rag and daubs a bloody scratch on my shoulder through a tear in my shirt.

"Yikes."

"Pain killer?"

"Not that kind."

He whips the rag back into his green gardening pants.

"What's wrong," he asks. "You in *love?*"

Phillip waves me to the greenhouse.

"Here," he says. He hands me a shovel and points to a wheelbarrow. By the greenhouse is a mound of chicken manure.

"Shovel it."

"Where?"

"Over there."

He points to a trellis at the edge of the yard.

"There's a crazy man in the woods," he says. He laughs. A gold crown glints in the morning son. "Watch out."

I shovel chicken shit.

Over my shoulder I hear someone moving in the woods, an intonation accompanying the rustling, a hoarse Gregorian pitch drifting through the trees.

When we moved to The Magic City Mother wanted to live Mountain Brook old money up. She was tired of the post-bellum poverty aristocracy of Virginia planters FFVs pretended for a hundred years. When she saw the Burke estate overlooking the small valley where the Country Club golf course unrolled like an invitation to the highest circles of Birmingham, she bought it. Written in the terms of sale was a clause that kept Phillip officially employed as landscape architect.

Caspar Burke was one of the original Birmingham steel

brokers. He was a thief and a liar and had impeccable manners. He built with Yankee husbandry a fortune his grandson Henry spent with the extravagance of an ante-bellum cotton baron. Grandson Henry, given to epileptic seizures, transformed himself into an Alabama gentleman and claimed Confederate ancestry and ownership of several pieces of the rebel flag from the battle of Murfreesboro; over his fireplace was hung the sword Beauregard surrendered at Memphis. So he said, through a rasp of Tennessee sour mash and cigar smoke.

In the 1930's Henry had built a Southern Colonial mansion in Mountain Brook vaguely modeled on Jefferson Davis' house in Montgomery and in the second World War served as a Major in the same division where Phillip was private first-class and welterweight boxing champion. Together they made a D-Day march across France, a mop-up job that ended eight months later in Paris, the week of V-E day. After the war, Major Burgess with flawless patrician timing offered Phillip a job as a yardman and imitating generations of Southern gentry who felt a paternal kinship and responsibility for their Negro help, stipulated in his will that his children would not sell his stately manor without first guaranteeing Phillip's employ as the estate's landscape architect. One thing blacks have only begun to do is lie about their lineage. The Burkes were as bogus as the Piltdown Skull, but Henry's kids didn't contest the will. Maybe they took to the notion of Phillip as a possession.

I walk the wheelbarrow over to the trellis. Downwind the ammonia rot of manure is a wall of stench.

Hattie and Claire and Mother lean out the kitchen window.

"Are you hurt?" Mother asks.

"No," I shout back. I dump the manure in a pile and walk with the wheelbarrow to the kitchen window.

I look up at Claire. I heard the lock click after I stumbled out of her room.

123

"What were you doing?" she asks.

"Last night?"

"Climbing out the window," she says.

"Your door was shut tight."

The joke doesn't take. She looks at Hattie. Their heads disappear.

"Smoke between you two," Phillip says.

He offers the flask. I wave it off.

"Back for good I guess."

"I don't know. I guess so."

Phillip sips.

"How's the gym?" I ask.

"Got a lightweight coming up, but that's about it. There's more for a kid to do these days beside box. A few mean business. Come on down and have a look."

"Box?"

"In your condition? You'd get a hernia."

"Gardens look great, Phillip. No kidding."

"We need a big rain, and we'll get it tonight. A cold rain. Hailstones. Frost."

"How can you tell? Bunions or something?"

He puts the flask in his back pocket.

"Satellites, dumbass."

He hands me a pair of shears. I trim the broken bush.

After Phillip fought in the second World War and spent a month in Paris after V-E day and travelled to Italy and Belgium a hero and liberator, he returned to The Heart of Dixie an Al'bama Nigrah. He's shown me a dozen times a crinkled photograph of a Parisian woman with big calves and black hair standing with him in front of a cafe in 1945. They're arm in arm, surrounded by a group of wine-drunk soldiers hoisting bottles like liberty torches. He said in France a black man was treated like a man. A week before he was shipped stateside, he received a letter from his wife stating the bank without explanation foreclosed the mortgage on their house and served an eviction notice through the city sheriff. When he arrived in Birmingham, his four children were parceled out to relatives, and his wife had been jailed for assaulting a police officer. His house was boarded up and a week later the block was leveled to build a warehouse. The same week his wife hemorrhaged and died on the way from the jail to the county hospital. The coroner said she was four months pregnant and had miscarried. I blamed myself, he said. Stepping out. I killed for them, so they could kill her. She was no more pregnant than Hitler's widow.

Phillip rolls the mower into the gardening shed. I hear the sound of an another engine starting. He rides out of the shed on a gardening tractor. As he rides by I hand him the shears.

He rolls to a stop.

"You think you're done?"

"I've got to get to the hospital."

"Webb."

"Yes."

"I'm sorry about Docie."

He lets out the clutch and rides off.

Claire and Hattie and Anna Ruth finish their coffee at the breakfast table. Brett squirms in his highchair.

Morning sunlight swims in the room. Birds flutter and perch on the window feeder and peck with mechanical animation. A light wind lifts the curtains.

Anna Ruth and Claire and Hattie discuss Phillip's garden and how extraordinary the flowers are this year compared to last, when a long winter and a cold spring kept the blooms low and dull.

"Ice saints," Claire says. "Iron nights."

"What are those?" Hattie asks.

"Cold weather in May."

Claire looks at me, and then looks at the glass of orange juice in her hand.

"We should get to the hospital," Hattie says.

"Let's go." Claire says.

"Webb," Hattie says.

"What?"

"What day is it?"

"Quit treating me like one of your patients."

"What day is it?"

"May Day."

"Did you hit your head?"

"I'm fine."

"Were you drinking with Phillip?"

"Not on your life."

"I'll bet."

"How much?"

Claire lifts Brett out of the highchair.

"Good boy," she says.

"Wait," I say.

I stand up and through the hallway catch my reflection in the dining room mirror. My shirt is ripped and streaked with green from the bush and dried blood runs along the scratch on my side.

"Get cleaned up," Hattie says, "and meet us later." She hands Brett to Claire, who doesn't look at me.

"I'll be ready in a minute," I say.

"We're gone," Hattie says.

I shower and change and go downstairs.

Anna Ruth sits at the breakfast table reading the paper.

"Anna Ruth, why did I leave?"

"You ain't gone yet."

"I mean, why did I leave Birmingham?"

"I don't know."

"Why do you think I left? What did everybody say?"

She folds the editorial page into quarters and without looking up reaches for her coffee.

"There was talk about you not knowing who you were and having to find yourself. Hattie-talk, mostly. She did most of the figuring."

"Not knowing who I was?"

"You heard. Hattie-talk."

"What did Father say?"

"He doesn't talk much."

"Did he think I'd come back?"

"When it didn't matter."

"When what didn't matter?"

"Ask him. Your mother was arguing with him about Aunt Clara and Bellewood. Your name came up and that's when he said you'd come back when it didn't matter."

"When was this?"

"Before he went off to the woods."

"What did mother say?"

"She said he was crazy. You heard her last night."

"I mean, when I left?"

She looks up.

"Webb, *nobody* was surprised when you disappeared. You weren't ready for any justice of the peace to sign a marriage license."

"Priest."

"Besides, youngest always slowest to grow up."

"I had six months to back out. Why did I bolt in December?"

"Lord, Webb, I don't know."

She folds the paper and yawns.

"Everybody figured it was best to leave well enough alone and let you to make your own mistakes."

"I'll bet."

"You know what I reckon?"

"What?"

"Something's troubling your conscience. Hattie told me you have a girlfriend in New York. Is that why you ran off?"

"I made that up. I mean, nothing serious. I just met her a month ago."

"After five years? You *are* a slow learner."

"The first in a while. I don't have much leverage. No cellular phone. No stock options. No career. No apartment."

"Well, are you going to tell me?"

"Tell you what?"

"You stormed into your mother's room, raising Cain, and then you vanished. Your mother looked like she was having a heart attack."

"No."

"Why not?"

"Because I don't know."

She gives me a pleasant, focused look.

"You're lying."

"Probably."

Phillip knocks on the kitchen door. Anna Ruth takes his pitcher and fills it with ice from the refrigerator door.

"Don't drip in here," she says. When she turns to the sink to fill the pitcher he takes a pop from the flask.

She hands him the pitcher. He kisses her hand and says something in French.

"What did he say?"

"Something about the next generation."

She backs him out the door.

We hear a crash on the back steps.

Phillip has kicked a over a tray left on the stoop.

"Watch where you're going," Anna Ruth says.

"It wasn't there two minutes ago," Phillip says.

"Mr. Clayborne's breakfast," she says.

I pick up the scattered plates and find a papery palm frond

tied into a Chi-rho cross. Beside it are ashes. I put the cross in my shirt pocket.

"I asked him not to leave the plates in the middle of the steps."

"You've spoken to him?"

"I've talked *at* him."

We sit at the breakfast table.

"I told him I was going to start using paper plates and he could bury them on the bluff if he didn't stop laying trays around for everybody to trip over. And you know what he said?"

"No."

"'They will eat their flesh like it was fire.'"

"What?"

"All I know is his daughter's laying in the hospital and he thinks praying in the woods is going to bring her back Lazarus-like. Maybe you can talk some sense into him. But he doesn't say a word except some phrase out of the Bible."

"I thought you said at dinner he wasn't crazy?"

"He *ain't*, exactly. He's touched all right, but times he acts more like he's filled with the devil."

She goes to the kitchen counter and opens a drawer and takes out a yellowed slip of paper.

"A few days after he burned his suits a flatbed truck pulled up and drove out over the back lawn. Phillip chased it down with one those hoes shaped like a half-moon, readying to kill whoever was driving over his grass. Two young men got out and unloaded enough tools and supplies for a small army and carried them along the path that runs to the bluff. Your mother stood at the kitchen window.

"After nearly two hours one of the men came to the back door with a clipboard. Your mother asked me to sign for it."

Anna Ruth hands me a sales receipt from Crestline Hardware. It lists as charged to the Clayborne account an axe, pick, five kinds of saws, two shovels, a wheelbarrow, a stump spud, a sledgehammer, wood chisels, crowbars, three bags of mortar, a miter box, planer, tinsnips, a roll of sheet metal, a T-square, a pitchfork, levels, hammers and nails, two sawhorses, a half-ton of bricks, four cases of paraffin, lanterns, kerosene, and a ten dozen boxes of Large Diamond Strike Anywhere matches.

"For the next three months he's in those woods *chopping* trees down, not even bothering with a chain saw, and cutting the trees into logs and building a cabin and hewing a table and chair and bed right out of the wood. By this time his hair and beard are as wild as weeds and he's wearing nothing but rags and sandals he cut out of old tires and roped to his feet. For four years he's lived out there on the bluff without speaking more than a few words to anyone and those he says directly from the Bible. When Docie had her wreck I went down the path to the bluff and found him at the edge of the cliff addressing a flock of blue jays perched in the pines. I said, 'Docie's had a terrible accident.' He turned to me with this wild look and said, 'For if they do these things in a green tree, what shall be done in the dry? I lay down my life for the sheep.' Pardon? I was on the road and I've seen the light, no doubt about it, but I don't think the right place for a believer is hiding out in the woods wearing rags and putting ashes on his head and acting like he's the only one who ever sinned or had a bad conscience in the whole wide world.

"What's more your mother never complained of it for a minute, even from the first day when they unloaded the truck to the day he moved from upstairs into the woods and started roaming the bluff like a beggar. She acted glad of it."

"Maybe she was."

"It doesn't seem natural."

Anna Ruth returns to the *Post-Herald*.

"Then again," she says, "why should it."

* * *

I pour a glass of milk and sit in the den.

Once in a Sunday CCD class a girl with a small nose and a spray of freckles and braces on her overbite asked Father O'Connor why so many of the saints began as terrible sinners. Father O'Connor was not a priest from our parish; he was old and retired and traveled the diocese visiting catechism classes. He was not aware that Jennifer's father had shot himself.

"Of all God's children," he said, "such loathsome sinners are the most qualified to testify to the grace of God.

"Saul, who became the apostle Paul, made havoc of the church and consented to the stoning of Stephen and was full of lechery and drunkenness, and on the road to Damascus the Lord shined all around him a light from heaven and blinded him with the truth of Our Lord Jesus Christ."

Father O'Connors's waddled neck swelled over his clerical collar.

"St. Augustine was a whoremonger full of the toys and trifles of his vanity when God, lashing him with shame, set before his eyes the whole mess of his sinfulness, and he repented. Why are saints such miserable sinners? Such worms? Such dungheaps? Why? Because they testify to the everlasting and infinite grace of God. They are no different than you or I, but that they were vessels chosen by divine will to sow the seed of the Word and bring forth the fruit of eternal salvation, lacking which our barren and miserable souls will blister like wieners on a redhot gridiron."

We were trying not to laugh at the word *wieners*, when we realized Jennifer was crying.

"Is my father in hell," she asked, "or is he a saint? Is he a saint?"

"My little flower, God has infinite, infinite mercy. His ways are mysterious; no human, saint or sinner, can comprehend his infinite love of frail, mortal man."

"Tell me. Is my father in hell? Is my father in hell? Is he burning in hell?"

A young nun hurried from another classroom and put her arm around Jennifer and led her out of the room. The nun looked back at Father O'Connor before the door clicked behind them. Father O'Connor cleared his throat and continued.

"My children," he said, "hell is a very real place."

He blessed us and left.

Weiners. We screamed with laughter and threw textbooks out the window.

So, according to Anna Ruth, Father had a road-to-Damascus experience. The only other explanation for his bluff retreat is that he's nuts, in which case he may as well say he's a poached egg as a saint.

From what I understand Father was fairly wild when he was young, looking as he did like Rudolph Valentino when looking like Valentino was not a bad way to look. He drank and womanized and spent his twenties in New York and Hollywood, back in the Thirties, where he took dozens of screen tests and had bit parts in movies I've never seen, except one, a RKO gangster release near the end of which he tells a henchman's moll to button up, and then the head of the bootlegger gangsters tells *him* to shut up, or else. It was an awful movie, with mannequin acting, and orchestra music that sounded like a swarm of bees on amphetamines.

I saw it by accident, at an art theatre downtown, where film festivals in the upstairs theatre were paid for by the porn flics shown in the basement. The legitimate theatre always had clever-by-half theme runs, like a week of Godzilla or spaghetti westerns.

When I went The Biograph was hosting gangster week, not the classics like *Scarface* or *Key Largo*, but the B-movies studios turned out by the hundreds. I'd skipped football practice with a couple of friends and we smoked some pot and sat in the back of the theater, giggling like girls, trying to muster enough nerve to sneak downstairs for a glimpse. At fifteen I was a dope novitiate, and before pot started giving me the cold dreads, it made me laugh until I groaned, like that guy in Mary Poppins who floats around the room laughing himself to tears.

Bill and I were slopping cokes and spilling popcorn, laughing at everything and nothing, daring each other to follow Donnie downstairs, where he'd lingered for half an hour, when he came back up and told us a guy with nothing but *skis* on was screwing a woman downhill-squat on a bear rug.

Right then I looked up and saw my father on the screen; his face was as tall as a billboard, with a fedora hat bent gangster-style over his unblinking eyes. The soundtrack warbled, scratchy close-ups cut back and forth his three-line delivery to the bootlegger, then a long-shot put him back in the crowd of dark-tailored gangsters standing beside a Harlow moll batting her eyes like they were butterflies readying to fly off a shrub. I wondered if the actress was still alive. I howled so loud the usher asked us to leave if we couldn't hold it down. I tried to tell Donnie and Bill that was my *father* up there, but I was laughing so hard they figured I was stoned out of my mind. When the credits rolled the name Max Clayton around, I knew I hadn't hallucinated. Mother said that was one of Father's screen names. The next day I asked her about the film.

"Do not ever again mention it," she said.

I gathered his first wife had something to do with it. She outwhored him in every category, so the story goes, and then divorced him.

Pappy doesn't know I know he was married before, but I've seen the divorce papers, and I know too that means more than just separation from a woman who left him for a man who had twenty bit parts instead of seventeen, a woman who banked, in Mother's version, on the expectation that if *she* couldn't make it, the new beau would rise to the top of the Hollywood glitz and become a *star*. No, divorce meant too that he was excommunicated forever, cut off from the sacraments, exiled forever from God and Church. For a Catholic, however wayward, and however much headed that way anyway, because of youthful vanity and general rakishness and every other mortal sin under the sun, it meant the ultimate serious business. *Non gratis*, turned away at the gates, damnation as perdurable as the God who'd put you there.

Catholics don't believe much of that anymore, seeing as how they'd rather feel good than imagine themselves doing the funky chicken or St. Vitus two-step on the superheated brickways of hell, or sizzling for an eternity like a Ball Park Frank on a back-yard grill or *wieners on a redhot gridiron,* and I don't blame them a bit, but for people who once believed it in their heart and soul, excommunication meant life was little more than a throwaway whipped here and there by the wind.

He was nearly thirty and about to be drafted, so he joined the Navy and was commissioned a second lieutenant. He promptly volunteered for and led what was called the Suicide Squad, a group of frogmen who defused floating mines in the South Pacific and dynamited beachheads to make way for amphibious assaults and American fleets headed to Guam and Iwo Jima, men who felt daredevil due to the not-so-lady-like women whose freedom to treat their men however they wished the men defended with their lives. Or so it seemed to Mother. Her version must contain some thread of truth. Twice decorated, he came out of the war not accomplishing the one thing he went for, that is, to fail to fulfill his wellness potential, i.e., get blown to smithereens, be-cause the Suicide Squad was just that; a lot of the frogmen got fed to the fish, so if you joined up you as much said to the world you didn't care much for living, and coming back alive might be viewed crazily as another kind of failure. Men with heartaches or damned souls make good soldiers; women to this day claim their Dear John letter sent a corporal or captain into the line of fire, where he took out German machine gun nest with hand grenades and a .45. For Father, perhaps nothing was better for his soulache than defusing floating mines in the shark-infested waters of the South Pacific, even if he survived. The war was worth a hundred years of psychotherapy. He returned home rid of the reason he volunteered in the first place. He married my mother in the post-war moment, and up until his bluff retreat was a faithful excommunicant, and a regular dad type, though strict and untalkative. And if he's undergone a real conversion, it doesn't surprise me, since he's always acted monklike to start, as if he were wearing a hairshirt for the sins of his youth. I've often thought that might explain why, and where I came from, too.

And wondered if once in twenty-six years he's ever wondered who *I* am.

What I know of Father's past I learned third-hand from Mother, who in turn learned most of it from Rosa the first year of Father's second marriage, long before Mother discovered Rosa Clayborne was Neapolitan wop and banished her forever from Virginia peerage. Rosa claimed to have never met Father's first wife. The day he shipped into New York Rosa met him at the port and took him straight to see the assistant to the Bishop of the New York Diocese and said a war hero shouldn't be shut out of the embrace of his faith because of one mistake. But divorce was divorce; the excommunication stuck. That explains why Father went to Mass at dawn in rags like a bum and knelt in the back of the church and knocked his hand to his heart and said *mea culpas* the way a Buddhist *nam myoho renge kyos* and begged for mercy, and why he never took communion or went to confession, because the moment after the war he turned to reembrace his childhood faith he realized Church law had cut him off from sacramental grace. After Vatican II when they allowed the divorced flock back into the fold, he declined, preferring to be excommunicated under the old rules. And why, I imagine, he's retreated to the woods, because now there is no longer even a Church to be excommunicated *from*.

* * *

135

I finish the milk and rinse the glass and put it in the kitchen sink.

I pick up the kitchen phone to call the hospital. I hear a voice say, "Steroids minimize brain swelling."

Anna Ruth backs the '65 Impala convertible out of the carport and points it down the drive.

"Let's put down the top," I say.

"I'm wearing a hat," she says, adjusting her hair beneath it, a bobby pin between her teeth.

We drive down Mountain Brook Parkway. The leafy May trees splinter sunlight over the newly paved blacktop. An idle steamroller sits off the road under a thicket of beech trees overgrown with kudzu. Purple poke berries, poisonous grapes, shade the deep green of woods, where a flat creek runs, its dark copper rocks washed smooth with water and softened with moss. The odor of fresh tar thickens the air.

Anna Ruth's powder white and veiny hands hang on the oversized steering wheel. She wears a flowery hat. A large black patent leather purse sits on the seat beside her. She looks like she's bound for Sunday service.

"So what's Claire's problem," I say.

"Problem?"

"She looks at me like I have a worm hanging out of my nose. One of those brown oozy nightcrawlers that looks like Frankenstein's idea of snot."

"If you were any more self-centered you'd be invisible."

"It's nothing personal, then, the earthworm look."

"Didn't Hattie tell you?"

"Tell me what?"

"Claire had a miscarriage."

"The power of prayer."

"Lordy Webb to say something so deliberately wicked. Sometimes you have the tongue of an adder."

"Who was the father?

"I suspect it was her husband, Webb."

"So she really is divorcing the judge."

"'Irreconcilable differences,' Hattie said."

"Sounds redundant."

"Pardon?"

"Nothing in common but spliced genes. Children."

"They were married, Webb. Doesn't that count for something?"

"No."

Like her sisters, Docie was raised Episcopal, which means to accommodate Mother she dressed up for Easter and spent the remaining fifty-one Sundays at home eating donuts and drinking coffee with Amelia and Hattie, while Father rousted T.E. and me out of bed every Sunday at dawn and took us to the six-thirty Mass. Once at Sunday dinner Father said Charity is the responsibility of churches, not welfare government. Docie said, All I see in Vatican City is a billion dollars worth of art treasures in the middle of a three-thousand-year-old Roman boneyard. Another empire hording gold as it declines. And who'll believe these myths in a hundred years? A Virgin Birth, Heaven and Hell? Immaculate Conception?

Brookwood Hospital is near where Docie wrecked so that's where the ambulance brought her. The building is modern and consequently has no outward marks to distinguish it from a shopping emporium or a minimum-security prison. A tip-off that it's a health center is the glow of television screens in the same place in every window ten floors up and down. Probably Father would have preferred Docie to be at St. Vincent's, the Catholic ward where I recovered from my bluff slip; it was an old Romanesque building with winged nuns and a holy smell and priests striding the halls in sanctified black. Over every bed was a graphic crucifix depicting Christ's agony on the Skull.

St. Vincent's was bought by a philanthropist. To replace the facility the Diocese built a modern monstrosity not even the Pope has the authority to bless. The Catholic Wellness Center. It's aquamarine. Broken sea shells buried in the mortar surround an abstract window so stained no light penetrates into the lobby. It looks like a place where you're not expected to die, or welcome to.

The philanthropist turned his Romanesque purchase into an art museum for his private collection. I toured the remodeled building; the museum brochure noted that artists and collectors everywhere were buying up abandoned churches. The former wards were now gallery wings hung with splattered canvases and overblown lithographs of movie and sports star supermench. In one room a wooden ring filled with sawdust sat beneath a television screen that played continuously a video of pitbulls fighting. The cool stone hallways smelled vaguely of myrrh, like sanctuaries for the sick.

Brookwood is the sort of modern building that gives me the heebie-jeebies. It's hermetically sealed, a sterile cube of metal glares and plastic sheens, with pneumatic electric-eye doors that *hsss* and florescent lights that turn skin corpse green. In the lobby the light is garish and the floors are buffed by ruminative janitors to a blinding shine and the staff in menacing white coats like behavioral scientists pretend oblivion to messages delivered by an omniscient-sounding voice over the PA system. Department store *pings* sound all around. There are no death-threats in the air, nor a countenancing of dust unto dust, much less a flattering unction for the soul, but an all-around numbness, like there isn't any life here either, but business-as-usual at the body shop.

Off to the side of the main lobby is a small door marked Chapel. It opens into a room the size of a broom closet. Anything more than a generic chapel might give patients the wrong idea. If they croak it's a medical mistake, not a crack in their hourglass; the Grim Reaper doesn't carry a scythe but wears a stethoscope and a yellow *Smile!* button on his white lapel.

We take the escalator upstairs. At the second floor we make way for an elderly lady, her head lolling forward, wheeled to the elevator by a nurse whose face is creased by a firm, habitual smile.

Hattie sits outside Intensive Care holding Brett. Down the hall through swinging doors is Emergency Surgery. A doctor in a surgical mask with her hands in the air backs through an operating room door.

"Two at a time," Hattie says.

Claire comes out of the I.C. unit. She looks wrung out.

"Go ahead," I say to Anna Ruth.

"You go. I was here yesterday."

"Hattie?"

"Let's go."

In Docie's room a large bed banked by instruments sits on oversized wheels. The floor slopes to where a drain opens. Crib-like, the bed railings are raised.

Docie's head is shaved and wrapped in gauze and bruised the color of old grapefruit where blood has spread under scalp. The right side of her face is as purple as a birthmark. A small table light makes the hematoma bruise an even blacker purple; the huge swelling looks alien, attached like a parasite to her skull, where it shines with its own malevolent, draining life. Electrode wires coil to Docie's head and intravenous tubing runs under the sheet and out. A bag of urine hangs from side of the bed, beside which a green heart monitor *blips* and an electroencephalo-graph's green screen reveals Docie's brain waves, a deep sea silence of tiny quivers. Her belly is like a big egg. She looks dead.

"Rosa," I say.

I wake up looking up at florescent lights. Hattie helps me sit up. The room whirs. I have a rush of cold sweats.

Rosa is somewhere in the room.

"Roads?" Hattie says.

"What?"

"When you fainted you said, 'Roads.'"

"Rhodes?"

"Maybe we'd better go," Hattie says.

"Not yet."

A nurse hands me a glass of water.

I stand up and lean against the railing. Hattie talks to Docie as if they were sitting together drinking coffee and watching a soap opera. She smoothes the sheet and gently lifts Docie's head and puffs the pillow.

The nurse unjigs the I.V. from a joint close to Docie's arm. A spout of blood arcs out of the tube. I hold Docie's hand and look away as the nurse changes the I.V. bag.

When I was nine one Saturday in July all of us but Mother drove to Virginia Beach for the day. A squall roared up. The wind was high and the waves churned and smashed our inflatable rafts and styrofoam kick boards into the swarming foam. The Coast Guard issued a small craft warning and scores of surfers turned out for the six-foot waves.

I floated waist-high in the surf. Father and Docie waved for me to get out of the water. Father looked mad. I saw him yelling but I couldn't hear him over the crash of the surf. He motioned for Docie to fetch me so she ran down like she was mad too and just before everything roars black and quiet I see Docie leap into a wave as it rolls onto the beach.

I wake up in the back of the car with my head in Docie's lap and the taste of saltwater in my throat. Amelia and T.E. and Hattie peer down at me and Docie's saying, Wake up, Webb, wake up.

The car rocks back and forth and the blare of horns fades in and out. I feel a warm spot on the back of my head against the cold water matting my hair and then I see there's blood everywhere, all over Docie's bathing suit and all over the towels and all over the back seat. Docie holds me down and then everything goes black again.

I come to in a hospital bed with remote control TV. Docie tells me I got El-Kabonged in the back of the head by a runaway surfboard.

"You were a goner," she says.

"Docie carried you all the way to the car," Hattie says.

"You got twenty-five stitches," Amelia says.

"So don't smile or laugh or cry," Hattie says.

"Or move," Docie says, and tickles my feet.

"Stop it," T.E. says.

Father stood by the bed. Hattie's look told me he was mad.

"He had it coming," he said. The year before I'd put my arm through a pane of glass and took a hundred fifty stitches.

"Had it coming?" Docie says.

"Next time he'll do what I say."

Hattie and Docie and T.E. and Amelia were excited because they had to stay in a hotel overnight and that meant dessert.

The next morning Hattie and Docie and Amelia came into the hospital room just as I finished peeing in a pan.

"We put fire ants in his sneakers," Docie says.

"Father's?"

"Surfer boy's."

"He said he was sorry," Hattie says.

"You know what he did?" Docie asks. She brought a box from behind her back. It was a model of a Messerschmitt, glue and paint included.

Back home I built the plane and Docie and I set it on fire in the backyard.

"Had it coming," Docie said.

The heart monitor blips and Docie breathes. The lines of the electroencephalograph waver, small identical troughs and valleys all but lifeless.

My spine tingles.

Rosa circles to the ceiling and down again. She hovers over Docie.

"What are you looking at?" Hattie's spooked. The down on her forearm is raised up. "It's cold in here."

"Is she going to wake up?" I ask the ghost.

"Stop it *now*," Hattie says.

In the waiting room Anna Ruth sits with Claire. Anna Ruth visits Docie. Claire and I wait while Hattie calls home.

"She looks peaceful," Claire says. "And awful."

"Extreme Unction."

"Don't say that."

"I didn't say Last Rites."

"What's the difference?"

"What will happen to them happen to them if she doesn't make it?" Claire asks.

"The twins?"

"Yes."

"We'd rear them. Some Clayborne would."

"What if Dr. Valentine wants them?"

"I'll drive a stake through his heart."

"Docie has to take *some* responsibility for this, no matter what happens."

"Not so. Not yet."

"Once in Richmond after a teen-age bully gave me a going over without a word Docie walked to the garage and sawed off a broom stick and marched down the street with the stick like it was a baton she was twirling for the majorettes. I watched from the living room window. She made a b-line to where he was bent over with a rock writing *niger* in big letters on the street. She hit him like she was beating dirt out of a rug. Then she marched back up the street to the house as pulled together as somebody about to conduct a symphony."

"What did he do?"

"Billy? Blew up our mailbox."

"His father caught him setting fire to their driveway with a can of gasoline."

"Sounds like you."

"Let him set the drive way on fire *again*."

"What for?"

"Therapy. His father was a psychiatrist. Two weeks later a house under construction in Cherokee Bend burned to the ground. It wasn't me, either."

"Docie was protective," I say. "She had an awful temper too. I got goose bumps like I'd been plucked when she'd have one of her fits. It was as if some animal part of her screamed, and not the human."

"I saw her once," Claire says. "She looked like Linda Blair in *The Exorcist*."

"Before the exorcism, you mean."

"I mean."

"One time Amelia and I heard her bang through the back door after school. We read the signs of a knockdown mood so we hid behind the sofa. She knew we were *somewhere*, and wouldn't let up until she found us. We heard her getting screwier and screwier. *Amelia! Webb!* We held onto each other like you would to a tree in a gale. She pulled the sofa back. *Why are you afraid of me? What have I ever done?* Her face reminded me of a neighborhood scare we'd had, when a rabid dog was on the loose. Nobody had seen it, but we knew what it looked like. Head the size of a pumpkin, bear-trap jaws, red eyes. Nobody fucking *move,* Docie said. She whipped off her Villager belt and started snapping out windows with the buckle. After about twenty she got calm as Sunday morning, put on her belt, and walked away. Now you tell me."

"Hormones."

"Mother thought a psychiatrist could help."

"Like Dr. Valentine?"

"Undertakers need corpses. Lawyers make their own work, like pyromaniac firemen. Psychiatrists drive people insane. It's their business."

A nurse offers us a drink of water. Claire and I share a conical paper cup.

"In high school she put hinges on her screen. Every night she went to bed at nine, obedient and sweet, Mother thought. By midnight she was out the window, riding around with whoever had a car. She'd come back by dawn, get up an hour later for school. With only an hour of sleep every night she made the National Honor Society and shot the lights out on the SAT's."

"Housewife speed?"

"Coke."

"*Coke?*"

"Cola, I mean. Sorry. Seven-ounce thick green glass. Kept a case under her bed. Contraband. Rots your teeth, gut, bowels, and brain, according to Father."

"My father drank R.C."

"Figures."

"You're right. For once."

* * *

"One fall Docie persuaded a friend of hers to have a party at her parents' summer house on the James River. In the middle of the night the boathouse burned down. When the fire trucks arrived the road to river front was so crowded with cars the woods caught on fire and half the river property was destroyed. Lucky for her the house was untouched. The girl told her mother the party was Docie's idea and Docie had bullied her into it. The mother believed her. She told Mother Docie was no longer allowed to associate with her daughter. The girl's mother was an influential garden club type. The accusation that Docie was a troublemaker, even though she didn't believe it, pissed Mother off because it knocked her down a social peg in this woman's eyes, at least for the moment. Then it made her suspicious.

"Mother waited outside her window. When Docie crawled out Mother asked her if she was interested in burning down another boathouse.

"I hid on the stairs and listened. Father dragged her inside and Mother wanted to know how long this had been going on, because they might have to consider selling the house and moving to Mississippi, if a daughter of theirs prowled around at night with any fool boy who had a car. Then Father said Send her to St. Theresa's and Mother said we'd move to Mississippi first and Father said If I had raised her Catholic and Mother said Catholic? No gigolo is going to raise my daughter a Catholic and then I heard a *slap* and I heard Mother cry for the first time in my life."

"Good Lord."

"Mother took Docie to see a psychiatrist. Docie told me the first doctor told her the reason she forced herself to have a miscarriage was out of unresolved hostilities towards her mother."

"Miscarriage?"

"Hold on. Docie didn't like him, she told Mother. He touched her. Mother sat up and said, Where? The second doctor said she had deep-seated hostilities towards her father. Docie didn't like him either; he smelled like licorice.

"Then she started reading books on psychiatry. The third doctor said she was manic depressive because one week she would sit in a sullen stupor looking pale and hopeless and the next week she'd breeze in with flowers in her hair saying how she loved the world and life and hug herself and give a shriek of pleasure about all the wonders of the world. The next doctor said she suffered from conversion hysteria because she complained about pains in her breasts and blinding headaches and a burning sensation in her womb. The next said Docie was a compulsive neurotic because she washed her hands thirty times a day and used geometry to talk about her emotions. Another said Docie was a borderline personality because Docie assumed the mannerisms of movie actresses and television personalities and told the doctor when she was a kid she was convinced she was Mata Hari.

"Then we moved to Birmingham and Mother thought a psychologist might do the trick. She had given up on psychiatrists because every doctor had a different diagnoses and some wanted three sessions a week and one told Docie after meeting Mother and Father it was not surprising she was a troubled girl because it was apparent to him after one conversation that her parents were insane. He tried to touch her too. Yet another said Docie's fits were epileptic seizures.

"Before we moved Father consulted a Catholic priest who had written a book on possession. It was after Docie had run away and come back and forced herself to miscarry by having a friend throw a bastketball at her stomach."

"No."

"Father and Docie were arguing during Sunday dinner, and Docie went into a fit and stood up and ripped the tablecloth off the dining room table. The roast beef tumbled across the floor like a decapitated head. Mashed potatoes dripped from the chandelier. Food was all over everybody, on our clothes and in our hair and on our faces. I was eleven and thought this was incredibly funny but I remember out of nowhere Docie made those inhuman sounds, animal screams that twisted her face like she was only a mouthpiece for them. Father tried to restrain her and she knocked him down. Later Mother said he slipped on green beans. What I remember most, besides Father getting floored, is the way she spat across the room. She must have had a gumball in her mouth because she cracked the glass on a frame holding a portrait photograph of my mother's great uncle. She ran out of the room and ran outside and ran for an hour until she was so exhausted she lay down in the yard and fell asleep. Father wanted to take Docie to see the priest. Mother said we'd move to Mississippi first. Then we moved to Birmingham.

"The psychologist in Birmingham asked her if she'd been molested as a child and Docie said Yes, by her brother and father and uncle. The psychologist explained that was the reason why she tried to seduce all of her doctors in Virginia. The therapist, a woman, asked her how far it went, and Docie said They touched me and the therapist said, Where? and Docie said, You know, on the breasts, and stuff. And stuff? the therapist asked. Do you ever wonder why you don't have a more positive self-image? Do you have any idea what this has done to you? Now, where else did they touch you? You know, she said, all over. And the doctor said, No, I don't. Docie slid back in her chair and touching herself said Here, and the doctor looked at her.

"The next visit Docie told the therapist she'd lied about being molested and didn't want to see her anymore, but the doctor said pretending it never happened wouldn't make it go away, so Docie told Mother what she'd told the therapist, and said it was what the lesbian bitch wanted to hear *anyway*. Docie said she was sorry she lied. Mother was upset and said we might have to move again. She never took Docie to another doctor again."

"Do you think she's crazy?" Claire asks.

"Mother?"

"Docie."

"No. She just thinks she is."

"Maybe something did happen to her."

"She was a daughter who had a mother. They all drive each other nuts."

"Not mine."

"Sorry."

"I think Docie *is* crazy," Claire whispers.

"Possessed?"

"A chemical imbalance, I think. We talked about it once. Those moody rages, the strength she had! Like an attack of mania, or a seizure. And I don't think the wreck was an accident."

"An impulse?"

"An impulse she had all the time."

"How many pregnant women commit suicide?"

Claire's father must still be as big a bastard as I remember, past fifty and vain as a teenager and quiet on purpose, like he had nothing to say to me because I was a bum from Alabama, or so he reckoned when Claire told him I hailed from The Magic City, which is neither magical nor much of a city, I grant him that. When Claire was growing up he was a good-old-boy bourbon lush but now he exercises to keep trim and gets facials and wears make-up to important business meetings and last I heard was checking into the hospital for a butt tuck. I can see why he didn't like me. He wanted to social climb Charleston with Claire's lovely hand.

Harry Hunter is from jerkwater south Georgia, near Black-shear, where the Satilla River and Hurricane Creek meet not far from the Okefenokee Swamp, and where his parents still run a feed-and-seed store and farm slash pine. Claire's visited her grandparents only twice in her life, as if Daddy Hunter were ashamed of his roots. Harry wound up at Fort Jackson in Columbia after serving in Korea. He thought about becoming a career officer but he got into real estate and made a killing in commercial development and took early retirement. The only thing he was lacking that he couldn't acquire with money, at least not the way he greased the palms of city council and rented out favorable zoning laws, was respectability, so he married a faded debutante from a Columbia family with Charleston connections. Her relations nearly took to the streets in protest, even though she was almost a decade his senior, widowed, and supposedly touched in the head.

He started to make himself Columbia respectable, planning an assault on the bluebloods of Charleston the city hadn't seen since Fort Sumter, but the richer the gaudier and grimmer he got. Claire's Mother converted to Catholicism, and when it became apparent the marriage was an embarrassment and wasn't going to work, she moved with Claire to Charleston to live with her aunt. She sent Claire to a Catholic grade school and took her to Mass every Sunday while her husband was in Columbia banging his secretaries and playing golf with business partners in plaid pants, packing Tampas, and heading to the bar for noon bourbons.

It's a subject of wonder how a child can love the biggest bastard on earth, and put up with him, hell, even *forgive* him for being what he is, just because he's Daddy. When Claire was ten her mother died of cancer. The Charleston aunt kept Claire for a year but Claire wanted to live with Daddy Hunter in Columbia, so the aunt had no choice but to let her. In the meantime Harry—now *Harold*—went from plaid spandex to cotton khaki, polyester open-collar to cotton button-down, golf spikes to docksides, and learned to mouth Charlestonian vowels like a Confederate general. But to no avail; he exuded south Georgia like swamp gas, and circled the upper reaches of Charleston like a buzzard without a perch. Claire's marriage to a judge was a coup, so he can't be very pleased with her divorce. Not, I know, as happy as it makes me, if only because it'll force the moonshiner to remember his roots at crumpet time.

I turn into the drive. We're half-way up the hill when a lime-green Bug flies through the gates and pulls up behind us.

"Who the hell is that?"

Anna Ruth turns around.

"Amelia."

I check the rearview mirror to see if she has any dagger-headed Buddhists in tow. She's alone. She waves and beeps the horn crazily.

I pull into the carport. She zips in beside us, waving.

"*Webb*," she shouts.

She climbs out of the VW, jangling and chiming. Over her jeans and blouse hangs enough hammered metal and eastern mystical jewelry to make you wish you were temporarily deaf and when you greet her.

Since I've been back I haven't asked where she is. As a kid she had a way of wandering in and out of the house looking as abstracted as the year before last, and like she'd just come to after fainting. We might not see her for a while, and then she'd appear in the den looking for a book or a Barbie doll like a ghost who drifted through the wall. When she got older, she'd disappear for days, but no one worried; we knew she'd make an appearance as sure as next year's Crimson Tide.

We hug and break. Anna Ruth, screwing up her eyes, gives Amelia a look and goes inside.

"How's Buddha?" I ask.

"Where've you been?" It doesn't surprise me Amelia hasn't the foggiest notion where I've spent the last five years.

"New York. Are you still playing?"

"I have a recital next week."

"Chopin?" As soon as I ask I remember before I left she'd gotten into a row with Mother because her music professor said she had enough gift to play concerts. Instead, she wanted to play experimental music that's enough to make your skin crawl, like you've walked into a dark room full of spiders, or else it's all jarring noises, like an interstate pile-up in the fog.

"They're not really *pieces* I'm playing. More like improvised tonal modes."

"How do you practice for that?"

"I can't, really. I mediate and play and see what happens.

Right before dawn I think I really hit on some unheard-of chromatic arrangements."

"I didn't hear anything."

"I wasn't *here*. There's negative energy in this house. I was at Birmingham-Southern. Will you come to the recital?"

"Absolutely."

I tell her about a concert I attended in an East Village basement. The musician sat in front of strobe lights and beat an aluminum-bodied guitar with spoons and rattled keys and made noises like he hadn't taken a dump in six months. I sat there trying not to bust out laughing. Above us was a transom window that gave out onto the street. Three black kids walk by and one of them leans down to listen. He calls his friends over, saying That *white* dude's making these *noises*, man, and they're actually people sitting there *listning*, and they poke their heads in the window and start howling so everybody can hear. From the mouths of babes. Turtle-neck bearded types and punks with liberty crown spikes and meditative sorts sitting there like God Himself was speaking, probably all of them saying to themselves, This is horseshit, but afraid not to get the point that wasn't there. We had to leave; I was laughing so hard I almost farted. To drown out the kids guitar-man picked up the volume. Out on the street we heard wailing and banging that sounded like an idiot on LSD.

"Can I bring a date?"

"A date. What an antique notion."

"She's a music lover."

A lot of experimental music *is* awful. It's not music, but performance art. But what I'm doing is different."

"Don't get defensive."

"You're making fun of me."

"Relax."

"You haven't changed a bit. Still stuck in the space-time continuum of western metaphysics. That's why you like Beethoven and Chopin. And football, where you always have to go *forward* or else you'll *lose.*"

"You finally learned the rules."

"A dumb, violent sport. At least you've outgrown that."

"Don't jump to any conclusions."

"It's the only exercise I get," she says, and gives me another hug.

"Have you seen Docie?"

"Yesterday."

"She's not crying wolf, this time."

The den smells like stale bourbon.

"Did somebody throw up?" Amelia asks.

"Webb got drunk," Anna Ruth says, "his first night home."

"Understandable," Amelia says. "I thought you smelled funny. Like moth balls."

"Boilin drunk," Anna Ruth says.

"Enough," I say.

"You should chant," Amelia says, clicking on the television with the remote control and racing through the stations. "Try acupuncture. Biofeedback. Homeopathy. Alcohol dams up your chakras."

"No kidding."

"Typical. Nothing's on." She watches a documentary about African fire ants. They pick an elephant's bones clean.

As far as I'm concerned, Amelia's been out to lunch as long as I can remember, but in a way that truly charms the hell out of people. She comforts bankers and corporate lawyers and other tax-break warriors with the illusion that they really *are* sane, unlike citizens of Amelia's ilk, so she's always invited to fund raisers and corporate-sponsored concerts and art shows and put on display like a beautiful rare gypsy freak of God's glorious animal kingdom, and in their own way her admirers are right. She's as preposterous looking as a drag queen by daylight and as giddy as a nun on a bungee jump and doesn't give a damn what anybody thinks of her, as long as she's left to her music. She's a year older than I am, but we didn't grow up close. Amelia always wanted to be off by herself. Mother and Father worried how little she cared for company of any kind, so they forced her to share a room with Hattie. When she built a scaffold for her Barbie dolls and hanged them for various offenses, like talking at night when she was trying to sleep, Mother and Father figured she was better off living in her world undisturbed, so they gave her a room of her own. She dropped the executions, and started playing the piano when she was six; she's lived by it like water ever since. Her hands on the keys are her only tether to the earth; without the manual dexterities of music she'd blow away like a dandelion pod. Apparently, though, Amelia went a little overboard with the chanting when I was gone.

Hattie told me Amelia's ashram friends would bicycle over the mountain from the Southside in the spring, where they lived in a commune, and pitch their lean-to's on the back lawn and blow their tinkly pipes and pump the same-sounding notes off the bellows, a drone enough to make you saw logs, and chant and chant and chant. One April Saturday when they made their Mountain Brook pilgrimage Anna Ruth fried up some chicken and instead of appreciating her hospitality they lectured her about sentient beings and animal cruelty and the unsanitary conditions of poultry farms, while they packed down twenty pounds of her bacon-flavored potato salad and littered Phillip's lawn with paper plates. The rest of the time they spent berating Amelia for living in Mountain Brook and being a crypto-fascist bourgeois ideologue and spiritually untuned, but Hattie said they drank beer like everybody else, only imports, and smoked too, only Indian clove-scented cigarettes, and drove cars, only old Volvos and vintage Mercedes of the sort seized, they claimed, by revolutionaries from imperialist diplomats in Central America. They sunbathed their shaved heads on the lawn all afternoon, and then took hot showers two by two, like they owned the place and the Randolph property was another roadside shrine on their way to Nirvana. Most of them were Mountain Brook kids themselves, with trust funds to bankroll their material loathing of the world, and plain lost souls who couldn't meditate in August unless they were air-conditioned into a proper state of tranquility.

Hattie says Amelia felt so guilty and inadequate after they left that she locked herself in her meditation room. All day they heard a mournful chanting. Clouds of incense bellowed from the third-floor window. Anna Ruth took up plates of food and tried to persuade Amelia to eat, but she never answered anybody at the door, just chanted and chanted day and night. On the morning of the fourth day Anna Ruth pries open the door with a crowbar. Amelia comes out of her meditation room, her eyes spinning like pinwheels, and walks down the stairs as disoriented as somebody beaned on the head, and says 'The light, the light,' and she goes down the front yard and out into the street, saying 'The light, the light,' head cocked like an Irish setter's, looking lopey-dopey and confused, spreading the Buddhist and Hindu cheer from door to door, and without even knocking walking into the Johnson's house and saying 'The light, the light' to a group of old ladies having a book club meeting in the living room. Mrs. Johnson nearly fainted.

She calls the police, but not before Hattie rings up a five-star nuthouse and they haul her downtown in a straight jacket. The doctors say she's having a fit of mania brought on by the fasting, and the sado-masochists sedate her with thorazine, a pig tranquilizer, Docie told Hattie. After a month of confinement and observation and straps and padded rooms and psychiatric cages, like she's King Kong's nearest relation, the doctors diagnose her a manic-depressive and "stabilize her mood" with lithium and release her into Mother's custody. Back at home she's stabilized all right; it's like she's brain-dead, or lobotomized. She drifts around the house, not humming a note or going to Birmingham-Southern to play a single chord on the piano. One morning she flushes the lithium down the toilet; everyone waits for another episode, but instead of an attack of mania she plays Bach's Sixth Partita three times through, gets up from the Yamaha exhausted, and goes to bed. The next morning she woke up cursing with joy. She hasn't had an episode since. She still chants, but no more fasting, Hattie said, just macrobiotic brown rice and soybean pizza, red wine by the jug, and an occasional Klonopin she cops from Docie.

I suppose her friends are still the same, deadbeats and bummers living on the sweet fat of the land without a pang of conscience, like maybe they should do something besides moan all the time. Once I overheard a bullet-head at a party trying to persuade Amelia to have her parents committed, since it was obvious to him they were mad as hatters. No doubt he was chewing the food of a sweet bilk, with Amelia testifying against her parents for mental cruelty, just for having been the instruments of her reincarnation. It was back when Amelia was so suggestible she might have agreed to try it. In fact, it was back when the psycho-shysters and metaphysical chiselers that Docie, Hattie, and Amelia consulted at various times about their problems with interpersonal relating and conceptualization of optimum self-image and the extraterrestrial search for inner space, it was then the monumental chord was strummed in their hearts that it was their *parents'* fault they were so miserable and aggrieved and unfulfilled, and not the result of anything they might have done, for which they presently suffered. The shrinks and gurus and therapists persuaded them (Docie, Hattie, and Amelia compared notes; they each had different spiritual and mental health mentors, depending on the fashion of the day, and paraded the particulars of method like costumes) that it was their mother and father who messed up their chances of happiness forever, like ham-handed surgeons who'd damaged their feel-good lobes past repairing. T.E. was a holdout from the therapy whitewash, and over dinner gave me half-blind, speechless looks when the blame-game got out of hand.

Anyway, those Pecksniffs and frauds didn't mind picking up where my parents left off, because they diddled my sisters and swindled my family out of tens of thousands of dollars for blob games and astral projections and scream therapy and spiritual umbilicals and assorted pills and talk-out sessions clocked by the quarter-hour, and every one of my sisters went from animal to vegetable to mineral overnight. They all wised up, I see, except Docie, who was the veteran and instigator, and who, because of her experience with doctors as a teenager, considered therapy recreational, amateur hour and a week at the beach combined, and time off from the pharmacology conferences and laboratory research.

Docie's a *scientist*, and she understands the world around her in terms of physics and chemistry, but I always had the impression she didn't understand herself very well, because she'd think she was crazy when everybody knew she was just bulldogged and refused to get her priorities straight out of the sheer perverse pleasure of being wrongheaded. And she liked attention she could terminate like a contract, without any emotional obligations, so she used psychology types because she figured they were thick, and not scientific, she said, only they pretend to be, so they're easy to dupe. But then she'd fall in love with every one of them, and when the romance and all the breathlessness of new love gave out, in other words, when she got tired of this or that particular method of amative healing, the therapy was over. She had a way of convincing them they were the one and only, and then she wondered why they came to pieces when she gave them the axe. She shared every deep secret and intimacy possible. At first they wanted her as a *patient* too. She had a feverish imagination that made her problems seem more astonishing than really they were, and for which she had them convinced they held the cure. Then she complained they didn't "understand" her. It's hard to figure. It's like she went out of her way to spite herself, and not the shrinks. And that's not insane, it's just plain dense, like her head was so abstracted from her heart she could persuade herself of anything, or saw relations like she would a pharmacology problem. It's hard to figure there *aren't* any solvable equations in sex, or spiritual chemistries you can break down or explain. With her head ringing clear with science and her cloudy heart from so much fretful effort enlarged like an athlete's, Docie wound up a total mystery to herself. Which is why, if she tried to kill herself by swerving off the road and rolling damn near to the bottom of a steep ravine, she least of all knows why.

What's worse, since she was fourteen Docie has possessed the kind of looks that'll knock a guy's socks off when she walks into a room. She's not a classic model type, no, it's much worse than that; she has an indefinable quality that either scares a man senseless or gives him horns and goathoofs. Women instinctively hate her. It's as if she has that quality enough for ten women, and it's all an accident of fate, the way you're born with a curved spine or a clubfoot. Her power over men was something she never cultivated, so she never trusted the snap results she got. She was proud because she's smart as shit, not because men were thralled on first look. Once on a research job her co-workers thought she advanced so fast because she slept with her boss, and that made her madder than being raped. That was *her* phrase for it. But with the shrinks and therapists it was psychological striptease from first blush.

I always felt sorry for the faker who'd be sitting in his office, day after day bored out of his mind by endless confessions of wallflowers too timid to scratch themselves in public, who thought they'd committed universal crimes only hypnosis could reconstruct, survivors of Satanic sex abuse committed on Uncle's Lazy Boy, mopey depressives who hated themselves enough to pay someone to secretly agree with them, phobic housewives armored in car coats and plastic rain scarves in mid-July possessed by unexplainable fits of weeping, eating-disordered college students who turned their dorm rooms into vomitoriums, lonely unmarrieds weary of want-ads and goofy males soaked in combustible nightmares, when in through the door walks this gorgeous statuesque girl-woman giving off the violent green heat of spring, like she's Diana, hands-off, but daring him to sport in the woods nevertheless, and no amount of rationalizing can gainsay who's in control from the start. Everything the poor fellow learned in every textbook lining the wall is blown right out the window like so many blank pages. He feels his scrotum tighten and his mouth dry up and his Adam's apple bob when he tries to swallow before he says, in a voice he already recognizes as too weak, Please, sit down.

Most of the time she didn't even pay, because she had a way of reminding the therapist about professional ethics, when most of them had wives and children on top of the trouble Docie managed to give them. But before you imagine Docie calculating and cruel, let me repeat that above all she believed, if only for a day or a month or a year, that she was truly love with these swindlers. When we talked about a particular affair, I encouraged her with bad advice, like sure, He's the right one for you, knowing the guy I'd just met in her apartment on a Sunday afternoon, when Docie was stoned from burning lungfuls of hashish or narcotized from smoking opium-tinctured cigarettes, was not only married and battened down with obligations, but a sensitive Ph.D type, a liar in a button-down shirt with a sweaty forehead and nervous underarms as smelly as his sincerity, with all the right weepiness about women, and a deep embarrassment, when I shook his humid palm, about his crazy lust for my sister. Or maybe the victim was a shaggy-browed authoritarian M.D. with scrubbed nails, alligator loafers, and combed hand-mink, who viewed me as part of his family case study in clinical psychiatry, but once alone with Docie, trembled over his prescription pad with parching anticipation whenever she demanded beforehand the Schedule One drugs that could land him in Wetumpka for five to fifteen. His brains fucked out, she left him for dead, and drove straight to the local People's.

In either case, she wanted to see how far she could go. If he was a therapist, she'd wring him dry in bed and force him to sit in his office for hours listening to her *problem*—by the third week Docie would flatten out to repeating herself—until he was ready to throw himself out the nearest window. She'd intentionally chew away at his patience until his eyes turned to glass; the moment she'd notice a suppressed yawn or a fidget of restlessness, she'd threaten to withdraw the sex she dispensed like placebos, and then the guy'd want to hang himself if he couldn't have another ten minutes of body-talk. Hell, she could persuade a guy to take a bath in acid and he'd scream till he melted and he was a hunk of burning love.

She drove one psychologist nuts enough to move his practice to Atlanta. One afternoon before he left I saw him in Brookwood Mall. He tried to avoid me but I cornered him in front of Sweet Temptations, a bakery. I asked him how he was. He looked spooked, like he'd seen his own ghost. He'd nearly busted up his marriage and lost his job because of his affair with Docie, when she started calling him at home and telling his wife she was possessed by the devil and *that's* why she was a nymphomaniac. He went to court and got an injunction against her saying she'd be arrested if she called his house or came within five hundred feet of his family. At that point he didn't care if she ratted on him; he just wanted to hide under a rock and recover. Standing in front of the bakery, with a yeasty sweetness in the air between us, he flinched like I might pop him one, just before he said my sister was a *witch* as far as he was concerned. He looked like the sort of modern lame-brain who doesn't even believe he has a soul, so for Docie to convince him she summoned the spirits of the night and had sex with incubi was a real feat. At the time I was proud of her.

If her fling was an M.D., she'd push him farther and farther into the land of forbidden prescriptions, starting with codeine and Demerol, and work her way up through Percodans to the felony heights of morphine and heroin. She supplied a lot of her lowlife friends with recreational narcotics on the weekends, even as the doctor, in the sobering fold of his family, questioned his sanity for handing over to a madwoman enough ammunition to blast his career a hundred times over. But Docie knew she had a long distance rope around his cajones; once he gave in, she could reel in favors on a whim, with unspoken understandings about medical ethics and the AMA.

And damn if she didn't think she was in love every time, even as she practically turned whomever into a human sacrifice. Docie's a hard one to figure, because she can tell you anything you want to know about organic chemistry, biology, physics, metallurgy, astrophysics, mathematics, and especially pharmacology, and lately astrology, according to Hattie, but when it comes to some idea of herself, she hasn't a clue. Maybe that's why she could mimic symptoms like last year's Academy actress. And whatever idea she happened to be entertaining about herself at any given time, she'd do whatever she damn well pleased, and to hell with the consequences.

For whatever reason, she always sought me out to talk about her most recent entanglement, maybe because her sisters were up to their eyeteeth with her craziness, not to mention their own psycho-dramas, and I always encouraged her, if only because she was so much older than I was, and it all seemed so grown-up. I hate to think I helped her along the wrong direction, even if it's been five years since I saw her last, the time it has taken her to accelerate to where she found herself, last week, literally flying off the road.

Amelia's brass bracelets ring and chime as sits in a rose-patterned wing chair turning the pages of the newspaper. On the floor Brett plays with old plastic soldiers, WWII vintage, the same ones I directed against a division of Panzers in the back yard, while a lit Spitfire dropped blobs of burning plastic from the sky.

"When will ya'll be back?" she asks.

"When do you want us back?"

"No head," Brett says, holding up a soldier.
"Take your time," she says, and looks at me over the paper.
"Space time?"
"That too."
"No leg," Brett says.
"You call this a *newspaper*?" Amelia says.

I take down the convertible top and drive the Impala along Overton Road and Country Club Lane. To the left and right are fake Tudor mansions and mock castles with long sloping lawns shaded with towering oaks and maples and trimmed with bushes and flowerbeds.

As a kid I was banished from this particular neighborhood because I accidentally set the Erland's yard on fire playing with gasoline and matches and not even three firetrucks could save the arbor in the backyard. That was two months after a BB gun I pumped misfired and shattered the Robert's Caddy windshield as the old guy backed down his drive.

That run of bad luck that made me look like I acted with bad intention. I was labeled a delinquent forever thereafter.

It's true I was with Rusty when his parents' diesel Mercedes smashed through their picture window and rolled into the living room, but he was the one who let off the parking brake. He jumped out and I had to scramble into the front seat to put on the brakes, but it was too late. When his mother came running into the living room, I was sitting behind the wheel. What could I say? She'd never believe me.

A week later I spotted Rusty walking up the path in the woods near his house, where a creek runs. He saw me and bolted, but I caught up with him and knocked him into the creek. I held him under water for a good minute. He came up gasping and screaming for daddy. He told his parents I tried to drown him. Even though Mother had patched up relations by paying for the picture window, his *momma* called mine and said I wasn't to set foot on their property again. I wasn't even *on* their property when I dunked the dumbass.

When Rusty was fifteen he hanged himself; half the tenth grade class attended the funeral. After the memorial service his mother approached me dazedly and said she was glad Rusty and I had been such good friends.

As for delinquency status, it's true too David Dothan and I would dress up like Marvel Comic Book heroes and break into houses and eat cold fried chicken out of refrigerators and swipe a few Cokes, but it was always done in the name of law and order. When we got caught in the Howard's house, we told them we'd seen a prowler in the yard and came to investigate, but that didn't wash. We may as well have been talking to mounted policemen. They didn't like the fact we were breaking and entering on the Sabbath. David told me they'd be downtown all day, since they were First Baptists of Birmingham and a regular service wasn't punishment enough, but they needed the livelong day to flagellate themselves for sins their ancestors hadn't even had the balls to commit. I don't know how the hell they got so well-to-do, if they were free of everyday dirt.

They had a boy a few years older we nicknamed Happy, because he was the somberest starched-shirt down-in-the-mouth kid in Mountain Brook; the Howard daddy and momma were mean-spirited righteous types, who didn't think Happy's teeth were clean unless he brushed until his gums bled, and who must have sandblasted their house once a week, because even the toilets bowls looked like part of a monumental display of pioneer china, and not for use. They were filthy rich and stingy as sober drunks; when they caught us they had us hauled off to jail to give us a scare. Happy looked petrified, as if his parents would blame *him* for what *we'd* done.

At the station, the cops played along, until old muletanner Mr. Howard launched into a stump sermon about damnation and prison. The sergeant winked at us through the bars. The Howard clan looked like refugees from the Dust Bowl, and like the Great Depression was still on; David and I were dressed like Flash Gordon and Spiderman, so a Mountain Brook police sergeant with a cushy job could hardly keep a straight face when the coot said we were the prison-bound scions of Satan. Five years later Happy, high on microdot, was busted on his eighteenth birthday for pedalling acid in the parking lot of Mountain Brook High School, and spent a year in prison himself. The only time I ever saw Happy smile was when he was tripping, which is how he spent most of his parole, until he saw Jesus chasing a dragon across the coke-stained screen at the Shades Valley drive-in. The last I heard he had joined an interdenominational missionary in Chile.

I pull into Mountain Brook Village.

Henri's is a wine and cheese cafe with little round tables the size of hubcaps and spindly chairs with legs that feel like they might snap if you sit forward too pointedly. I've never felt comfortable in places like *Henri's*, not only because I might cross my leg the wrong way and knock a table over, but more because hip winehead joints make you feel like a Yahoo unless you cough up a fifty bucks for tiny appetizers and an even more for a split of champagne, all to feel *European* in the Alabama mug and humidity, with mosquitoes dive-bombing the outdoor patrons sporting French berets and swamp fever from the heat soaking their fashion-name shirts. It's all so papery fake and powdered around the bobtail, everybody eyes everybody else, to see how just to behave, when no one has a clue, so everybody drinks wine out of tulip glasses or sips espresso out of dinky cups, and eats toe-jam cheese and imported crackers that would give a billygoat gas, all the while trying to look as proprietary as English Lords, when they'll get in their Buick boats and float home and watch videos and eat popcorn like everybody else in suburban manor USA.

I never met a woman who didn't like places like Henri's, and Claire's no exception. To be selfish about it, I'd rather be in a downtown sports bar over a dozen raw and cold mugs all around, where I can forget whatever's bothering me, but instead I've got to recognize Anna Ruth's right. What she said reminds me of what the only priest I ever liked said in a CCD class, that life is undergone, and eventually we have to acquiesce, endure God's acts, make the best, not the worst of it, and it's better undergone together. That was back when priests came out of the closet and started acting as secular as transvestites, or played Jesus rock during Mass, and grooved on youth and peace, when we're all as good as dead anyway, and the reason you might listen to a priest is because he was in a hard-earned and privileged relation to God's truth, and understood the stations of the cross and the Catholic histories of spiritual agony and millenniums of martyrs and saints and a lot about the poor passing fact called human life. The new kind of priest is a fashionable sort, the jack of every kind of parade, and stuffed to his chops with slogans about problems that seem fairly short term, considering his vocation. But Father Carnahan always got down to the hard facts of faith, and let us know our souls were in daily peril, even as a divine gentleness withheld from us the true revelation, the home truth our life holds and can't hold bared, that life is always already cordially evil. To miss this, or to be in any way sentimental about the thoroughgoing hideousness of our hearts, of what becomes of our souls in dragonish climes, was for Father Carnahan to be double damned. But in spite the of Catholic hardball, he was the kindest priest I ever met, more ready to forgive than kick ass with incantations of the pit. Besides, he'd played linebacker for Notre Dame, and that didn't hurt, like maybe there's nothing wrong with being a little manly and thick-skinned about the world, when it makes gentleness and compassion all the more convincing. But when he talked about acquiescing, I didn't know what he meant, because I thought *hell no*, I'll go down fighting first. I should have learned by now all that is, like Anna Ruth said, is thinking about yourself.

In blue shorts and an oversized shirt knotted at the waist,

Claire sits crosslegged at a table under the outdoor canopy. She watches shoppers walk up and down the avenue and linger in front of boutiques and specialty shops. They bend and peer in, moving idly from one window to the next. Mountain Brook Village is supposed to look Lake Country rural, with some Tudor thrown in to make it quaint. The sidewalks are stone, and the main streets cobbled. Even the Sunoco down the street is in architectural sync. You expect to see haywagons and milkmaids, but instead imported sports cars jockey in the lots for places to park, and nut-brown tennis wives make Saturday tours of the import shops branched clear from Rodeo Drive.

Seeing her from a distance reminds me of a rutting moose I read about that mooned after a cow in a pasture. The cow stood across the field with not a whit's worth of what was going on, with a ruminative munch and a lowering head, looking blankly around, while the moose longed in the distance, all impossible hope and watery eyed. Heaven knows there's nothing cowy about Claire, but I'll be damned if I don't feel like that moose sometimes, mooning after the wrong species.

I order a thimbleful of coffee. Claire drinks an English tea.

Between us sits Pete Ledbetter. He has his arm around me.

"New New *York*," he says. He lifts his Bloody Mary and stirs it with the celery stick. "Takes balls to live in that third world dump. Now what do you do?"

"Market analyst for Goldman Sachs."

"No kidding. I thought you majored in English."

"Business English."

"See this little lady here?" He points his drink at Claire. People at adjoining tables watch us. Last night's bourbon thins in my blood; my heart pounds in my head. "You should have *married* this little lady, Webbo. I hear every guy at C.U. was after her. Why, do you ask? And why *you*, you big dumb ox." He lifts his drink to his temple, spilling it on his tuxedo. "Why—," he says, making a wide gesture at Claire, "just *look* at her."

"Where's the wedding?" Claire asks. She hands him her napkin.

"St. Luke's." He says to me, "You remember *Beasley*, don't you?"

"Sure." Beasley was a porker. In junior high he ate pate de foie on Graham Crackers with liverwurst sandwiches and sour buttermilk. He never bathed. His breath smelled like shoe sweat.

"He's marrying Sarah. Daddy's giving her away in less than an hour. Come to the reception. It's at Highland Park." He looks sloppily at Claire as he daubs the lapel of his tuxedo. "Next time we'll go there for dinner."

He drains his drink and stands up, then leans over and kisses Claire on the chin.

"Good to see you, old Webbo." He pounds me on the back. "I'll look you up when I'm in New York. Say hello to that looney-tune family of yours."

"I'll do that."

He stands there.

"Say," he says, "when are you leaving town? We could play the back nine." I watch the last belt wash over his eyes. He sways.

"I'm flying out this afternoon."

He winks at Claire. She looks at me, then turns up her eyes.

"I offered Claire a thousand dollars to pose for a painting. She turned me down. Claire, is it true you were a topless dancer in D.C.? Bad joke. Am I drunk?"

He moves off, tilted, and tacks into the wind.

I look at Claire, who's redfaced.

"Next time?"

"I went out with him once."

"I thought you were married."

"I *was*. He got so drunk he fell down at the 21 Club and I had to drive him home. His daddy paid for a taxi back."

"He lives at home."

"He spent four years at some academy des Beaux Arts study-ing painting. He's crummy. His nude studies gave me the creeps. The way he paints the female body made me feel like I was in the same room with a serial killer. Then he had a scheme to import pecans."

"Where?"

"France. Daddy financed the deal and lost a bundle. Now he can't get a nickel out of Daddy, so he lives in the garage apart-ment and paints. And drinks."

"Great date."

"He said you were buddies."

"Once. We were potheads then. Now I guess he's a drunk."

"He's drunk. A drunk usher. Let's go watch."

"I've seen enough."

"So have I," she says.

A maroon BMW with tinted windows idles by. Inside a guilty soul navigates the shopping village streets, observing the crepus-cular landscape through windshield sunglasses. Guilty because in every shaded car is a ghost steering down the black infernal Styx, river of New World hate, only this breed of ghost hates himself but does not know it, feels good, brims with depression, turns up the volume on his coaxial cacodemon cassette deck sighing High-tech High Priestly Hymns for Castrated Yappies. The car is equipped with an alarm.

"Did Hattie tell you about Docie's criminal friend?"

"I thought they were all criminals."

"Felon friend."

"Which?"

Claire sits up.

"A while back ago Docie started hanging out with what she called a 'street person,' but he was really a dishwasher in the hospital cafeteria. After a month he quit his job and moved into her apartment. Weekends Docie would supply the drugs and they would stay high from Friday until Sunday."

"So."

"One Sunday they had a fight. He wanted to keep going, but Docie was disciplined about the drugs. She had to show up at UAB Monday morning with a halfway clear head. He completely lost it. He beat her up and robbed her. He disappeared for a few weeks, but one night he showed up and threatened to kill her. She called the police and had her locks changed and got an unlisted number, but once a week he would show up at her door at four in the morning. Then she found out she was pregnant. She got high and had an abortion. She got a terrible infection and spent two weeks in the hospital. When the doctors figured out that she was strung out, they wanted to have her committed, but she claimed she had been shot up and raped. The police were contacted and Docie worked up a composite of the suspect. Two days later the police returned and said so and so, alias so and so, aka so and so—he had about twenty different names—was wanted in six states for armed robbery, assault, credit card fraud, and distribution of narcotics. I didn't meet him, but even Amelia said he looked like a phrenologist's idea of a sociopath. I asked Docie why she would go out with such a lowlife. You know what she said?"

"No."

"'I thought I could help him. After all, I went to University of Virginia, I was advantaged. I wanted to share it.' As if there'd been nothing between them but philanthropy! No needles, no speedballs, no smack, nothing. In the meantime, he broke into her apartment and charged his way to Chicago on her VISA. Later he was found murdered. Stabbed fifty-seven times. Karma. Case closed."

"Hattie said I should ask you about Docie. Is this what she meant?"

"How can someone so gifted as a researcher be so stupid

when it comes to judging character? Why mess around with narcotics for weekend recreation?"

"Legalize the stuff and she'd lose interest *snap* just like that."

I order another espresso.

"Yes," Claire says, draining her teacup, "that's what Hattie meant."

"Why ask you?"

"I held her hand through the entire stay in the hospital. No one else knew until it was over."

"You?"

"She ran out of immediate family."

It's a green day, with no threats in it, and pink and white dogwoods bloom up and down the avenue.

But Docie's condition, like a sudden eclipse, casts a shadow over the table.

"There's nothing on earth we can do," Claire says. "Not yet."

We drive out Old Leeds Road and head back on Route 4 past Par 3 Golf and Eastwood Mall. We pass a block of fast food chains, stores with obese boys in overalls holding triple-decker hamburgers on high, drive-thru egg-roll shops, arches and mansard roofs, Dairy Queens, Burger Kings, Houses of Pancakes, Churches, White Towers.

"Have you ever tried to eat donuts on LSD?"

"I never eat donuts," Claire says.

"In high school I went to Krispy Kreme tripping on a four-way hit of orange barrel acid. Four in the morning. After a dozen glazed I went outside threw up in the dumpster. By the vapor lights I saw thousands of donuts stacked in the garbage. Flies the size of thumbs swarmed over the rotting pile. I swore I'd never take acid again."

"Or eat donuts."

"Nary another."

"I took mescaline once."

"I don't believe you."

"My sophomore year I bartended weekends at The Senate." She leans towards me. "A club for congressional parasites in Washington. My Dad and I weren't getting along and I stopped cashing the checks he sent me, out of principle I guess. Believe me, I needed the money. Anyway, one night a congressional aide offered me some mescaline. It was crazy but I took it. Nothing happened for a while and I thought Big Deal, but then all of a sudden every glass on the bar racks looked as luminous as the night sky. I was writing a paper that semester on the birth of galaxies and I *felt* like the glowing flung-off part of aboriginal creation. Then a crazy equation popped into my head. I had it all figured out! I told the manager I was having my period. I took a cab back to campus. I wrote the equation down and took a long walk. I had it all reconciled: math, zoology, platonic love, chemistry, sex, quarks, personal happiness, white dwarfs, heaven and hell, superstrings, menstrual cycles, solar flares, black holes, wimps, all of it. Just before dawn I fell asleep. The next afternoon when I woke up I looked at the equation. It made perfect nonsense."

"Wimps? Weakly interacting massive particles?"

"What do you expect, after you practically ditched me at the church door?"

"You sound angry. Why does that make me happy?"

"I'm *not* angry. Not at you. Personally."

A pick-up in front of us hauling a rickety horse loses a bale of hay. It tumbles to the side of the road, exploding straw. The old mare looks melancholy. Her owner, she has long known, is incompetent.

"That's the *scientific* definition," Claire says. "Wimps also describes a subclass of males in the animal kingdom, the kind who refuse to protect their mates from predators, or fail to honor the monogamous bond, or abandon their brides at the altar."

"Don't exaggerate."

"Among *homo sapiens* they are commonly referred to as

scaredy-cats, jelly-fish, yellow-bellies, chicken shits. In my most recent encounter, in the form of a husband, I discovered a sub-order of *Rodentia*, The Mouse of the House.

"I don't remember The Senate."

"It was a private club."

"Your husband was a mouse?"

"In the house. On the bench, a lion.

"Anna Ruth told me you had a miscarriage."

"The fetus had too many chromosomes. Trisomy."

"I'm sorry."

"With Brett I was so afraid of S.I.D.S. I didn't sleep soundly first six months after he was born. A miscarriage is benign by comparison. Ask any woman whose child has died."

"Any man?"

"I'm sorry. Of course."

Claire is more stoic—more *scientific*—about her second miscarriage than she was about ours. She was always level-headed. Being around her was like having insurance against a world of therapy swindlers who cook the books to make you feel good, even as they rip you blind, or spiritual pickpockets of the sort Hattie admires, who'll swear you're the messiah as they shove you headlong into the jaws of hell. She doesn't run around pulling her hair out because she doesn't have enough boyfriends, or orgasms, or clothes, or because she's convinced she's too fat, like some women, when to look at them you think they'd like to die, they're so bony. She doesn't punish herself by reading self-help books, or stuff like *Self* that implies if you read it you don't have one to start with; she doesn't moon at the movies or talk about hunks, and she wouldn't have affairs to make her marriage work. She acts more Catholic than anybody I knew at St Francis' Church, though she couldn't tell a mortal sin from a maniple; but she'd no sooner have an abortion than commit suicide, not because she fears the inferno, but out of natural regard for her insides.

* * *

We drive by Mountain Brook Jr. High. The school is deserted. The main building has been gutted by a fire. Sky shows through the burned-out roof.

"Lightening?" I ask.

"Arson."

The school was built in the twenties, and had ceiling-high windows that lent themselves to idle trances and fanciful loafing and encouraged spring dreams about the cheerleader two rows to your left, but the rebuilding indicates a climate controlled labyrinth is in the works, a windowless cinderblock maze with nothing to do in each room but watch the clock and gnash your teeth. It's no wonder kids get crazier by the minute, having to go to school in bomb shelters.

The football field is cleated from spring practice. Blocking sleds sit under the goalposts. Poorly laid lime hashmarks line the field. One-third of the hundred yards is the grassless inside of the baseball diamond. Left field is gridded with ten-yard lines. During hot summer practices, the dugouts became the only relief from the unrelenting sun.

Once in late August the ninth-grade varsity was taking a breather from a lethargic scrimmage, and when the cheerleaders lined up in the end-zone for their practice, we wilted, mooning dumbstruck at lean-shanked, goosenecked girls in braces and pleated skirts doing cartwheels and chorus-girl cheers in the August heat. Who are they? What are they? There they are! We sat in the cool dugouts, unbudgeable, sweating to boil, our helmets dangling by their facemasks from our disbelieving hands.

Our coach was an Eskimo, and we called him Ski, but he was as Alabama redneck as any Coosa County farmer. We had trouble figuring he grew up in an igloo. He chewed tobacco and from fifteen paces *tck*ed at his spittoon. His teeth were as black and yellow as Indian corn. At Alabama he'd played second-string fullback for Bear Bryant, so we admired him for that.

When he saw us doting over the cheerleaders, he stood on the pitcher's mound and shouted at us. *Eleven* men on a team make an *army*. Add one *girl* and you'll end up with eight dead men, the king and his queen, and two *qwurrs*. But *we're* a team, a fighting machine, we're a killing footbawl dream of death! We don't need no girls!

We looked at one another. What the fuck was he talking about? We were too hot and tired to kill anybody. We just wanted to dote.

Then Ski took another tack. He said: don't sit there *shuffling* your feet, and *staring*. Prove you mean it! Prove it to them! Show them! Show them you'll give your last drop of blood and sweat, for them! They want boys with *hide*, not a bunch of *dawgs* laying around with their tongues lolling out. Protect them from the other team! Show them what team they can believe in! Give it to them!

Well, I didn't think anybody was worth my last drop of blood, but he's getting us worked up, since he's worked up about it himself, and we start feeling fearless and cool in the infernal heat. He gets us growling and doing our team chants and warwoops, and pretty soon we're worked up to murder. We start butting heads and slapping helmets and knocking shoulder pads, and when we head back to scrimmage, we're iron-boned, steel-eyed, indestructible, and fleet. Or so it felt. We execute our plays like pros, drop-backs and blocks and trap-plays and wide-outs and bone-crunching tackles, all of them so perfectly timed we felt like we were playing under a spell. Each side responded like eleven people coordinated into one body of an indivisible will; at the same time, each of us wanted to impress one of the girls enough to make her beam back in the hall. We knew, too, deep in our eager hearts, that they wanted to cheer at fall games so everybody would be watching *them*, not us, and we agreed to the pact, because on game days, when we wore our jerseys to school, the angels in saddle oxfords and cheerleading skirts and billowy blouses under sleeveless Shetlands were as excitable as we were, and that meant close dancing after the game, slipping away from whoever's party for necking out under the night sky dewed with autumn stars, and if we won, hands daring every damp, warm place for a guaranteed sleepless night, no matter how many times you might pull yourself off for a little peace of mind.

Claire takes off her sandals and pulls her long legs up along side and slides toward me. In college when we took spring drives to the Blue Ridge Mountains she sat that way. It stirs me up something awful. To make things worse, she rubs my shoulder. I look over. She gets me wrong.

"You're shaking, Webb. Take a deep breath."

"I need a drink."

"Don't."

She takes a flat plastic box out of her purse and starts to assemble a variety of vitamins. We pull into a Piggly Wiggly and she hops out barefoot. Her long legs and graceful walk with just the right ratio of carelessness to assertiveness make her own whatever place she enters. She talks with the clerk, who looks outside to see if she's alone. She's a foot taller than he is.

She comes out with a diet Coke, an *Elle*, and a bottle of mineral water.

I spend five minutes in the parking lot washing down a dozen vitamin pills with the fizzy water, white ones that taste like chalk, yellow sour ones that pucker my tongue, green ones that smell like fish, and brown ones that look like baby poop.

When I finish, Claire sits up like she has a great idea.

"Let's go up on Red Mountain."

I wish it were dark, because that's where couples have parked since there were cars. It's a sight to sit up there at night and look out over Birmingham, the twinkling lights like constellations refracted in beautiful patterns through the dense pollution, or if you drive up at dusk, industrial sunsets that take your breath away.

It's early afternoon, and a soft and skyey spring day, with

breezes in the heavy leaves, and honeyed sunlight coming through the giant old trees along the steep road up the mountain. Here on the ridge of Red Mountain overlooking Birmingham is where the iron and steel fatcats and city developers built their first baronial splendors. The mansions have all the exaggeration of sudden money, but nearly a century has given them a seasoned dignity they wouldn't otherwise have. Heavy pollution has done to the masonry what the weather would have taken a thousand years to accomplish. It makes Birmingham seem older than it is, like it was *built* as a ruin, and was never new.

We park and sit on the stone wall that runs the length of the ridge. The air is surprisingly clean. Since I left for New York, the last of the mills have shut down. The difference is amazing. The air used to be a perpetual sulphury pink, day and night. When Claire flew to Birmingham the first time, she said just as she woke the plane descended through a salmon-colored cloud. She thought she was dreaming. Now the air is clear blue.

In the distance, summery cumuli climb to bright peaks and float stockstill over the city, a sleepy procession that relaxes you just to look at it. We can see the shadows they cast on the city blocks below.

We sit in easy silence for a while, sunning on the warm stones and feeling drowsy. What with the little sleep, a drop in the bushes, the trip to the hospital and the afternoon nearness of Claire, and the fact that forty-eight hours ago I was balled up like a hedgehog in the cover of New York—jail, the bomb about Claire, ignoramus drunk, Docie's wreck—I'm worn out. I stretch out on the wall and put my head on Claire's lap, and start to drift.

I think about Docie and then about a couple I knew in college who lost their first baby to crib death. She'd fed it at midnight and put it in the crib. Two hours later John got up to feed it again. It was a very tiny baby. When he picked it up it was already cold, like a stone. Amy said John fell to the floor and lay there. He didn't cry. He turned bright purple. She thought, he is having a heart attack.

I went to the funeral, and none of what happened sank in until I saw the coffin. It was a simple, very small coffin. Seeing the coffin is what made everybody cry. Amy said after the funeral they stayed in bed for three days. They smoked cigarettes, or took tranquilizers, or one of them got up and fixed something to eat, or took a shower, but mostly they cried, and made love, and slept, and made love, and slept, and cried and made love, or cried in their sleep, or cried when they made love, or made love in their sleep and woke up crying. They confused all of what they were feeling, and didn't want to stop and sort it all out, even if they could have. They just rode it out, like a fever. Then they got up for good. Five weeks later Amy says she's pregnant. They had two children in two years. Whenever I saw them, if she mentioned the first born, John would leave the room.

I fall into a blank sleep, and when I wake the angle of light looks like hours have passed. Claire's jacket is under my head. She is sitting under a tree reading a magazine. She gives me a small smile.

I roll off the wall and crawl over on all fours. Before she can move I kiss her.

"We'd better get back," she says.

IV

We drive down Red Mountain. On a ridge above us stands Vulcan, Birmingham's ten-story monument to metal-working and a classical-god emblem of the millstacks. Bandy-legged, he looks north over the Magic City, so his copper brown can, recently refurbished, faces south to Mountain Brook, where all the steel money's gone for more than sixty years. According to Roman myth, Vulcan was fifty-fold a cuckold. In Birmingham, he faces Northeast, homage to Birmingham's carpetbagger bankers who invented wholecloth the biggest city in The Heart of Dixie.

We stop at the museum of steel making, where the Sloss Blast Furnace sleeps like an iron giant. Massive steam shovels painted brown sit in suspended animation. Worker pride is evident in the huge air blowers, in every brick laid, in cauldrons once filled with 3,000 degree molten pig iron, limestone, and coke we saw at night seethe like lava from Red Mountain lookouts as the workers poured the living magma into molds from the tremendous buckets. Steam-powered piston engines sit idle. Under the steel mill's pavilion a podium stands before a hundred unfolded chairs. A speech by the Birmingham Symphony's new conductor has been cancelled. A steel plaque tells us that the mill is haunted by the ghost of a phantom foundryman who fell into the blast furnace and vanished without a trace. Are his atoms still stirring in some far flung girder or bridge span? His ghost roams the grounds, crying for comfort from the molten sun.

* * *

"New Orleans," I say.
  "Not yet."
  "Botanical Gardens?"
  "We ought to get back."
  "We'll stop by the zoo."
  "Okay," Claire says.

We tour the hot house and then sit in the Japanese Gardens outside.
  "So what *did* you do at The Senate anyway? Tend bar?" We're sitting side by side on a cool stone bench. Our knees graze.
  "Stripped," she says.

We walk to Jimmy Morgan Zoo. We tour the cats, snakes, ruminant mammals. We watch a hippopotamus pack his hide with dungy mud.
  At the primate cages a crowd has gathered. An orangutan is trying to couple with a bright navel orange; his pink dagger pokes it up and down the concrete floor. The crowd, mostly children, jeer. The ape, though embarrassed, thrusts in earnest.
  "Is that what you did in New York?" Claire asks.
  "Times Square," I say.

In the car I gently hold Claire by the back of the neck and lay her flat on the front seat. I kiss her ear.
  "You shouldn't have done that."
  "Strip," I say.
  "Not quite."
  I bite her neck.
  "You missed again," she says.

* * *

A pale green sixty-five Chevy truck, its tail-gate laden with baskets of tomatoes, sits under roadside pine shade. A woman in jeans and a western shirt leans against the truck smoking a cigarette and pulls at the rim of her straw hat. Pink-scarfed, a Mountain Brook matron hands her a bill and tucks a basket of tomatoes under her arm. The matron climbs into her Mercedes convertible and raises both tinted windows at once.

"When I walked out on stage, they looked up at me."
  "With what?"
  "Not lust. Admiration. Almost love."
  "With what?"
  "*Awe.*"

"I was nineteen."

"My father was grooming me for a Charleston match. Harvest Ball debut. Pedigree breeding. The works. It was my private protest. His shining light, his prized daughter, Aphrodite dancing for degenerate Senators. Even Venus was a virgin once."
  "Why didn't you tell me?"
  "It might have made a difference."
  "Might have. Might not have."
  "Might have. I never told anyone."
  "Why now?"
  "We have something in common." She laughs.
  "I don't follow."
  "For the five years you thought you were hiding out?"
  "Yes."
  "Your mother knew exactly where you were and what you

were doing."

A lit-up fire truck blasting its horn approaches.

"How?"

"A private detective. Mrs. Clayborne paid dearly to know what circle of hell you were touring."

"They knew?"

The truck screams past.

"We all knew. *Fay ce que voudras.* Sounded like a lot of bad fun."

"I could a tale unfold whose lightest word would harrow up thy soul, freeze thy young blood, make thy two eyes, like stars, start from their spheres."

"*I* did that."

I turn down a shady block.

"Thy knotted and combined locks to part, and each particular hair to stand an end, like quills upon the fretful porcupine."

"I prefer country and western."

A purple boom car passes, defying the Doppler effect.

Last night I fabled a glamorous stint in Gotham. Now Claire knows the foxhole jobs I took, the battles I lost, the hasty retreats I beat, always on the run down a haunted block of Brooklyn, down downtown, West Side, wherever I woke up spooked.

Good. I too love New York, the part I only *saw*, the most fortifying part, the lucre sexiness I coveted through swinging doors, behind a mop, in upscale eateries.

"What exactly did you do at the Live Sex Emporium on Broadway?"

"Bounced."

* * *

"Tell me about The Senate."
"When I was on stage?"
"That'll do."
"Binary stars."
"I see."
"Webb, you just ran a red light."

"A wealthy businessman in his early sixties. Impeccably dressed. An affected English accent. Weekend after weekend he paid me a thousand dollars to sit at his table and talk."
"Dressed?"
"One night he went to his knee and slipped a huge sparkling thousand-faceted stone on my ringfinger. 'Diana,' he said—"
"Diana?"
"My work name. 'Diana,' he said, 'virgin goddess of the moon, swift deity of the hunt, whom no mortal man has espied bathing in the deep wood—' 'I was dancing for a Republican cheese lobbyist from Wisconsin twenty minutes ago,' I said. 'Diana, moon-goddess,'—"
"Bullshit."
"Serious."
"'Will you marry me?'"
"Yes."
"What happened?"
"As Diana, virgin goddess of the moon, what could I do? I told him no."
"Well?"
"He asked me every night. For two months of Saturdays I sat at his table and held his hand. The last night I saw him he drank double scotches. Two by two. I took a napkin and rubbed his glasses and wiped the tears off his face. 'It's just a club,' I said, 'and I'm just a dancer.' But I wasn't, I now know. I really *was* a goddess to those middle-aged sorrowful men, so full of hormones and aggression and weariness and disappointment. And my suitor

believed in Diana. My God, he worshiped her, this goddess of his psyche. It was moving. And sad. "

"Well, and then?"

"He said, 'Keep the ring.' I gave it back, but when I got home that night, I found it in my purse. A few weeks later I quit. I had the ring appraised. The jeweler said the diamond alone was worth thirty-five thousand dollars."

"What did you do with it?"

"What do you think I did with it?"

"Kept it?"

A band of skateboarders race down the steep turn in the road, their aquamarine tank-tops and MTV accouterments flapping in the upward breeze. A Mohawk rudders with his menace of bristled hair, a minimum foot high in the stiff wind. His grin is simple; he looks like a human buzz saw.

"The Senate didn't make me *bitter* about men. I felt bad for them, in a way. Our government run by emotional retards with the weight of the world on their shoulders. Five-year-olds crying for Mommy in their Bloomingdale diapers. Others were what one girl called 'shortdicked motherfucker *jerks.*' 'What do they think we are,' she'd say, 'their *secretaries? We* run this goddamned show. This is *our* Congress, *our* House of Representatives. We're the fourth branch of government. The anarchy branch! We *repeal* the laws in here!'

"A lot of patrons scowled because they thought *we* were immoral. Midwestern surveyors of sin and New England calculators of spiritual abasement. Texas Statisticians of Babylon and God's accountants of whoredom from North Dakota. One regular even gave me a Bible. King James. He sat there night after night, his eyes gone in the light of dozens of beautiful breasts of every imaginable variety, then had the nerve to tell me *I* was a lost sheep, headed for hellfire, etc., one of St. Augustine's dancing whores."

"Why were you ever attracted to me?"

"You looked lovable."

"How so?"

"Gullible?"

"You performed in these live sex show?" Claire says.

"Nope. I told you I was a *bouncer*."

"It's not *that* funny," I say.

"The hell it isn't."

"You never felt guilty about The Senate?"

"Brazilian bathing suits? Reckless mischief mostly. The night I took mescaline. Whoa. Getting off on stage with five hundred eyes licking your skin like it was sweet butter. About freaked me out."

"No Catholic guilt?"

"That."

"I *said* I was nineteen. Possessed of considerable power."

"Considerable."

"Possessed also."

"That too. Power?"

"The world-class curves sixty thousand years of evolution bestow on a nineteen-year-old Caucasian female."

"I see."

"I didn't realize that's all it was, exactly. But the sanctimony of some of the clients pretty near made me self-righteous about the job, which was, after all, fairly innocent."

"Innocent?"

"Awe," Claire says.

Rain clouds gather. The temperature drops.

⁎

"How long did you bounce?"

"A week," I say.

"You quit?"

"Never looked back. Why would I work in a dump like that?"

"Money?"

"The night I quit I walked to Riverside Park determined to throw myself in the Hudson. I went to a bench I'd spent a few nights on a couple of years earlier and sat in the dark. For hours I watched the lights breathe on the murky Hudson. I was feeling fairly sorry for myself, sitting in the dark with nowhere in the world to go, hoping in my sleep I'd drain out of the world. And pissed off too I didn't have the nerve to jump. I lay down on the cold bench and fell asleep.

"The next morning sunlight filled the air. I felt the sweet sensation on my scalp that told me Rosa was there. The eastern light made the river a breathing pink, as if it were teeming with life, and flowed for some purpose I didn't need to understand. Pigeons fluttered and made fat gurgles on the sidewalk, pecking for crumbs. I sat up and another bum a few benches down said, Top of the morning to you, sir, and I felt like I'd known him from before I was born. I was never so happy to see anyone, never happier to be alive, when only a few hours earlier I'd wanted to die. I walked over to Broadway and bought coffees and hot pretzels and walked back. We sat a couple of benches apart and ate in easy silence."

"Rosa?"

"My guardian angel."

"Well now."

Claire pats my right knee, the one I injured, and for which she bade me get well with a card that sent me hobbling to her dorm room. It's the tiny tendernesses you remember that affect you so, and not the grand passion. She used to massage my knee when it was sore and forecasting rain.

I head up the winding drive. Phillip trims a bush in the front yard. He waves with the cutters.

Claire turns to climb out of the car, but I take her gently under the elbow.

"What?" she asks.

"Virgin goddess of the moon—"

"Yes?"

As I pass through the kitchen the phone rings. I answer it.

"Hello," a long distance voice says, "this is Dr. Valentine. Who's this?"

"Joe."

"Joe, I'm calling from Atlanta. I understand there's been no change in Docie's condition."

"Docie died this morning."

"Oh god."

"*What* are you talking about?" Anna Ruth asks.

I smell cornbread and ham. On the stove in a cast iron pot collard greens simmer.

"Mother homesick?"

"Worse I've seen her yet," Anna Ruth says. "She wanted terrapin and Chesapeake oysters. I said, 'Where in Birmingham am I going to find turtles and oysters from Chesapeake Bay?' Smithfield ham will have to do."

By the time we sit down to dinner the sky is a black mass of rain cloud. The galvanic odor of a thunderstorm sweeps the air. The barometer falls. My knee throbs.

Anna Ruth and Hattie bring out of the kitchen the traditional

Virginia fare. The ham butt sits like fleshy transmission on the serving plate. Steam rises from the corncakes and collard greens.

Hattie pours Mother a sherry and Claire snaps Brett squirming behind a highchair tray. Amelia plays piano chords on the tablecloth and murmurs *Myohos*.

We reach around and hold hands. Mother says a brief grace.

I carve and serve. The plates go around and around heaped with steaming food. Whenever Mother gets the Virginia blues, she weaves Richmond fiction about our Randolph lineage and ramifies it hundredfold into Ancient American History. Tonight, lightning and claps of thunder punctuate her story. We sit silently and eat. The rain is so loud we can barely hear her. Hail drums the roof, taps the windowpanes.

"What about Father?" Amelia asks.

"He has a lightning rod. He'll be fine," Mother says.

The lights sputter and blink out. Amelia retrieves from her bedroom meditation wicks that smell like sandalwood. Anna Ruth comes in from the living room with a ghostly candelabra.

The phone rings.

"Docile's boyfriend," I say.

Hattie struggles up out of her chair and goes into the kitchen.

"She's awake," Hattie says.

Anna Ruth gives me a hug.

"I told you praying would work."

"Sure enough." With iced tea I toast Rosa, who hovers nowhere in the room.

The phone rings again.

"They need to decide on a C-section fast," Hattie says to Mother. She orchestrates cars and drivers. Her face shines with purpose.

"Claire, Webb, and Amelia, take the Impala. Mother and I will take my car. Anna Ruth, stay here with Brett. For godsake's pray, and watch after Father. We'll call from the hospital."

I take a candle off the candelabra and go into the kitchen. My heart jumps into my throat. In a flashpop of lightning I see Father standing outside the breakfast room bay window making the sign of the cross. His sackcloth is drenched, and the white wisps of his hair fall in funnels of water. In the second flash of lightning, his enormous beard looks like a cloud. He smiles up at the rain. It falls like needles, angled steeply in the wind.

Claire comes into the kitchen with a candle.

"What are you looking at?" she asks. She looks at the black window.

"Nothing."

Another singeing white of lightning flashes, turning the backyard into a floodlit blue.

Father's face is pressed to the window.

"What on *earth*," she says. "Why in hell doesn't he get out of the storm? He'll get killed."

She hands me the candle and heads to the back stoop. When the lightning pulses again, he's gone.

"Where is he?" Claire asks.

"Forget him," I say. "Let's go."

The wipers are useless. We creep forward, following a cloud of rainy headlight cast ahead of us. The ink of dark explodes with white.

Amelia *renge-kyos*. For the first time I understand the chant's calming effect.

When we reach the hospital Claire and Amelia get out at the lobby entrance. I park. Hattie drops Mother off and pulls in beside me. I wait for her but she waves me on.

I run through the rain to the main entrance. Just as I reach the pneumatic doors, a simultaneous explosion of light and thunder knocks me headlong. Every light in the hospital blinks out. I try to stop my momentum but deaf and blind I slide on the wet walkway into the jammed doors. My good knee breaks glass. The generator kicks in and the doors hiss open. A wedge of the glass leaps out of the door and shatters next to me. Hattie flies out of the rain from the parking lot.

"Are you all right?"

"I think."

"Look at that *tree*." A pine tree in the parking lot is split from top to bottom. Smoke rises from the fissure.

Nurses have come to the door. One helps me up. "Your hand is cut."

"I'm fine," I say.

Outside the I.C. unit I see Amelia steadying Mother. Claire gives me a straight look.

A nurse and two doctors knock a rolling bed through the swinging doors. I see beneath the oxygen mask the patient on the bed is Docie.

One of the doctors yells to a nurse, "She's fibrillating." The other says, "Prep for a C-section."

They wheel her down the hall into emergency surgery. My hand is covered with blood. The floor tilts, like a ship rolling on a wave. I follow the bed to the surgery door. Amelia grabs me. Her piano-practiced hands are as strong as vise-grips.

"No," she says.

I run back the way we came. The emergency lights make the corridors a low, ghostly blue. I go down the up escalator to the first floor.

The chaplain's door is open. He reclines in a swivel chair, his black leather dress boots propped on the desk. He's reading *People*.

"Are you a priest?" He looks up, startled. I must have shouted.

"Yes. I mean, no. I'm a chaplain. All denominations."

He stands up. He's wearing an all-purpose collar loosely buttoned. His face is a fleshy, well-fed pink. His mink mustache is combed. He flashes a snaggletoothed smile and extends a hand. I shake it. Unclasping, I note his cologne on my own. I whip up my cut hand to point and blood sprays across his face.

"What can I do for you?" he asks. I notice a sudden film of sweat on his forehead. He looks past me into the lobby and wipes his face with a handkerchief. I point out the door.

"My sister's dying."

"Relax. Let me call a nurse." He puts down the magazine. His hands are shaking.

"I want last rites." I'm out of breath.

"You'll be fine. Just stay calm."

"My sister's dying."

"Now?"

I grab him by the throat.

"Final *god*damn last rites *now. In Latin.*"

His face is squeeze-red, puffed like a bullfrog's.

"Son, please," he squeaks.

"Let's go."

"Let go."

I drag him from behind the desk and yank him to the escalator. "*Hurry.*"

We head down the hall to the I.C. unit. Two nurses see us and wave to a third. One blocks our way.

"Sir, no one but authorized personnel allowed in surgery."

I knock her aside and pull the chaplain down the hall to the operating room. I shove him through the swinging doors. I am aware of Hattie and Amelia and Claire shouting.

"Here," I say.

A masked surgeon looks up and gives a muffled command.

"Get them the hell *out* of here," the other says to a nurse. Blood is splattered on his surgery green. The first doctor holds up one baby and then the other as the nurse cuts the umbilical cords and hands the babies to a nurse waiting behind her. The second surgeon applies the metal plates of a defibrillator to Docie's chest.

"Dear Lord—" the chaplain says. I've got him by the back of his neck. I'm trying not to faint. I hear the *Ddtt* of the defibrillator. "In *Latin*." I knock him down and climb over him and pin his arms back. The nurses from the hall pull at my hair, my shirt, my arms. I can hear Claire saying my name.

"*Suadente diablo dominoe nabisco*," the chaplain says. He looks terrified. His eyelids twitch crazily. Tears fall into his eyes. "*Non sequitur exemplum gratis.*"

"In English then, but *say* it."

"On earth as it is in heaven."

I feel a sharp pinch on my shoulder. An icy wave moves up and down my spine and washes over my scalp to my eyes and flexes my face like a fit of crying. I hear someone saying *Docie*.

Two nurses untangle us. I roll over on my back in waves and look up at the florescent lights over the surgery table. A black mass like a tornado funnels out of Docie and rips upward and, screaming like an animal tossed into a chasm, vanishes.

I see a woman clothed in sun hovering overhead. She's surrounded by sunbright snow. It's Rosa. She's holding a dead baby. It's a boy.

I come to in the back seat of the Impala. My hand is bandaged. Claire is driving. Mother sits in the passenger seat. For a few minutes I can't move. I can't remember why I'm lying in the back of the Impala on a rainy night with Claire driving and Mother in the front seat. Then everything implodes into place, like an explosion run in reverse.

I sit up groggily. Claire and Mother's conversation blurs. They stop mid-sentence.

"Dos?" I say. Full sentences are marshaled in my head, but my tongue is numb.

"She made it," Mother says.

I pass out again.

* * *

"Twins?" I say.

"The boy was stillborn," Mother says. She is crying quietly. "The girl is doing just fine."

I flop back and fall into another drugged sleep.

Claire tugs my arm.

"We're home."

"Sleep here," I say.

"Anna Ruth is making some coffee."

She helps me through the kitchen door. Hattie and Amelia sit at the breakfast table eating sandwiches and drinking milk.

Anna Ruth takes me by the arm and sits me at the table. Claire hands me coffee.

I pace around the kitchen. The clock over the stove says four.

"Seven hours?" I ask.

"Out cold," Claire says.

"What happened?"

"You manhandled the poor chaplain," Amelia says.

"Forgive me Father."

"Do you remember?" Hattie asks.

"Yes. But after that?"

"He was scared shitless," Amelia says.

"They tranquilized you," Hattie says. "Like big game."

"It was like you were on PCP," Amelia says. She takes her plate to the sink. "The doctor said we're lucky all the commotion didn't interfere with the operation."

"Did it?"

"The baby was stillborn," Hattie says.

"His heart was so small, and poorly formed," Claire says. "He didn't have a chance."

"Oh Webb," Hattie says, "the baby was born without part of his brain."

I lean against the refrigerator.

"Just before I blacked out from the shot, I saw something

incredible."

"What?"

"An angel carrying that newborn baby away."

"Stop," Hattie says.

I stop Claire in the dark front hall.

"I'm exhausted," she says. "So are you."

"How could I have slept for seven hours?"

"Sleep is not the word I'd use."

"Do you believe me?"

"About what?"

"About the angel."

"When I had my wisdom teeth out," Claire says, "the dentist gave me intravenous sodium pentothal. The nurse asked me to count backwards from ten to zero. Seven is the last number I remember."

"You passed out?"

"I looked up into the dentist's lamp and saw a green field of flowers. My mouth was wadded with cotton and wedged open with clamps. I pointed at the light and said 'Ook.'"

"You don't believe me."

"Hold on. The nurse lowered my arm. She asked if I was all right. She thought I was crying because of the pain. The dentist was cutting my gums and pulling out my wisdom teeth with what amounted to a utility knife and a pair of pliers. I didn't feel a thing. All I saw was this field."

"You don't believe me."

"Of course not."

Beside my mother's bed a dim table lamp casts her shadow on the ceiling. She looks out the window. The storm is fading, but when the wind comes over the bluff the pines sway and the sound of rain begins again.

"She knew you were there," Mother says.

"Who?" I sit on a hassock next to the dresser.

"Eudora. She knew you came to see her."

"During surgery?"

"No. Earlier. Yesterday."

"We were all there."

"When you were born, she would stroll you around the neighborhood and say, 'Look at my little boy.'

"Mother—"

"Don't."

"Don't what?"

"Don't say that."

"Say what?"

Distant lightning glimmers in the window. In the back yard I see Father, his arms upraised, wandering at the edge of the woods in the dwindling rain.

"When I was a young girl I pretended I was like my sister. That I was my sister. I wore her dresses, I imitated her gestures, I pretended her boyfriends were mine."

"Mother—"

"That boy will never know who his mother was."

"Mother."

"Don't."

"Who's my father?"

"Mothers ought to know, sons ought to know."

"Know what?"

"He'll never know his mother or his father."

"Mother—"

"*Don't.*"

"Don't what?"

"I won't, I tell you."

"Mother, who's my father?"

"No, I tell you."

"No what?"

"He'll never know. I know it. That will suffice. I know it, he

doesn't and never will."
  "*Mother, w*ho the hell's my father?"
  "I'm not your mother," she says.

V

"Who."

"Clara."

"Your sister. My aunt."

"My sister. Your mother."

"My aunt?"

"Your mother. I'm your aunt." She wipes her eyes.

"Who's my father?"

"When you were born, when you cut your arm, up until she had to be taken care of, I never believed *her*. It was the way your father behaved. I checked the blood types. It's possible."

"Possible?"

"Clara was fifty, I tell you. She came to me and said, 'I'm pregnant.' I asked her if she might make an educated guess and tell me who the father was? She said, 'I know who the father is.' I said, 'Will he marry you?' 'He can't. He's already married.' Wasn't I surprised by that? I said, 'Who's the lucky father?'"

She presses her hand to her forehead.

"She said, 'Edison is.'"

"Who?"

"Your father."

"My father?"

"Him." She points to the window.

* * *

195

"Was she trying to provoke me? I asked him. He said, 'Your sister is a liar and a drunk.' I tested Clara. I said, 'We'll find a doctor.' 'No, I'll have it,' she said.

"Another?"

"'Then I'll raise it,' I said, 'it's half mine.' 'Fine,' she said. Edison said 'all right.' It was the way he said it. Clara was right. She wasn't lying, I thought. But now I'm not so sure."

"Why?"

"With all the blood tests in the world there was still a chance she was wrong or lying or just undone. I decided not to care. Clara *is* your mother, we know that much, and we raised you like you were our own. Could it matter much now?"

"No."

"The conversion," I say.

"What?"

"The conversion. When did it happen?"

"Not long after you left."

"He knew I knew?"

"About the blood types? Yes."

"Why did you?"

"Why *shouldn't* we rear you like you were our own? We could bother ourselves with the paternity problem until kingdom come."

"So Aunt Clara gave me up that easily?"

"She did not."

"What do you mean?"

"We won you."

"Won me?"

"I sued for custody."

"Is that why I never saw her much?"

"We thought it best."

"How did she think it?"

"Do you remember when she visited you in the hospital?"

"Maybe."

"After that she said, 'You're right. I couldn't have done it alone. He needs brothers and sisters.' Later she claimed I stole you. Towards the end every time she was arrested for vagrancy or picked up for lying drunk in Byrd Park or thrown out of a rooming house she wanted to press charges. Kidnapping, she informed the police."

"Well?"

"An unmarried fifty-year-old alcoholic woman with a psychiatric history of drug addiction and nervous breakdowns? The custody case never even went to court. Maybe today. But things were very different then."

I look out the window.

"Psychiatric history?"

"Depression. Drink."

"Hallucinations?"

"The last few years she lived on the street. She claimed to see angels. Then she lost her speech."

"Were things so different then that a woman couldn't keep her own child?"

"Haven't I just now suggested to you she wasn't up to it?"

"Even if you knew, you wouldn't say."

"Knew what?"

"If Edison Woosley Clayborne really *is* my father. Then you would have another Randolph *scandal* on your hands. As if anybody gives a damn!"

"If I would tell you now, if I knew, I tell you I would. I do not know. In spite of yourself you will one day find it a privilege and a responsibility to be numbered among the descendants of Edmund Randolph."

"Is Aunt Clara the reason we left Richmond?"

"Absolutely not."

"Who else knows all this?"

"Who have I told? I told Anna Ruth fifteen years ago."

"But why did Father let me stay?"

"He could either stay or leave. But you were staying."

"He stayed."

"He was harder on you than the rest."

"Yeah. I'm a mistake, *his* mistake."

"You'll have to ask him that yourself."

"And what?"

"You're not illegitimate. We adopted you."

"But born a bastard."

"If that's the way you choose to think of it," she says, and looks out the window. "But you will change your mind."

I stand up to leave.

"Wait," she says. She rummages through a stack of papers on the bed. She hands me a yellowed sheet of paper. It almost crumbles in my hand.

"What is it?"

"Short of a DNA test, the closest thing to proof about paternity you're very likely ever to get."

At the top of the poorly typed page is written in meticulous script *The History of Luminescence*. After you were born Clara started writing what she called 'stories,' more symptoms of mania than literary inspiration. None make much sense. That in your hand is the last she wrote, not long before her final episode. I think you have a right to see it."

"Her last episode?"

"She thought she was Greta Garbo."

"I showed them to her psychiatrist. He said patients suffering from mania often have delusions, but that delusions contain some truth distorted by the illness. On the other hand," she says, smiling, "delusions might be exaggerated daydreams, or fantasy."

"Delusions?"

"She was a bag lady in Byrd Park."

"If she *did* know Edison Clayborne, it was before he met *me*," Mother says.

"In New York."

"I suppose."

"Father's first wife?" I ask.

"Impossible."

"He was an actor. Wasn't Aunt Clara a model?"

"So she said. She had two jobs in two years."

She looks through a pile of magazines stacked by her bed. She hands me a Vogue magazine from 1939.

"Page 67. And the next."

Aunt Clara stands under the cabled span of Brooklyn Bridge holding a white parasol, flanked by two other women wearing identical dresses of different color. Their shoes are black half-heel clunkers. Broad-shouldered dresses fall mid-calve. On the next page the same women dressed in Easter white are arranged like mannequins under the Washington Square arch. Aunt Clara wears a broad-brimmed hat and given the occasion looks too daringly into the camera. She is stunning but not in the way a fashion plate is required to be. Her black hair is too black and her skin talcum white. There is something reckless in her look, even slightly crazed, an expression both joyfully buoyant and grim.

"I've often wondered if she's the reason he came to Richmond," Mother says.

"Read this."

"What is it?"

She hands me a bulky manuscript bound in imitation leather and gold thread.

"I write too," she says.

I press Aunt Clara's typescript between the pages of the manuscript like a leaf.

"Why tell me now, and not five years ago?"

"Everything has changed."

I turn to go.

"Wait."

She hands me an envelope.

"Your birth certificate."

I look at it. The heading says Medical College of Virginia Hospital. Under *Mother* it says Clara Randolph. Under *Father* it says *unknown*.

"What about the one I took to Little League tryouts and football sign-ups?"

"It was forged. Doctored, I mean. Changed in small but important ways."

"To protect the guilty?"

"And the innocent."

"When your mother dies, you will be the sole beneficiary of her estate."

"A bag lady's?"

"Seven million dollars. Mostly tobacco stocks, a trust fund."

"And the rest?"

"Dividends, interest. After you were born she lived like an indigent."

"That's why we never saw her."

"Yes."

"Didn't you try and help her?"

"She didn't want any help. Believe me."

"Do I have any choice?"

* * *

"My half-sisters," I say.

"Cousins."

"Should I tell them about Aunt Clara?"

"It is your decision."

"What should I call you?"

"Aunt. Mother. You decide."

"Aunt Mother?"

"If you wish," she says.

I close the door quietly behind me. I feel breezy, in skyey spirits, like I just stepped out of a Saturday confessional. I walk to the kitchen.

Amelia and Hattie sit at the breakfast table drinking hot chocolate.

"Cousins," I say.

I tell them the whole story.

They kiss me.

I sneak into Claire's bedroom and slip my hand under her nightgown and gingerly cup her breast.

"Starlight," I say.

"Goodnight," she says. I climb the third floor stairs and go to bed.

I lie awake. The sky is a dark blue plane edging to grey. Birds are stirring.

I pick up Aunt Mother's manuscript and open it. On the first page is printed in Gothic script the title *Dark House, A Romance of Olde Virginia*. Centered below is *Marybelle Randolph*. I flip fifty pages and read from a chapter entitled "Wedding Night at Belvidere Mansion."

One summer twilight she had walked with her lady-in-waiting to a spring where the cool waters refreshed her alabaster skin and brought a finer blush to her delicate face. Passing a field, she saw him standing, naked from the waist up, lashing a black stallion held by the reins. The animal reared; with a whip he lashed and cursed it with a fury that left her trembling. He mounted the majestic animal, and striding its furious rearing and violent prancing, rode it into a graceful and obedient gallop. When he cantered by the fence where she stood in a fever of fearful joy, she swooned.

She woke in his arms. The horse grazed on a grassy knoll. She looked into his dark eyes and attempted to cry out. As in a dream, she could not.

At the ceremony, when he lifted her veil and leaned down to kiss his bride, and again at the wedding reception, when she watched him graciously and slightly bowing as he greeted each guest, she found his eyes fixed on the locket at the end of the gold chain that encircled her neck, the locket that held the key to the chest in which her family's ancestral gold sovereigns and silver services were stored. When his face turned with the slightest imperceptibility to a look of mockery, she felt a faint chill, as though the beginnings of a strange delirium engulfed her in its feverish tide. When she looked into his eyes, a deep and horrible panic struck her, as if her beating heart would burst beneath her corset. That chill had deepened as they drove to his ancestral mansion.

Now she stood at the massive oak door, her prized husband beside her, whom she dare not now look in the eye, so violently did she dread his gaze. A servant whose ashen face sent a quiver of fear through her heart took her custom-made luggage from the carriage, and, placing it on the portico, opened the giant door. Her husband lifted her and carried her over the threshold.

"My dear," he said with utmost civility as he put her down, "since we are both tired, should we not retire for an hour, and dine at eight?" She was restored to her earlier happiness by his kind expression, but only briefly, for as he turned to walk down the western hall toward the wing of ancestral portraits he had recently engaged a winter afternoon touring her through, with a subdued and charming pride in his expression, while snow like a confusion of souls whirled outside the windows, as he exclaimed, before each one, that there not a single descendant of his time-honored family to compare with the constellation of *hers*, she caught his reflection in a gilded mirror that hung over an English escritoire. Her heart started at his expression, for she could not be entirely certain that his eyes had not, for an instant, glowed with the glassy light that wolves reflect when startled by the bright lanterns of a passing carriage.

As she ascended the dark stairway, accompanied by the crooked servant whom she could tell, even as he looked directly ahead, laid the unyielding gaze of a wandering eye upon her bosom, a maelstrom of horror swept over her. She *knew* in an instant of terror the mistake of her life was irreversibly made, no, not the mistake of her life, for there was no life *here*, she sensed, only the pall of dust and gloomy must of secrets long forgotten yet sensate beneath the dark impenetrable walls she felt had eyes all their own which watched her as she moved from room to room, just as she sensed, upon entering the boudoir, the heat of the person who, hearing her footsteps, had quickly left the bedside where the negro servant, now bowing, now turning, drew the heavy curtains against the blaze of the setting sun.

The room had a sharp odor, like camphor. She undressed and lay on the bed. Exhausted from the ceremony and reception, and with nerves weakened by the increasing sense of apprehension that seem to seep from the walls like a contagion, she fell into a drugged sleep.

I take Aunt Clara's yellowed sheet of paper out of the manuscript. The typescript looks like rows of crooked teeth.

A History of Luminescence

* * *

From street corners under grey fedoras they watched me tap the wide walk with stiletto heels. I was seventeen and my body was a garden: tightly furled rosebud and broadleaf abelia, beautybush and chaste tree, creeping fig and trumpet creeper.

Over the river my sister leaned like a blighted tree. No leaves from her hands, her palms and heels were broken shells.

At night I crept with boys into alleyways, behind carriage-houses. The gardens were alive with fireflies and June beetles crunched beneath our feet. Under a linden tree I kissed my lover. On a white bench beneath a wide oak my sister sat, waiting. I held my lover behind his neck and pulled him down. My sister said, What are you doing. Over his shoulder I saw her on the wide bench, sitting. We rolled onto the ground. My teeth slid down his neck. What are you doing, my sister asked. She walked through the iron gate into the alleyway. His tongue turned in furrows like a root, burrowing, uprooting, and there poured forth its luminous milk.

The next week, at the soda fountain, I saw her with him. At night we met under the linden tree. During the day they rowed boats in the park. I saw them at matinees on balcony rows, hands twined. At night we met under the linden tree. When the moon sailed out, we watched the brace of constellations turn, a radiant inlay of lights, fruits hung from a heavenly tree. I planted my heart in the roof of stars.

Under the linden tree my belly filled, a luminescence, bone-white, heavy with blood, sloped like a pear, taut as a bulb. I went to my sister and said, Where do you think he is every night? With me, under the linden tree.

Out of the bulb tendrils shot. I lay in the cool water and held the warm breathing.

I dreamt of heaven's body, every tiny star a baby's head, every constellation a child.

My sleep was stolen. I woke and the baby was gone. I lay in

the wet of the broken sac.

From under the linden tree my sister stole the son. The baby. From under the linden tree my sister stole the baby. From under the linden tree.

I look out the window. In grey light on the golf course below a tiny figure jogs. I hear the drone of a small plane. A blue jays dive out of the pines and wheel down to perches on the iron-work love seat in Phillip's flower garden.

Father's lantern burning in the bluff woods brightens for a second, and then goes out.

Aunt Mother's manuscript falls from my hands onto the floor. I drift into sleep, startled awake by a sudden recollection. When I was seven, lying deliriously awake in the hospital after the blood transfusion, the person who appeared at the end of the bed like a vision was not Aunt Mother, but Aunt Clara, my mother. Then I realize that that was, without a doubt, the last time I saw her.

I turn off the light. The sun is up. I draw the curtains and sleep.

VI

A knock at my door. Claire peeks in.

"The hospital called," she says. "Docie wants to see us."

"She's talking?"

"Sort of."

Claire wears a sky-blue flowery dress with a small lace collar. She sits down on the bed and hands me a cup of coffee. Her stockings *swish* when she crosses her legs.

"Going to church?" I ask.

"I felt like dressing up."

"Hattie said you had something to tell me," she says.

I tell her the whole story.

"Webb," she says.

Claire leans over and looks out the window.

"So who is that crazy man in the woods?" she asks.

"Who else?"

"Maybe we're all somebody else's children," I say.

"Sometimes we wish we were," Claire says.

"When we first moved to Birmingham some country club Baptist bitch dropped by for a housewarming visit. 'Oou*wee* my, you have such lovely children, Mrs. Clayborne.' Then she looked out the window and saw Amelia playing in the yard. 'And that youngun' is the cutest little pickaninny. I a-wished my kids had a little colored playmate around the house.' Mother turned pale and left the room. It couldn't have been easy for Amelia, going to school with Mountain Brook cotton balls. What is she? Gypsy, jew, Indian, Mexican? Surrounded by all these Alabama Baptists white as worms. Aunt Mother probably told her she was the great granddaughter of Sally Hemings."

"Aunt Mother? That's nice. I like that."

"Anything else?"

Amelia stands in the doorway. I turn off the movie projector.

"We saw a midget," she says, "dressed like Uncle Sam walking sideways up a pine tree. Then a tremendous bird with a wingspan as wide as the house flew over the roof."

"How old were you?" Claire asks.

"Six."

"Then I was seven," Amelia says, blowing steam off her coffee.

"We fanned our arms," I say, "and flew around the room."

"It was very early Saturday morning," Amelia says. "We were watching the farm reports on TV, waiting for the cartoons to begin. Webb jumped up and pointed out the window. 'Look!' he shouted. A little man walked up the tree, and then the bird flew by. We flapped our arms and took off."

"I told you she'd remember," I say to Claire.

"When Docie and Hattie and T.E. woke up," Amelia says, "we said, 'we can fly!' T.E. got the movie camera. We flapped and fanned like penguins and didn't get an inch off the ground." I turn on the projector back on. "That's what we're doing here."

On the film Amelia and I wave our arms, then look at each other, embarrassed.

"It happened," I say.

"I remember," Amelia says.

"We flew," I say.

"In our heads," Amelia says.

"Not on film," Claire says.

"In the air," I say.

Claire says, "Maybe you saw *Peter Pan* too many times."

"Shit. We flew. I *remember*."

"Not on film," Claire says.

"In our minds," Amelia says.

"That's not good enough," I say.

"It's not?" Claire asks.

"It's not on film," Amelia says.

"Last night," I say, "just before the shot put me under, I saw Grandmother Rosa holding Docie's baby boy."

"Sodium pentothal," Claire says.

"That's not good enough. Before that I saw something fly out of her body, like a magnetic field. It was dark, and shaped like a cyclone. It screamed, vanished."

"Beelzebub," Claire says.

"The doctor told us they gave you enough sedative to knock out an elephant," Amelia says.

"He wanted to know," Claire says, "if you had a history of mania. Depression."

"Who doesn't?"

"Seriously."

"My mother does," I say.

"You had the strength of five people. That's a symptom," Claire says.

"Or angel dust," Amelia says.

"Are you depressed?" Claire asks.

"Right now?"

"Did you have any problems in New York?"

"Always broke."

"Any attacks?" Claire asks.

"Of homesickness? Occasionally."

"I don't think you're aware of what you did last night,"

Amelia says.

"I'm fully aware."

"The chaplain was scared out of his mind," Claire says.

"Easily done."

"You were *brilliant*," Amelia says, "now that I think about it."

"A guy's sister is dying. What is he supposed to do? What if the mechanics can't put her back together? What about her soul?"

"Her soul?" Claire asks.

"Grandmother Rosa swung low," I say, "and took that still-born baby back."

"Why not," Amelia says.

"First manned flight without a ship," Claire says.

"And no parachute," Amelia says. She pauses, leans dizzily into the door jamb, appraising me in some new light.

"Never mind," I say.

"We'd better get to the hospital," Claire says.

"I have an errand to run," I say. "I'll meet you there later."

"We won't be there long," Amelia says. "T.E.'s plane gets in at 11:00."

"See you Sunday dinner then."

I stop them before they go.

"Ask Anna Ruth to set three extra places."

"Who for?" Amelia asks.

"My mother. And T.E. of course."

"The other?"

"A ghost."

I fan my arms.

"There's a phrase for that," Claire says.

"Flying," I say.

"For what we thought was flight," she says.

"What?"

"*Folie à deux*."

"What does that mean?" Amelia asks.

"The madness of two," Claire says. "When two people, especially children, convince each other of an illusion. Like telling ghost stories, getting scared, then seeing a ghost. Or believing you can fly. Without a plane."

"Not possible?"

"Not yet."

"What about seeing the ghost of your grandmother?"

"That's the madness of one," she says, and closes the door behind her.

The backyard garden has a stone terrace with two ironwork glasstop tables. A potted plant sits on each. Ironwork love benches are arranged under hundred-year-old oaks. Stone Grecian vases holding plants and vines sit atop square brick fence posts that support the elaborate iron grillwork surrounding the terrace.

Boxwood, ilex, cherry laurel, sweetshrub, and witch hazel encircle the flagstone patio, sculpted bushes I wouldn't know one from the other if Phillip hadn't taught me, and the trees in the flourishing yard too: plum, hawthorn, crab apple, magnolia, dogwood, black gum. The garden is woven together with espaliered dwarf fruit, bittersweet vine, fire thorn, euonymus. Along one side of the flagged terrace a long, narrow lily pool runs to the edge of the lawn, fed by a series of rills and cascades of water pumped from the garden greenhouse.

Last night's rain has made the woodland paths that move over the yard a burgeoning, growing bloom of white and purple flowers. The air has been wrung clean; the sky is a high cold blue scattered with cirrus.

I pass out of the terrace gardens and walk along the banks of flowerbeds that cradle the wide yard. The putting-green lawn slopes to the green blackness of pines. The path to the bluff is a tunnel.

I step into it. Woods-cool breathes over me, like entering a cave.

Birds make their morning noise, blue jays and thrashers flapping and pivoting overhead, dropping through the sunlit rooftop of trees. A Lord-God hammers in the pines.

Down the path the sagging ax-hewn cabin leans up the slope to the bluff. The hut looks like a mushroom sprouted from the ground.

The path is thickly strewn with pine needles. I stop and listen. I hear only birds and distant golfers.

The door of the cabin is open. I walk across the warped planks of the floor to the desk under the only window. Down rises on my neck.

On the desk lies a *Roman Missal*, a paperweight letter-opener, a battered *Catholic Bible*, a King James, *The Confessions of St. Augustine*. A dozen well-worn spiral-ringed notebooks are stacked against the wall. A blackened kerosene lantern hangs from the window over the sunken army cot. On the bedside table sits a yellowed paperback, a pocket-sized New Testament. A dried palm-frond cross hangs over the desk.

A rustling in the woods. I walk out to the path and see Father moving where sunlight splinters through the thick growth of vines and trees. He's headed towards the bluff where the pine crucifix overlooks the links.

I angle to a side path and cut him off. He stops and looks at me, placid, unsurprised, rapidly reciting Latin like a priest in a confessional.

"*Dies Pentecostos erant omnes discipuli pariter in eodem loco.*"

He wears a home-made monk's robe sewn out of burlap sacks. The white shock of his hair stands on end, as if raised up by static. His face floats in the white bloom of his beard. His eyes are crazy. It occurs to me that he might have been grazed by lightning.

"Are you my father?"

"*Lucis tuae radium.*"

"What?"

"Tell the fox, behold, I cast out devils. *Pater pauperum.*"

"Go on."

"They shall dwell safely in the wilderness, and sleep in the woods."

I step closer.

"*Loqui variis linguis, Spiritus Sancto dabat eloqui.* Let children first be filled," he says, "for it is not meet to take the children's bread, and cast it to the dogs."

"*Are* you my *father?*"

"Out of his belly shall flow rivers of living water. *Lumen cordium Nihil est innoxium. Flecte quod est rigidum Alleluja.*"

I don't know whether to kneel or knock the son of a bitch down. I grab him by his robe-rags.

"Are you my goddamned *father?*"

"If you are without chastisement, then you are bastards, not sons."

"Don't freaking talk to *me* about chastisement. Or *bastards* either." I hear the distant *swick* of a golfer on the teeing green a hundred feet below. Father looks at me blankly. His breath is sweet and stale.

"Who the hell is my *father?*"

"Your father is in heaven."

"He's dead? Who was he?"

He raises his arms.

"Your Father is in Heaven."

"You're not my father?"

"Your Father is in Heaven."

"What about my mother?"

"Hateful birds. She hath lived deliciously. Seven heads. A scarlet beast. Ten horns shall hate the whore, and make her desolate and naked."

"Where's my tricycle?"

"Voices and lightning. A lake of fire. Gog and Magog."

I let go of his rags. I look out over the bluff.

Golfers walk on the green river of a fairway. I see an iron shot arc up and down and bounce quietly to the flag below. On a stone bridge over the creek that winds along the golf course two blacks with canepoles stand and fish. One of the golfers waves at them with his driver.

"The devil is cast out of thy daughter."

I turn around and walk back up the path. He says "*Dispertita linguae tamquam ignis.*"

I hear a golfer yell, "Fore."

"*Repleti sunt omnes Spiritu Sancto.*"

"Hell," I say.

Claire stands on the garden terrace. Anna Ruth and Aunt Mother look out the breakfast room bay window. They crane their heads as they watch me walk up the garden path.

"I thought you left," I say to Claire.

"I heard you shouting. Are you all right?"

"What do you mean, am *I* all right?"

"Is he all right?"

"You mean, did I knock him off the bluff? No. But somebody ought."

"Don't say that."

I sit on an iron chair. I'm happy enough to enjoy how unpleasant it feels.

"What did he say?" Claire asks.

"Gibberish."

"Nothing?"

"Zilch."

We sit for a moment in silence.

"*Is* he bats? A retired executive gone lunatic in the pastoral suburbs?"

"Is he your father?"

"Doubtful. Probably. Impossible. Conceivably."

"How badly *do* you want to know? There's genetic testing."

"Not that bad."

"He was out in a hell of a storm last night."

"He got singed by a thunderbolt."

"How is he, really?"

"He's fucking nuts," I say. "Really. And so what?"

Mother sits at the breakfast table reading the Sunday paper.

"Well?" she says.

"One last witness," I say.

"No. Not today."

"Call Bellewood."

"She hasn't uttered a word in ten years."

"I'll call."

"No. Tomorrow."

"No. Today."

She calls on the hall phone.

"This is Mrs. Clayborne. Clara Randolph will have a visitor today."

"Webb," she says, "her son," and hangs up.

"So, what did he say?" Aunt Mother asks.

"He was speaking in tongues."

"How many?" Amelia asks.

Hattie calls from the hospital.

"Docie wants one of her dolls," she says. "The landlady will let you in."

"One of her dolls?"

"One," Hattie says.

I stop by Docie's apartment in the Southside. It's the second story of a brick house in a neighborhood built at the turn of the century by the gentrified steel czars, until their own smokestacks drove them over the mountain to Mountain Brook.

I ring on the first floor bell. The stereo is turned up. "I Am Woman" shakes the windowpanes.

The stereo stops mid-refrain. The landlady, mid-thirties, wrapped tight in a black Danskin, answers the door. She shines with sweat. In each hand she holds a ten-pound dumbbell, her breasts pumped to chest muscle. Blue tubes of veins run down her thin arms. She's tanned dark as an acorn.

"I'm Docie's brother," I say.

"How *is* she?" She puts down the weights and towels off. On the wall by the fireplace is a poster of a female bodybuilder. Slick and hard, she stands in shadowy light, her ropy swimsuit tied like tourniquets around her waist and breasts. Her legs are grooved with muscle; she holds her hands behind her neck and flexes her stomach. The caption says, "Power and Grace."

"She regained consciousness last night," I say. "She's going to be fine."

"Webb, right?"

"And?"

"I'm sorry. Carrie."

I explain to her why I'm here.

"The *babies*," she says suddenly.

I tell her what happened.

She takes the stairs two at a time and unlocks Docie's apartment. On every shelf and in every chair in the front room sits a different doll. All are girls. Most are antiques.

"Which one did she want?"

I recognize a Raggedy Ann.

"This one will do," I say, and pick it up.

Carrie gives me a sweaty half-hug.

"So the girl is going to be just fine."

At the hospital I'm given a minute to see Docie. She's half-asleep, drowsing in postpartum exhaustion and the aftermath of coma. A tiny light of consciousness shines in her eyes. She looks at turns amazed and confused.

She's aware of someone standing by her bed.

I lift her hand and lay the Raggedy Ann beneath it.

"Eudora," I say.

"Ball," she says.

At the premature infant ward I ask to see Docie's baby girl. A nurse points through a large window to a row of incubators. Nurses in sterilized masks go from one incubator to the next, checking clipboards. Docie's baby is third from the left.

She is a very tiny baby. Electrodes taped to her chest monitor breathing and heartrate. The tiny baby sleeps.

"How is she doing?" I ask. The nurse is young, with brown, friendly eyes.

"Very well," she says.

The baby kicks. I see her gumless mouth open and her face redden with wrinkles.

"Is she okay?" I ask.

"Exercising," she says. "This girl's got a voice. I've never heard such pipes on a preemie. She can *sing*."

The nurse laughs. She means what she says. I laugh too.

Bellewood is west of Birmingham, out past the old mills and coal mines. Soot lies like century-old carbon snow on scrap heaps and abandoned plants. The sulfurous air for decades corroded the mills that spewed it; now they look half-eaten by their own acid. Car graveyards glint from the roadside, the crushed and battered bodies randomly stacked, smashed headlights and crumpled grillwork still nosing forward as if knowing where to go.

When the steel desolation stops, Alabama pine green begins again. A few miles farther a sign for Bellewood.

I turn into the drive and give my name over the intercom.

The iron gates swing open and I drive up a winding road that levels out in front of a neo-colonial house.

Old folk in wheelchairs sit dumbly on the lawn, or sleep like infants on porch swings under the wide veranda, blankets pulled to their chins. A few scattered patients, attendants beside them, walk the grounds in robes.

Inside, the lobby looks like an old hotel's. Oriental throw rugs lie on the dark hardwood floor. Fan-backed wicker chairs are arranged around a marble coffee-table, where a rickety lady wrapped in a loose-knit shawl pours herself a cup of tea from a silver service. In the far corner sits a grand piano with a handicapped bar attached to its side. Through the high open windows breeze from the surrounding tree-shade moves through the room.

The head nurse, fiftyish, firm, and gracefully brisk, greets me at the front desk.

"You're Hub," she says.

"Who?" I say.

"Right this way."

A long, roll-out rug runs down the wooden hallway. The floor has a seasoned squeak. Along the walls wheelchairs form a crooked row of beat-up old heads, liver-spotted, bony domes that hang weakly over wilted pajamas, their skin papery as locust husks, their faces suck-cheeked and wrinkled like old paper bags. These are the ones too old or despondent to wheel outside to the May weather. I fear we'll penetrate another barrier, move into some deeper recess where the utterly hopeless sit in drooling stupors, cataract-blind, incontinent, unable to bathe or dress themselves, and there I'll find my mother, gape-faced, half-paralyzed, idiotized by age, mania, and forty years of pills and drink.

Instead, the nurse takes me through the large kitchen and out the back door to an enclosed garden, where a woman sits on a stone bench under a chinaberry tree.

The nurse takes my arm and walks me over.

"How long?" the nurse asks.

"Sunday dinner. I'll have her back tonight."

I sit down beside Mother Clara on the bench. She wears a dark flowery dress with a starched collar that sets off her face like a finely fractured gem of wrinkles.

Her head bolts forward. She's bony as a bird. Her elbows and knees are scaly knobs. Liver-spots cover her hands; milky-blue, bulby veins run down her finger bones. On her ring finger held by a gold band rests a tremendous sapphire. Crazy wrinkles spider down her neck. Her arms are sticks. Gravity's dragging her down the final few feet, but beneath the sag of her face her eyes gleam bright as dimes.

I look at her. She looks at me.

"Hueb," she says.

At the front desk I ask after any particulars I need to know.

"Physically she's fine," she nurse says. "She loves ice cream. Peach, strawberry, chocolate fudge. She'll eat a whole half-gallon if you let her." She smiles at Mother Clara, indulging the adult-child leaning on my arm. "She doesn't say much, but sometimes she sings."

I turn to go. I remember another question.

"What's Mrs. Randolph's blood type?"

The nurse does a rapid type-in on her desk computer.

"O," she says.

"So he *could* be my father," I say. Knowing it's possible, I discover I don't particularly give a damn.

"What?" the nurse says.

"Zero," I say. "My blood type is zero."

"O, you mean. There's no such type as zero."

"Not yet."

By her bony elbow I lead Mother Clara to the car. In the sunlight her face looks like a crazed jewel. She walks, stooped, certain of every step.

* * *

I drive east through town back to Mountain Brook.

I remember Hattie talking to comatose Docie, and why.

I tell Mother Clara about my adopted family, and lay out the question of paternity, and how even if she *could* explain the mystery, it no longer matters. I tell her about being raised by my perhaps-real-only-step-father, who begrudged me, I thought, because I was a boy, the way fathers beat up on their sons because *they* were beat up by *their* dads, all the way back to the first inseminator who reared up off his haunches and slapped the taste out of his son's mouth. I tell her too that he might have begrudged me because I reminded him every waking day of some mistake his wife had made him live with for twenty-six years, and that she adopted me not only because she thought you were unfit to raise a child but also for propriety's sake, some shame of her older sister in light of the unblinking look of Richmond's FFV sanctimonious inbred and neurasthenic pedigrees who would sooner spontaneously combust than fart within hearing of a hundred illustrious ancestors' ashes resting on mantels in urns like antique spittoons or scattered at restless angles inside moldy mausolea, and who would sooner bring an unsanctified pregnancy to term and drop it in the Chesapeake Bay before they would admit to having yielded for the several seconds it takes to get-with-child to the lust they pretended had been bred out of them by refinement built on tobacco trade and a hundred thousand slaves. No, I tell Aunt Mother I admire the way she dropped through the floor of social presumption and lived on the street, blue-blood baglady. I tell her I'll imagine my father a fellow vagrant who on a winter night wrapped himself in the same blanket over the same heating vent on Grace Street and there towards dawn left his genetic code whipping its flagellum towards your final fertile egg, and two days later was found frozen hard as bloodstone on a muddy bank of the James, was taken to the morgue from which, unidentified after three days, he was hauled to the city graveyard and buried, and did not rise again after three days or three years or three millenniums to kick his son in the pants or box his ears with the threat of hell or bark like a drill sergeant the Seven Catholic Graces or Seven Deadly Sins, which latter your sister once believed he was guilty of, at least one, but now that no longer obtains. I'll imagine my father a wart-nosed sterno drunk who picked you up passed out from an alley when a hard freeze blew down from Canada and took you to his flophouse where he fixed you a breakfast of gin and crackers and seduced you on his sprung sofa, and where, waking in the morning, he drew a bath in a rusty tub and washed your back. I won't imagine him a failed Hollywood actor and Valentino philanderer who met you in New York the year you modeled there. I won't suppose he had an affair and smelling money followed you to Richmond after the war, where he met your sister, ten years younger, at the Country Club of Virginia Harvest Ball and, knowing from what you said that she was naive and homely and bookish and rich, over a period of months seduced and married her for the tobacco fortune *you* wouldn't let him marry *you* for—or he wouldn't marry you? Did your drinking sprees and married boyfriends remind him too much of his first wife, the wife for whom he joined the mine-defusing frogman Suicide Squad in the Pacific theatre so he might get blown to hell already? And continued his affair with you for almost ten years while his five children by your sister were born and while he assumed your age and drinking and craziness made pregnancy almost impossible?

Did you both agree that the mistress's sister was to be his wife? Did you send him to that Country Club of Virginia dance, knowing postwar euphorias and war heroism would blind Aunt Mother to the fact that he was swart half-Italian from Brooklyn, New York? Did you plan the meeting out of some long-standing antagonism towards your sister? The same practical joking antagonism of the planeside photograph in the Richmond Times-Dispatch circa nineteen-thirty-nine, where you and Marybelle are standing beside the single-engine plane of the state senator you met while working at Valentine Auctioneers ten years after being expelled from Sweet Briar and Salem for generally raising hell and allegedly attempting to seduce a teacher—a woman, rumor had it—the auction house where Depression folk hocked heirloom silverware in order to keepsafe their family farms and houses, heirlooms which you sold to the people still rich enough to afford them, like the state senator with whom you were having an affair and arranged to have your picture taken with Clara in front of his plane and printed in the society column of the paper, where everyone recognized who took the picture and why, the brainy homely twenty-year-old younger sister fresh out of Chapel Hill, a cub reporter on the morning paper naively standing with her thirty-year-old sister in front of the plane everyone knew belonged to the state senator with whom she was having an affair? And when Aunt Mother discovered the joke, that her sister was involved in a sordid liaison with a public official, and that her sister had implied through the society column snapshot a lurid participation in the liaison—heady stuff for the times, Two Sisters Do Elected Official, now as routine as root canal—is it true she swore she would buy up the entire edition and have it destroyed? That from then on she wanted nothing on earth to do with you? That when you were arrested fifteen years later for vagrancy she wouldn't even post a ten-dollar bail? Or when you told her you were pregnant and with whom she didn't believe you, that her husband was no more interested in the bag-lady than the bag? Or was Father seeing you because Mother reined the purse-strings and you half-mad now were more generous, an indigent millionaire spendthrift who lived in a rooming house when she wasn't wandering the streets drunk out of her mind?

"Hueb," she says. Her head lolls with the rhythms of the road.

I tell her about Anna Ruth and football and college and Claire, about being raised Catholic and thinking her sister was my mother, and how I found out about the blood types and thought Aunt Mother had borne a bastard right under her husband's

221

nose, and how I busted out for New York, because it was one thing to grow up with the catfights and dog meanness and the family scrimmage, tolerable if you're some true-blue relation, but then to find out you hadn't *needed* to be stirred into this particular family pot, that life might have had you elsewhere, in some other configuration of mom and pop and brother and sis, all this made me run away and wander like a ghost through the concrete bog of Manhattan, park benches and down downtown drunks and houseboat drifts, living like a cipher amidst people I wrongly figured all added up in some way I didn't, when we're all just souls half-tethered to the bodies we carry, never ever ready to fly off when that fatal storm flashes out of nowhere, but cling to life like a castaway clings to a plank. I tell her I'm glad just this moment to be alive, and don't know why.

I pull into the Winn-Dixie. Sunday shoppers in their spangled imports jockey in the lot for places to park. I ease into the fire lane in front of the store.

"Wait here," I say.

The store is crowded. Couples mill down the aisles, assembling picnics and barbecues. A girl in a Roll Tide tanktop carries a bag of briquettes on her shoulder. Her boyfriend, a jock gone to malted pot, pulls up the rear. Beneath the beer fat is a 4.5 linebacker with the lateral quickness of a crab. He heaves a case of Busch out of the refrigerated bin.

Down the center aisle run the open freezers. A mist of cold air hovers over the frozen peas and ice cream. I pick up a half-gallon of peach.

"The nurse," a voice says, "forgot to tell you."

I look up. Rosa is leaning crook-backed over a grocery cart. Her blue-dyed hair is as wispy as a baby's. She's wearing a rosary I remember. It looks heavy on her frail body.

"Raspberry's her favorite," she says. I pick up a half-gallon.

Turning to ask her, I see she's gone. Instead, Miss Alabama

tanktop is reaching for a bag of frozen fries, her shirt made even more negligible by her leaning breasts. She smiles up at me.

"Roll Tide," I say. She knows I admire the pride she takes in her shape. Her boyfriend waits behind the cart. He gives me a *Don't even look* look. Ribs and potatoes and cabbage and charcoal and beer fill the cart to brim.

"Having a party?" I ask.

Linebacker's going to knock the heart out of a spring afternoon with six-packs and barbecue and that bountiful tan-legged football girl in high-riding cutoffs smiling at him from a lawn chair aside some emerald pool. I recognize the type. I was one, for a while. That's no better than Manhattan turnstile sprints and warehouse exile beside the choking flow of the East River. No solution at all. Standing in the express line, my hands numb from the blocks of ice cream, I know Rosa would have said *he's in heaven* too, whoever he is, so I'm glad I didn't ask. Come to think of it, she didn't even give me a chance to.

Back in the car, Mother Clara has tuned the radio to a big band nostalgia station. Her foot makes tiny taps. Her hands fumble for invisible cigarettes. Frank Sinatra sings. Her head lolls.

I drive home. As we round the road under the bluff, Mother Clara sits up.

"Home," she says.

"Not yet," I say.

I head up the winding drive and pull into the garage, startling Amelia's cat from its litter box.

"At," Mother Clara says.

I pick up the groceries and help her from the car and walk her through the kitchen door. T.E. sits at the kitchen table drinking scotch.

His barn owl eyes are bloodshot. His bald head reflects the

kitchen light.

"Edison," I say. T.E. is legally blind.

"Afternoon," he says. We shake hands clumsily. He cuts a stumped look in my direction.

"You remember Aunt Clara," I say.

"Yes."

"She's going to have Sunday dinner with us."

"Good," he says.

I seat her at the kitchen table and put the ice-cream in the freezer.

T.E. stands up and scratches his beard. I see now he's not puzzled; jet lag has knocked the wind out of him. He drains his scotch and feeling the counter puts the glass in the sink.

Aunt Mother flies into the room.

"I tell you, it's not true," she says. Mother waves a genealogical chart.

"What?" I ask.

"Not you," she says. She looks at T.E. and unrolls a computer sheet of family branches. Mother Clara looks dumbly on.

"William Randolph was *not* an indentured servant."

"Not *the* William Randolph," T.E. says, sitting down. "But our Randolph was. Born in Liverpool like Ringo Starr, indentured to William Byrd II of Westover, from whom he purchased his freedom stateside, 1747, Westover. Basically, he was a butler."

"It's not true, I tell you." Aunt Mother's face is crimson.

"After William Byrd the third, drunk and voluptuary, gambled away half of the Colonial Treasury, he divided his inherited estate into lots and raffled them off. Wilson Webb Randolph, scion of Byrd's butler, won an impressive piece of land in Shockoe Bottom, and went from wheelwright's apprentice to tobacco-trader overnight. And that, I'm afraid, is the extent of our neo-colonial prestige. Bingo aristocrats."

"*Quiet*," Mother shouts. "It's a lie. William Randolph was *the* William Randolph. He was no *house*boy. Grandson of Isham Randolph of Dungeness estate, Old Dominion. Grand nephew of Peyton the president of the first Continental Congress, second cousin of Edmund the governor of Virginia and a blood relation of jurist John Marshall. *The* Randolphs of Turkey Island! William and his wife Mary the Adam and Eve of Virginia! Thomas Jefferson's first cousin! A guest at Monticello and Washington's inaugural ball! He fought in the American Revolution beside Lafayette. Do you hear me?"

"Yes," T.E. says, "but you've got the wrong man."

"No," Aunt Mother says. "What do you know but atoms and equations? Damn fool calculations of emptiness! We are *Randolphs*. Don't you dare *ever* forget it."

"In my cosmogony seminar at Cal Tech there was a black student named Randolph. Are we related to him?"

Mother rolls up her genealogical scroll and flies out of the room.

"Bits," Mother Clara says.

Claire and Mother Clara and I walk in the garden.

"T.E. is odd," Claire says. "He and your mother have fought from the minute he got here."

"The clan lore is junk. He knows it. He's been proving her wrong for decades. Why else would a quantum mechanic relativity cosmologist give a shit about lineage?"

"Light," Mother Clara says, looking up.

"What did she say?" Claire asks.

"Light," I say.

We walk to the terrace and sit on the iron chairs.

"Every time he came home from whatever boy wonder school, he'd have a bag of gadgets that terrorized the neighborhood. Stinkbombs, rockets. Boxes that jammed the neighbors TV signals or made their phones ring at off the hook. He blinded cars with a telescope mirror and bugged the Jimson's dining room. Once he built a transmitter and tuned the neighbor's car radio to the broadcast frequency. Mr. Davies was a brimstone

Baptist, as strict as a whip. When he drove off the next morning, he heard T.E. thundering over his radio, 'Mr. Davies, I am Lucifer, Lord of Hellfire.' The old fart about had a stroke and drove off the road."

"Not cruel enough," Claire says, laughing, "but still cruel."

"T.E. was going blind. His eye therapist said all that mischief was panic. We went along with the pranks. He was a prodigy with failing eyesight."

"Sad."

"Once he made Hattie the star of a home movie. She put on Mother's stockings and make-up and a floppy sunhat. When T.E. rolled the camera, we jumped from behind boxwoods and hit her her with a dozen eggs. Hattie stood crying, splattered with yolk. It's all on film. Do you want to see it?"

"No."

"What's wrong?"

"I'm glad I was an only child."

"So was he."

"Another time he took the light bulb out of the basement toolroom and locked me in."

"What for?"

"T.E.'s absent-minded. I fell asleep on the floor. The next morning he opens the door and says, 'I found him!', even though he was blind as a post. A policeman was standing next to him. Father wanted to know if I'd locked myself in the basement for the sheer stupid pleasure of it."

"Well?"

"Why I said yes, of course."

Mother Clara points to the woods. Her flowery pagoda sleeve waves in the breeze.

"Crisco," she says.

"She must be hungry," Claire says.

"It wasn't that bad. I didn't rat on him so he bought me a

record. *The Emperor Concerto.* I still have it. He taught me how to make gunpowder. We built a Heathkit Shortwave once. I soldered. And it's nice to have a brother you can brag on. Ten years ago he and a French guy named Aspect proved some notion of Einstein's was wrong. I walked around wondering what it meant that I had a brother smarter than *Einstein.*"

"He's working on supersymmetry now."

"The origin of the universe."

"The big crunch. Black hole primordial."

"The time before no time."

"Baryons, anti-matter."

"Cosmic soup."

"A million million million million miles. Numero one followed by twenty-four zeros. The size of the observable universe."

She kisses me.

"Higgs Boson. Naked singularity."

"Quasars, solar wind. Red shift."

"X-rays. Light waves."

I touch her breast.

"A weave of cosmic forces: gravity, magnetism, sub-atomic mysteries."

"Superstrings."

"Shoestrings," Mother Clara says. She holds up a foot. One of her black orthopedic boots is unlaced. I kneel down and tie it.

"How do you know so much?" Claire asks me. Her question is a referential joke. She knows we sat in same astronomy class at C.U.

"I read the paper," I say. "And I know *you.*"

"Will the universe collapse, or expand forever?"

"Which universe?"

"Spanish," Mother Clara says.

"Why does he pick on your Mother when Docie's so sick?"

"My aunt, you mean."

"Sorry."

"He never got along with Docie. He doesn't think much of mainlining Demerol or seducing married doctors. His eyes went from bad to worse while Docie, faculties intact, went earth cult goat hoof."

"No excuse. Docie's his sister."

"Lines have been crossed. Moral standards violated. The pleasure principle reigns unchecked."

"Is he Catholic?"

"He'd no more go to Mass than light his own farts to fly to the moon."

"Would you?"

"Yes. For the icons."

"On the moon?"

"Bloody crown of thorns. The hands and feet spiked. The spear wound. The forsaken upward gaze. You remember, don't you?"

Claire shudders. "Afraid so."

"I liked the idea. When I was a kid I used to think about it during Mass. If I were crucified, I figured I was a shoe-in for heaven, like the criminal Jesus promised to take to paradise. Getting through the gate. The crux of the matter."

"A crock."

"Who knows?"

"Roam," Mother Clara says.

We walk around the garden. Phillip plants a fledgling bush. From a second-story window comes the sound of Amelia chanting. The sound is sustained, rapid, rhythmic.

"Phillip," I say, "this is my mother."

"Pleased to meet you," he says. He looks at Mother Clara.

"Bo-peep," she says.

"Yes ma'am," Phillip says, and steps aside. Head at a quizzical tilt, he stares at me.

"I *knew* you wasn't one of them," he says.

"Phillip," I ask, "are you my father?"

"Nor your brother neither."

* * *

I seat Mother Clara at the kitchen table. Claire fetches Brett. I watch Mother Clara move her head from side to side. She smiles at me.

She takes the sugar spoon out of the sugar bowl and licks it. She looks around the room.

"Surprise," she says. She laughs, frowns.

Anna Ruth comes in the back door with some parsley from her herb garden. She unwraps a leg of lamb from white butcher paper and rubs it with oil and wedges in cloves of garlic where she's sliced the fat. She sprinkles the lamb with salt and pepper and slides it in the oven.

"Would you help me for a minute?" she asks.

"Sure."

She hands me a grocery bag of pole beans and asks me to snap.

I fix the beans while Anna Ruth peels and cuts carrots and slices tomatoes and red onions for a salad. She breaks a head of lettuce in the sink.

I helped Anna Ruth one afternoon before a big game in high school. I was sixteen. It was a Friday afternoon. She handed me a pot of boiled potatoes and a saucepan of hot buttered milk and asked me to mash. Ten minutes later she touched my hand to stop.

"I didn't ask you to whip them till they float away." They looked like cotton candy. "Nervous about tonight?"

"No," I said.

"Relax," she said. "You'll do fine."

I didn't, but that was that. She went to the game. In the fourth quarter I muffed a simple wide-out. I turned on my route, cleats ripping the sodden turf. The quarterback tossed a wounded duck high and off his fingertips. I heard the galloping thud and war grunts of a linebacker approaching blindside. I caught the ball and turned upfield. With a classic face-mask-on-the-numbers tackle, the linebacker knocked the wind out of me.

The ball squirted loose. From the mud I watched the cornerback catch it mid-air and run untouched into the end zone.

In the locker room, a bench-warmer in his sparkling uniform gave me grief. I was covered with mud. "Hey guys, who's the white trash in the bleachers? Webbo's *Momma?*" Anna Ruth was the only non tennis-mom or golf-dad in the stands not hawking hot dogs or sweeping up popcorn boxes. "Webbo's mom is a live-in *maid.*"

In the car, Anna Ruth asked how I felt about being suspended for two games for giving a teammate a bloody lip.

"Better than I should," I said.

I pour the beans into a colander and run water over them.

I spoon a dollop of raspberry ice-cream for Mother Clara and sit at the table. She eats it in one bite. She winces, presses her finger against a molar.

"Old," she says.

I look at Anna Ruth and then at Mother Clara.

"So you knew the whole time," I say.

"Yes," she says.

I go out the back door. Phillip sits on a sagging beach lounger beside the greenhouse. He works his wiry hands into the dark soil of a flowerpot.

"Planting more?" I ask.

"Looking for night crawlers. Good bait if they're hooked right."

"When are you going?"

"Tomorrow morning. Brim."

"Where?"

"I'll show you."

"You don't mind?"

"Come by at four."

He hands me his flask. I take a burning bite and hand it back. The sunlight in the woods deepens to afternoon.

"Need any help around the gym?"

"No pay." He works a purple worm out of the pot. It curls, contracts. He drops it in a styrofoam cup and tosses dirt on it. From a pile of soil at his side he fills up the flower pot and works his fingers through it.

"Can you still work a speed bag?" he asks.

"Maybe."

"Got a kid stands real close and gets it going good. One time he worked up till he hit himself in the face. Reminded me of you. Rich white daddies these days want *fighting* sons. Stockbrokers want to see their kids' brains pouring out their ears. Can't figure it. Spend your life getting out of what makes you want to fight in the first place and here come the rich the other way. They pay good, though."

He works another curling worm out of the pot. He looks up at me.

"I'm glad of Docie," he says. "But sorry about the boy."

"I know," I say.

I stand for a minute and watch him worm.

"Birmingham's passable," he says. "Not like it used to be."

"The air's clean."

"You could do anything here you could do anywhere else."

"Like fuck up."

"Sure you can," he says. He puts a perforated top on the styrofoam cup.

"Find something you want to do and stick with it," he says.

"Ever thought about going back to Paris?"

"Every goddamn day."

"Webb."

"What?"

"From now on, use the stairs," he says.

"Webb." Mother calls me from the living room.
"That writing of your mother's I gave you last night."
"Yes."
"I'd like it back. With some editing perhaps I can publish it in *Vulcan Quarterly*."
"Don't lie."
She flushes.
"I was upset. Please give it back."
"No."
"Yes."
"I'm finished with yours, though."

I go upstairs to Claire's room and out of her jewel box take the Senate ring and put it in my top pocket.

I go into the kitchen. The brown smell of roasting lamb fills the air.
Phillip has one arm around Anna Ruth, the other on her hip.
"Oops."
"Dinner's about ready," Anna Ruth says, straightening her dress.

Upstairs I knock on T.E.'s door,
"Dinner's on," I say.
"The arrow of time," he says. I open the door. On his back he's half asleep.
"T.E.," I say.
He stirs and rubs his eyes.
"Time to eat."
"Tomorrow," he says, and rolls over.

* * *

The grandfather clock in the hall chimes Sunday three o'clock. We sit at the dining room table laden with spring potatoes and butter, parsley and snap beans, salad, lamb, brown bread, and red wine. Claire sits Mother Clara next to Anna Ruth, while Hattie pours Aunt Mother's sherry and opens a wickered bottle of Chianti.

"Where Edison?" Mother asks.

"Asleep," I say.

"Hattie, go and wake him up."

"Good luck," I say.

Hattie comes back holding Do Not Disturb signs in Japanese, German, and English.

I sit at the head of the table and carve. Settled, we say grace, reaching around to make a ring of twined fingers. Mid-way through the blessing I look up and see Rosa gliding through the room. She's in a playful mood. She makes a diving sweep over the table and blows out the candles. Hattie raises her head and gives me a puzzled look. She looks at the candle smoke.

"Why did you stop?" Claire asks. Everyone is looking. Amelia beams at me. I realize I halted mid-sentence.

"Forgot the words."

"Did someone turn the air conditioner on?" Hattie asks.

"And bless this food bestowed by Thee," Aunt Mother says.

"Swing low," Amelia says, toasting the air with an empty cup.

Hattie pours wine while I serve.

To my right sit Amelia and Hattie. At the end of the table sits Aunt Mother, and to her right Anna Ruth, then Mother Clara, and next to me Claire and Brett.

Brett bangs a spoon. Everyone talks at once. Docie is recovering. Father is praying. The earth is spinning. The universe is expanding.

"Why don't you go ask Father to join us?" Amelia asks.

"He's already eaten," Aunt Mother says.

"Ask him anyway."

"Has Phillip?" I ask.

"Wasn't hungry," Anna Ruth says.

I heap up a Blue Willow plate and pour a glass of wine and take them outside to the greenhouse.

"Anna Ruth says you were starving."

"Naa."

I put the plate down on the work bench. I hand him the glass of wine.

"Mercy," he says.

I walk down the path that goes through the woods to the cabin. I see a shadow moving through the trees.

"Pappy," I say.

The direction of the rustling tells me he's heading for the bluff.

"Father," I say.

The shadow fades, but I still hear rustling.

It stops. I pause. Birds flap overhead. I hear golfers' awe at a good shot.

"Yo," I say.

The rustling moves deeper into the woods.

"Never mind," I say.

I see father standing on the edge of the bluff beneath the cross, arms upraised, looking out over the golf course.

"Get behind me, Satan," he shouts.

"Fuck off," a golfer says.

I walk back up the path and across the yard. Phillip sits inside the door of the greenhouse eating. He waves. I go up the back steps.

"Webb."

I turn around. Father stands at the edge of the woods.

"The earth is clean dissolved."

"Earth my ass," Phillip says, smiling, grape-stained.

"Dead men shall live, together with my dead body shall they arise. Awake and sing, that dwell in dust: the earth shall cast out the dead."

"What was the name of that gangster movie you were in?"

"A light has come into the world."

"What about the Screen Actor's Guild?"

"The cock shall not crow, till thou hast denied me thrice. *Unitate.*"

"Did you meet my mother in New York?"

"The mistresses of witchcrafts, there is no end to their corpses. As thorns cut up they are burnt in the fire. Moab is destroyed. Nineveh is laid waste. The cankerworm flieth."

"Are you my father?"

"Yes." He disappears into the woods.

Claire puts small bites of food on a fork and guides Mother Clara's hand to her mouth.

"I ruined her appetite," I say.

Brett throws his spoon from the highchair. It sails by my ear.

"The nurse at Bellewood said she loves ice-cream."

Aunt Mother stares at Mother Clara.

Claire comes from the kitchen with a bowl of ice-cream. Mother Clara picks up her fork and eats.

We finish dinner. Hattie and I clear the table and Hattie opens another bottle of wine. Anna Ruth offers coffee. Amelia goes into the music room and plays for several minutes what sounds like Bach. She comes back to the table.

"Enjoying music again?" I ask. Her own compositions sound

like a stack of dishes smashed on slate.
"*Wer mich liebet, dir wird mein Wort halten.*" Her German
is a mouthful of bolts.
"I'm taking voice lessons."
She sings intentionally off-key.

O spare us the great disaster.
Tune ye strings and voices
In lively, joyful tone.

"Neither can we," I say, and pour wine all around.
The phone rings. I answer it in the hall.
"Webb." I recognize Docie. Her voice is slurred.
"Welcome home."
"Michael call?"
"Who?"
"Valentine."
"Yesterday. He's in Atlanta at a conference."
"Come by?"
"He's in Georgia."
"The boy?"
"He doesn't know. We'll call him if you want."
I hear a baby crying.
"Her?"
"Uh huh."
"What's her name?"
"Rhoda," she says. "It means rose."
She sounds doped. Her voice is thick. She sniffles.
"You in surgery?"
"I lost my head. Do you remember anything?"
"A dream. It's cloudy. See the little one?"
"Yes."
"Was it my fault?" The baby cries louder.

"No."

The line is silent.

"Docie?"

"Yes."

"He was gone before he got here."

"Okay." She blows her nose. She drifts off.

"You want to speak to Aunt Mother?"

"Who?"

"Mother."

"Yes."

"We'll see you later."

We sit around the cleared table. Aunt Mother comes from her wing of the house wearing a royal blue princess dress with bishop sleeves. She carries a barrel handbag. Arch-backed, she stands in front of the dining room mirror that hangs over the sideboard and adjusts a blue cloche hat over her combed hair. She seems braced, confident, even happy.

"I'm going to the hospital," she says. "No one must join me. I need a few moments alone with Eudora."

"We're not going anywhere," Amelia says, sipping wine.

Aunt Mother leaves. Hattie opens another bottle.

"More?" Claire asks.

"You'll have to drink my share," Hattie says, and rubs her rising belly.

"Not me," I say.

"I'm drunk," Amelia says. Hattie fills her glass.

"May as well too," Claire says. I fill hers.

Brett wants to play.

"Here," I say. I lift him out of the highchair and dandle him on my knee. He balls his fists and squirms. He punches me on the chin. I put him down and he crawls under the table.

"I propose a toast," I say. I raise a glass of iced tea.

"To what?" Claire asks.

"To everything. To nothing. To infinity. Anna Ruth, have a glass."

Reluctantly she lifts her cup. I pour.

"What's the toast?" Hattie asks.

"To the observable universe," I say, and look at Claire. Rosa zips around the room.

"I want some," T.E. says. He stands sleepily in the doorway rubbing his eyes. I take him a glass and pour.

"Alleluia," Hattie says.

"Hush up," Anna Ruth says.

"Curlylocks," Brett says under the table. "Bozo."

"See that long, lonesome road?" I ask.

"No," Claire says.

"There's enough heartbreak that way to last a thousand lifetimes. In the meantime, with wine and lamb and the vegetable bounty of spring, let's walk as if we all know where we're headed, destined to return to places we've never been before."

"Right," Hattie says.

"You're drunk," Claire says. Realizing she's drunk, she laughs.

"To the Dark Ages. And organ donors."

"To my next lover," she says.

"Ajax," Mother Clara says.

"To sharps and flats. Gregorian chants," Amelia says.

"Analog recording."

"To the music of the spheres," I say.

"Harmony in discord."

"To the C Major, blazing chords of *The Creation*, 'Let there be light.'"

"To my children," Anna Ruth says.

"To Rhoda," Hattie says. "And mine."

"To microwave towers," Claire says. "Aerodynamics and DNA. To fractals. To vasectomies and the National Endowment for the Humanities."

"Bullwinkle," Brett says.

"T.E.?" Claire asks.

"Spin," T.E. says, raising his glass. "To the eleven dimensions of space-time. To the speed of light. To public transportation and satellites. To space probes. Computers. To vacuums true and false, and cosmic horizons. To library fines and nuclear fusion."

"To Docie," Phillip says, standing in the hallway with his flask.

"And Rhoda."

We click our glasses and drink.

Afternoon sunlight splinters through the empty bottles on the table, a late spring cant of swimming white. Dust motes swirl in the windows.

"A stream of solar energy," Claire says, "which took a million years to penetrate from the sun's core to its surface and radiated into space as photons travelling 93 million miles from the sun's to the earth's surface in a little over eight minutes, lands on a mahogany table in a suburban dining room in the Magic City, Birmingham, Alabama, where several people sit, after a meal nourished by same rays, drunk on wine made from crushed grapes nourished by said sun."

"Fertilizer," I say.

"Photosynthesis for salad. Oxygen and grass converted to caloric energy, enabling the lamb to prance on a hillside before its appointed time with the butcher's bandsaw that runs on hydroelectric, coal, or nuclear energy, all derived, in one way or another, from the solar axis, our sun. Babies in wombs growing like seedlings in soil. What did we eat for dinner? Condensed light. We are congealed light ourselves."

"Sun," T.E. says, bumping into a chair.

"Starlight," I say.

"Typical," Claire says, "one of hundred million in the Milky way, a spiral galaxy among millions of others. Angular diameter of 32 minutes of arc. Condensed 5000 million years ago from interstellar gas. Present radius 696,000 kilometers. Luminosity

3.90 X 10 to the 26th power watts. Medium bulb. Absolute magnitude, 4.79. Composition: 75% hydrogen. 25% helium. Of its expected duration of 10,000 million years 4 1/2 thousand million have lapsed. When fusion has converted the sun's hydrogen into helium, gaseous orb will expand into red giant, a dispersing star whose luminosity will engulf the earth and utterly destroy organic life."

"As we know it," Amelia says.

"More wine?" I say. Claire reaches to put her hand over her glass. She knocks it over.

"How many astronomers does it take to change a light bulb?" T.E. asks.

"If the sun had more mass," Claire says, "it would burn, die sooner. Instead of expanding, it would collapse to such density the star would superheat from accelerated nuclear reaction."

"And then what?" Amelia asks.

"*Boom.*" Claire says, throwing up her hands.

"The Crab Nebulae, containing the only visible pulsar," T.E. says.

"Yes. Spectacular corpses. Remnants of supernovae," Claire says. "The cosmic A-bomb."

"Is there anything to look forward to?" Hattie asks.

"Bacon," Mother Clara says.

Amelia murmurs her chant. Anna Ruth and Hattie clear the table of empty bottles. Claire and Amelia drain the last of the wine from their cups. Sunlight deepens to late afternoon.

I go to the stairwell bathroom and wash up. Coming out, I bump into Claire.

"Describe star birth," she says.

"It's time to take a nap," I say.

"Almost," she says, and bites my ear.

I hold her tight.

She puts Brett in his crib. I ask Anna Ruth to watch Mother

Clara.

I follow Claire upstairs. On the tier where the stairway turns to the third floor there's a diamond-paned window that looks out over the backyard. Claire throws it open. I kiss her downy neck.

"Look at that *garden*," she says.

VII

I take Mother Clara back to Bellewood. We walk up the stairs to the front porch. The same nurse greets us.

"Did you enjoy your dinner?"

"See," she says.

"She liked the ice cream," I say.

I walk Mother Clara to the stone bench under the tree.

"Later," I say.

"Ebb," she says.

"Who was he?" I ask. She looks up at me and smiles.

"Alligator," she says.

I kiss her forehead and walk to the front desk down the hall of crooked wheelchairs.

"Come back," the nurse says.

The twilight sky is purple. The air is cool. I put up the convertible top and drive over Red Mountain. By the time I descend out of the roadcut, the sky is dark.

Claire comes into the dining room with a glass of tea.

"Need some aspirin?"

"No," I say.

"Let's walk."

* * *

Down the street we circle the cul-de-sac. Wooden-fenced and gated houses are flooded with yard lights, gaslamps, porch lights. Televisions glow in windows.

"Are you all right?" Claire asks.

"What are the three most frightening words in the English language?"

"'I love you.'"

"No. They're, 'Are you okay?'"

"No," Claire says.

"What are you thinking about?" I ask.

"Nothing," she says.

"You took the dark mood right out of me," I say. "Now it's yours."

"Thinking?"

"A nun."

"Becoming one?"

"My mother was sick with bone cancer. I hardly recognize her my last visit. She couldn't have weighed more than seventy pounds. Daddy said, 'When she gets better, we'll all go to Six Flags over Georgia,' but I knew that that was the last time I'd see her. I also knew why Mother Catherine summoned me from the playground. Still, I actually never believed Mama *would* die. I asked every saint in the canon for mercy and prayed to the Virgin Mary. God, I *believed*." I touch Claire's wrist.

"All Mother Catherine said was, 'She was young, but God chose her time and we must accept it.'"

"It? The time?"

"Wait."

She turns away. A honeycomb gaslamp at the end of a drive lights up her face.

"I looked out the window and watched my friends play field hockey. The sky was empty, except for a few birds. I tried to imagine what those birds *saw* from where they flew. Children playing, the church, school buildings, the neighborhood, trees, driveways, rooftops, what? The curve of the earth, of course. I remember thinking that if I could fly high and far enough I would get free of this heaviness. Forget my mother was dead. *Dead.*"

"Is that why you studied astrophysics?"

"What for?"

"So you could fly."

"Fly. Yes."

"See the curve of the earth."

"The curve of the earth. Yes. And further. The beginning of time."

"I thought it was because you were smart."

"It's *freezing*," Claire says.

"Not often we get hail in May."

"Not often? Not ever. There are no ice saints for Alabama."

We play an undergrad game, imagine the force of gravity turned off, heinous genius in lab, throw switch in hand flung. We all fall *up*. Off the face of the earth.

We brush, clutch. It's clumsy. It hardly matters.

Claire showers. I step out in the back yard.

My father is my father but may or may not be my father. My mother is my mother but is not my mother. My aunt is my mother and therefore is not my aunt at all. This much is clear.

First, I'll call myself *Clayborne*. Paternal surname or no, that's *what* I am, so I'll let the adopted name indicate the same.

I'll face the fact it's to late to be a quick-kick artist, punting on first down before I give whatever direction I'm going a chance to break into the open field. Figure out if Claire and Webb ought to figure out where they stand. Done. We'll figure it out.

What with the air clean and a new civic center and a blacks up late to yuppiedom from the downtown slums, even if they buy into the BMW bullshit, Birmingham isn't half bad, though Mountain Brook is still a clan of silly rich, whiter than white bread. If I stay I'll move out of the Heart of Dixie's fancy-pants suburb, maybe west to Homewood, or the Southside, cross whatever suburban river and live somewhere in Shades Valley, anywhere where money isn't a funhouse mirror making people look bigger than they are.

As for the tribe I was reared in, I think about Stanley in New York, a no-bones-about-it bum, an ex-radar man on a Navy bird-farm. His father was an oilrig drunk and his mother abandoned him with his sister in a Greyhound station in Banning, California, before she eloped to Mexico and disappeared forever. His crazy aunt in San Antonio raised them both. She died and he lied his way into the Navy at sixteen. His life was a hundred times rougher than mine. Dishonorably discharged after going AWOL in Manilla, he lived in proud beggary in warehouse Brooklyn off the East River, a sculptor with a foodstamp sinecure, ex-Texan snakeskin taxidermist who bred pitbulls in Waco before he moved to New York, at thirty-five broken open on Canal after he yelled "Geronimo" and leapt from the step-van.

I think about his difficult life. So I was tied to trees and packed in footlockers or locked in toolrooms, or tossed like Buster Keaton as a kid, when his vaudeville parents sewed a suitcase handle to the back of his pants and pitched him back and forth for rent-money. *He* grew up to have houses collapse around his head and received nary a scratch. So my alleged pop was rough on me, even then I knew I came from somewhere else, I didn't exactly know where, and all that time alone in the company of an alien family with time to think, when all I wanted to do is move through the world like everybody else, and yet, not like everybody else, since none of us wants *that*, but to breath free and have the occasional savor of peace. My lot's no larger than most. Don't we all hope, tripped up and falling, we'll stand on our own two feet till the end? Stanley had a freight of misfortune to his name and took it down, *down*, flooring misfortune over and again, until he didn't have a lick left. A body can take but so many blows, his more than others, until it drops. He told me once his name meant *dweller at the rocky meadow* and I'll be damned if it didn't. I imagine he knew when it was time to leap, bow out, give in to the accumulated weight of his fate.

As for dark moods, the sort that Docie's afflicted by, I'll write a letter: "Dear Depression: go fuck yourself," though sadness I'll welcome anytime, because there's a sweetness to it, like the cant of summer sunlight at dusk.

I knew a marine biologist whose parents were killed in a plane crash, when the pilot flew through a bank of fog into a Seattle mountainside. A week after the funeral he got a job as an observer on a Korean fishing boat. No one could understand a word he said, nor he they. For three months he lived on the wide expanse of the north Pacific, watching the ocean, reading, filling out the minutiae paperwork of fish hauls, species, oil slicks. He told me his parents were eighteen when he was born. He figured they'd live forever.

I think about Claire and *her* mother, fifteen years departed, emptied out by cancer to a breathing stick, who put the starch in Claire's spine that makes her such a fighter, as fleet of thought as swift of foot. And Claire's dad, who never liked me, but will, if Claire deems there's helpmeet potential in me. And I've got my *own* parents, adopted ones and all, for a few years yet.

We'll stay in the Magic City too, if we marry. We'll raise Docie's baby girl, if Docie's unable. That's all we have. That's all there is. And we'll help out with Hattie's, if the inseminator won't answer the family call.

That is, *if* Claire will join me at the Jefferson County Justice of the Peace, no St. Francis church bells or boozy Fathers slurring the nuptial vows. A civil ceremony. A mutual vow, till death undoes it, when we sleep until we wake. We'll settle for the domestic, children, the divine nimbus of gin on autumn afternoons. Summers we'll drive to the Gulf and dive for Holy Ghost shells. In spring, gardens and Sunday afternoon naps, and winter with bourbon and firelight.

Which troth Claire and I may not want to pledge. We've got time enough. We'll figure it out. I'm protoplasm yet, a teeming, shapeless life to offer, not yet ramified into sturdy husbandry. I could go it alone back in Gotham, take a shot at respectable profession, no Times Square dog shows, but clerking in one of the hundred thousand cubicled shoots rising out of the granite bog of Manhattan—Merrill Lynch, ABC, Aetna. Be a corporate soldier, hup-two.

No more gutter drunks, park bench conk-outs, or hot-tempered socks. Or weary one-nighters.

I'll cash in a fistful of tobacco stocks and go on an equipment spree for Twentieth Street Gym. Weights, Everlast heavy bags, skip-ropes. Medical insurance. Headgear, a new ring. An Oasis.

I take the Senate ring I swiped from Claire's jewelry box and hold it up to the houselights. It sparkles. I put it in my top pocket.

Enough of sport. Football was good under a green sun. The clack of pads, the thick ripping sound of grass torn up every hike by three hundred cleats, hot grass and sweat, punch-drunk fatigue from blocking dummies and tackling backs. The apple-shine of autumn air, girls in kneesock Shetland wool. The brief and unsurpassable sense of triumph as the team trots out under the spangle of a fall sky, butterflies in my stomach till that first good hit, or a twelve yard pass-run when I snag the ball and head-down knock a cornerback breathless on his back, while the rest of the defense swarms and wails me good. The perpetual sporting growl when the ball, *snapped*, starts the charge, then to see the play break open, when I pull and angle off-tackle in front of the halfback, feeling just right when I hammer the linebacker, and from the sweet sod see the runner break for daylight.

But enough of that.

Claire and I might even go to Mass, even if the Catholic fish-net couldn't haul a wahoo these days, and no one but no one takes the bait off the dogma hook, least of all priests. We'll make it museum tours of medieval remnants—frankincense censers, the holy hush of sainted candles, lyrical Latin sweetly intoned. But not even that anymore. A few years ago I stumbled into a church in Brooklyn during the dawn Mass, after an all-nighter of sheet-metal thieving with the Water Street sculptors. I felt like a fraud standing there, stinking drunk, but as I looked around I realized there was little to distinguish the church from a bingo parlor. No traceries of stained glass. Florescent lighting and a bright Astro-turf rug. No stations of the cross along the ambulatory, but sunrise posters captioned with greeting-card schmaltz. Beyond the Rattan pews, the crucifix over the alter as smooth as a washed stone, no replica of Golgotha, but a cross as plastic and flat as a credit card. We don't want to believe some immortal part of us hangs in the balance, that flesh is grass, and our mouths full of dust, and the choice is ours, paradise or peril, and who can blame us, now?

As for my alleged father, out there with the cliff swallows and hermit thrush, the cold world *will* do its worst, so maybe he was dead-on when he said all we want to do is to live safely in the wilderness and sleep in the woods. He's not half as baked as some pseudo-scientist types, mechanics who want to fine-tune the engine of the world with genes or genocide, or think we're just cerebral baboons, rats who'll twitch to any old response, suicidal as salmon, upstream swimmers struggling just to spawn, and die.

We're all manifestations of the divine, so some saint said, only in distressed form. She failed to emphasize how stressed, but I think of hurricane newsclips I saw as a kid, Camille bending palm trees head to sand, rooftops blasted off like hats by a gust, stormlit boardwalks smashed by thirty-foot waves. How many blows of fortune can anything take?

Maybe Father figures everywhere everyday divinity is

shortchanged. Maybe he's just making up for it. I can't say. I know they got the phrase backward. We're only *materials* in a spiritual world, never vice-versa. Angels flutter around our heads like bobwhites before an autumn storm. On good days I can feel them, like Rosa. Lightened up like that, I have to bank we're more than animated mud. Then I walk around feeling like I tossed a knapsack of bricks off my back, as long the weightlessness lasts.

So maybe all this talk about living waters isn't madman blather, just a conceit, sort of, he's carried to extremes. And if he's only my adopted pop, I guess he has his place, like other aging fathers, belonging nowhere but where a name puts them, Mr._____, son of _____, father of_____, husband of _____, distant, disagreeable, as selfish as a baby, bull-headed, ornery, ass-kicking, the older the angrier and quieter, sandblind, full of dying fears, sunk to the neck in the quicksand stepped in day-one, like all of us, but now more sunk. It may be a blessing to be blindsided by a bus, or do a Geronimo from a step-van.

I suppose too we're *all* bastards, foster children by default, since we're not too long born in the world not knowing whence we came, before we discover we have to leave one day, sooner or later, and no one, and nothing, has given us a glimpse of *wherefore*.

Claire comes out into the yard in jeans and a T-shirt. Her wet scented hair is combed. Through the trees a kerosene lantern burns.

I anchor myself on Claire's arm. We breathe in the garden.

"We'll have strawberry beds," I say. "Flower banks, corn rows, tomato vines. Zinia. Cat's paw, shooting star. Mock-orange and larkspur. The mauve and garden lilac of early morning."

"Why not," she says.

A crescent moon sets through the black pines. On the gold-white sliver seas and craters are shadowed by the sun.

I pick up the undergrad astronomy game, point to constellations.

"Lupus," I say. "Bootes."

"Cassiopeia," Claire says, "Vega."

"That's a star."

"I know. Where?"

"Lyra," I say, pointing.

"Cygnas the Swan."

"Denab. Crown of the Northern Cross, one of the brightest stars in the Northern hemisphere."

"None brighter?"

"Sirius."

"Canis Majorus. Corona Borealis."

"Draco."

"The nearest star?" I ask.

"The sun, you moron."

"*Imbecile*. Keener than a moron, but lacking an idiot's snap. I mean *star* star, Ms. Hunter."

"Alpha Centauri. With Proxima. Triple star."

"Remember what that Father-professor said the heavens were like?"

"'The shadow of celestial wings.'"

"'Signs of invisible empyreans, dancing joys, a harmony of souls."

"He also taught astronomy beyond Ptolemy. He said stars were very hot, and full of nuclear fusion."

"'Dens forever, a pasture of flocks, a joy of wild asses.'"

"He didn't say *that* about the magnitudes."

"Sure he did. Ninety percent of the cosmos is what?"

"Dark matter."

"Light we can't *see*," I say. "Visible to mystics. What were those arrows piercing St. Theresa?"

"Catholic fantasies."

"Cosmic numina."

"Doubtful."

"Doubtless."

"Learn to share."

An eventide maypole brush against the dark.

"Don't ever shave."

"Never again. Or you. Implants neither."

When we embrace there's a crinkling sound in my top pocket. She reaches in and takes out a Chi-rho frond. It's crumbled.

"What's that?"

"Palm tree. Aloha."

"And this?" She feels the diamond ring through the shirt pocket.

"Carbon."

I put the ring on her finger.

"It's gaudy," she says.

"It cost me an arm and a leg."

"It cost me more than that."

We look up.

"Where's Andromeda?" Claire asks, testing my memory of the seasonal skies. She takes off the ring and flings it into the woods. It flies, flung, sparkling, a diamond-white meteorite swallowed by the night sky.

"For a science reporter, Ms. Claire, you don't know much about the heavens. That's a winter constellation."

"We can wait on that," she says. "It's cold enough already."

"If you had had a daughter," I ask, "what would you have named her?"

"What are you talking about?"

"What would you have named her?"

"Lucy. After my mother."

Rosa over my shoulder. Claire's pregnant, a prickly scalp-code and dazzle of light. It's a girl.

"What are you smiling about?"

"Angles," I say. "Depths, heights, distances. Those stars. Angels."

"What was that?"

"Non-stop."

I draw her close.

"One of us is crazy," she says. "Why are we dying?" Claire asks.

"Progress."

She draws me down. "It's *freezing.*"

"Did I ever tell you what my grandmother said?"

"No. It can't be romantic, thank God. Your grandmother said it."

"That depends on how you think about it."

"No more, Webb, please. It's freezing."

"Every so often she sang a line from *Ave Maria.* She was dying. One morning she lifted a frail hand and motioned me over. 'Closer,' she said. I bent down. She smelled rank and sweet. She looked light, like she might levitate. She was smiling. She whispered up at me."

"What?"

"'You're gone before you get here.'"

"And dies."

"Hold on. She paused and took a breath. 'The morning stars.'"

"And died."

"No."

"Yes."

Claire steps back and hugs herself. "And died."

"And *flew.* Her body was so still I knew she had vanished. I pulled the covers up to her chin. No more sickbed television for her! I think she died in a state—"

"Of what? Oblivion? Nothingness? No more, Webb, please."

"Grace? Ecstasy?"

Claire's hand lightly touches the base of her throat.

"I don't know," she says.

"What?"

"About me. You. Practically everything."

"Neither do I. I had a few clues, for a while."

"Are you going back to New York?"

"Should I?"

"You should if you want."

"And leave you with these lunatics?"

"*These* lunatics? Don't stay on my account."

"I won't leave on your account."

"Do you have any reason to go back?"

"Do I need a reason?"

"No."

"You're right, though," she says.

"About what?"

"It depends on how you think about it."

"See the moon? The dark part?"

"Yes," Claire says.

"What did Father-professor call it, when you can make out the dark part? The ashy light?"

"Earthshine."

GEORGE WILLIAMS is the author of two novels, *Degenerate* and *Zoë*, and four collections of stories: *Gardens of Earthly Delight, The Valley of Happiness, Inferno* and *The Selected Letters of the Late Biagio Serafim Sciarra*. His stories and essays have appeared in *The Pushcart Prize, Boulevard,* and *The Hopkins Review,* among others. He is the recipient of a Michener Fellowship and a grant from the Christopher Isherwood Foundation and works as a consultant and writer for Corra Films.

On the following pages are a few
more great titles from the
Down & Out Books publishing family.

For a complete list of books and to
sign up for our newsletter,
go to DownAndOutBooks.com.

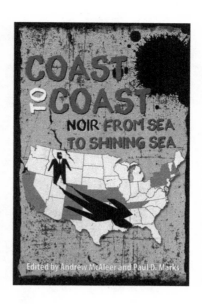

Coast to Coast Noir
Andrew McAleer and Paul D. Marks, editors

Down & Out Books
September 2020
978-1-64396-147-7

It doesn't have to be the dark of a rainy night for it to be noir. It doesn't have to be shadowy rooms of Venetian blinds. It doesn't even have to be a femme fatale. Noir is somebody tripping over their own faults, somebody who has an Achilles heel, some kind of greed, or want or desire that leads them down a dark path, from which there is sometimes no return.

No one is safe.

There's no place to hide in this collection of twelve stories from the dark side of the American Dream.

Permission Granted
Grant & McNulty Stories
Colin Campbell

Down & Out Books
September 2020
978-1-64396-127-9

Helping an old lady get her stolen glasses back and dangling the thief over a cliff is just the start of Jim Grant's tarnished career and these stories fill in some of the gaps between his other adventures.

But he's not the only Yorkshireman in America. Vince McNulty is a Yorkshire ex-cop working for a tinpot movie company in Boston. It would be a coincidence if these two men didn't know each other. Cops don't believe in coincidence. Neither should you.

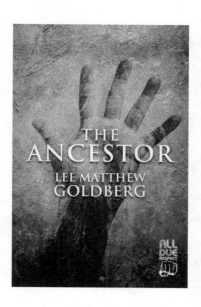

The Ancestor
Lee Matthew Goldberg

All Due Respect, an imprint of
Down & Out Books
August 2020
978-1-64396-114-9

A man wakes up in the Alaskan wilderness with no memory of who he is, except for the belief that he's was a prospector from the Gold Rush and has been frozen in ice for over a hundred years.

A meditation on love lost and unfulfilled dreams, *The Ancestor* is a thrilling page-turner in present day Alaska and a historical adventure about the perilous Gold Rush expeditions where prospectors left behind their lives for the promise of hope and a better future.

Deemer's Inlet
Stephen Burdick

Shotgun Honey, an imprint of
Down & Out Books
August 2020
978-1-64396-104-0

Far from the tourist meccas of Ft. Lauderdale and Miami Beach, a chief of police position in the quiet, picturesque town of Deemer's Inlet on the Gulf coast of Florida seemed ideal for Eldon Quick—until the first murder.

The crime and a subsequent killing force Quick to call upon his years of experience as a former homicide detective in Miami. Soon after, two more people are murdered and Quick believes a serial killer is on the loose. As Quick works to uncover the identity and motive of the killer, he must contend with an understaffed police force, small town politics, and curious residents.